EVERYMAN, I will go with thee,

and be thy guide,

In thy most need to go by thy side

sinecure
close
faute de mieux
precentor
deacon
canon
woolstapler
bedesman
bull
scion
emoluments

ANTHONY TROLLOPE

Born in London in 1815, the son of a barrister. Held important position in the Post Office, 1841–66. Visited America, Australia, South Africa and New Zealand. Died in 1882.

ANTHONY TROLLOPE

The Warden

INTRODUCTION BY
KATHLEEN TILLOTSON

AND AN ESSAY BY
MICHAEL SADLEIR

DENT: LONDON
EVERYMAN'S LIBRARY
DUTTON: NEW YORK

© *Introduction, J. M. Dent & Sons Ltd, 1957*
All rights reserved
Made in Great Britain
at the
Aldine Press · Letchworth · Herts
for
J. M. DENT & SONS LTD
Aldine House · Albemarle Street · London
This edition was first published in
Everyman's Library in 1907
Last reprinted 1977

Published in the U.S.A. by arrangement
with J. M. Dent & Sons Ltd

No. 182   Hardback ISBN 0 460 00182 5
No. 1182   Paperback ISBN 0 460 01182 0

INTRODUCTION

'My first success'—so Trollope entitles the chapter about *The Warden* in his *Autobiography*. He did not mean by that a popular or financial success. Published in December 1854, when he was nearly forty, *The Warden* took two years to sell 500 copies and to earn its author £20; as he says: 'stone-breaking would have been better.' Nevertheless, the book was indeed a success in contrast with the abject failure of his earlier efforts—his two Irish stories, his historical novel, and his unacted play—and it led to greater success, by showing him 'wherein lay whatever strength I did possess,' for the perception of that 'strength' marked the beginning of the Barsetshire series.

Yet the novel is not typical of the series. It is short, in the one-volume form which libraries did not favour (Trollope has a facetious allusion to its shortness in Chapter VI), but it took him longer to write than any other novel. *The Warden* occupied three years, from its first conception in the summer of 1851: 'in later days,' he says, it 'would have been completed in six weeks. No work that I ever did took up so much of my thoughts'; accordingly, he gives a particularly full account of its origins. It sprang from two impulses, a sense of scene and setting, and the wish to expose certain abuses. On a visit to Salisbury, early in his three-year tour of the western counties on behalf of the Post Office, he 'wandered' one midsummer evening 'round the purlieus of the Cathedral,' 'stood for an hour on the little bridge,' and 'made out to my own satisfaction

the spot on which Hiram's Hospital should stand.'
(Barchester is, nevertheless, not Salisbury, but a
composite of several cathedral towns.) He wished
to express his conviction that while the malversation
of charitable trusts was an evil, an evil equally
great was the severity of newspaper attacks on the
recipients of church incomes.

The Warden thus differs from the later Barsetshire
novels in being a 'novel with a purpose' in the
narrow sense: so much so that its controversial
content was what chiefly struck contemporary
readers. Like Trollope, who refers to these matters
in Chapter II, they had read Robert Whiston's
Cathedral Trusts and their Fulfilment (1849; 5th
edition, 1850), which led to a court case against the
Dean and Chapter of Rochester; they would share
his interest in the long-drawn case of the Hospital of
St Cross, near Winchester; and they had followed
the debates on the Charitable Trusts bill, which was
finally passed in 1853. Moreover, readers had in the
past ten years become well accustomed to the use of
fiction for such exposures; as Thackeray put it in his
'Plan for a Prize Novel' in 1851: 'Unless he writes
with a purpose, you know, a novelist in our days is
good for nothing. . . .' But Trollope did not
continue this sort of pamphleteering in later novels;
indeed, he mocked at it in Charley Tudor's novel in
The Three Clerks. *The Warden* seems to have shown
him that the 'purpose novel' was incompatible with
his temperament, for his ability to see both sides
militated against his contemporary effectiveness.
With some irony, he suggests that his readers would
have preferred him to satirize either the 'red-nosed
clerical cormorant' or the 'venomous assassin of the
journals.' He may have had in mind the *Athenaeum*
review, which found it a 'grave fault' that 'the right
or wrong of the subject was melted down into a

matter of perfect indifference' with exclusive
emphasis on 'the extreme hardship and *incon-
venience* to the parties in possession, caused by any
attempt to rectify their administration.' To a
modern reader, Trollope's moderation, his preference
of natural characterization to exaggerated types, is
part of the strength of the novel as a novel. He
shows how the acquiescence in and the exposure of
an abuse affects *individuals*; he uses the situation to
discriminate the shades of distinction between the
consciences of the warden and of the bishop, the
archdeacon, the reformer John Bold, and the editor
Tom Towers. And further, he deliberately inserted in one episode references to two writers of the
day that were immediately recognizable, Carlyle
(Dr Pessimist Anticant) and Dickens (Mr Popular
Sentiment); his vivacious parodies of a *Latter-day
Pamphlet* and a novel in shilling monthly numbers
are used to exemplify the very methods of violent
one-sided attack that he himself deliberately avoids.
Chapter XV is no excrescence; besides helping to
define Trollope's own method, it is designed to set a
sharp and truthful edge on Mr Harding's sufferings.
Henry James called *The Warden* 'simply the history of
an old man's conscience,' but it is not *simply* that; it
is also the study of an old man's sensibility to the
harshness of modern publicity, a theme that might
also be expected to appeal to James himself.

When Trollope, so often his own best critic, speci-
fied the merits of his novel, he picked out the characters of the warden, the bishop, the archdeacon and
his wife. He was especially pleased with Archdeacon
Grantly—'a simple effort of my moral consciousness'
which 'came whole from my brain.' But the really
outstanding characters may be reduced to two—
Archdeacon Grantly and Mr Harding, the warden.
The threat to the hospital sets them in inevitable

collision, and we see the initial contrast between the
formidable power of the one and the tremulous
timidity of the other, yielding, by natural steps, to
the victory of integrity and simplicity over worldli-
ness. This essentially is the 'plot,' and it is one of
the most satisfying that Trollope ever contrived.

The finest chapters of the novel are those leading to
Mr Harding's victory by renunciation, when he
eludes the archdeacon and travels alone to London,
only to find that he must wait all day before the
lawyer can see him, and so may be overtaken and
forestalled by his antagonist. In 'A Long Day in
London' (Chapter XVI) Trollope wonderfully con-
veys the slow passing of time, and in tracing Mr
Harding's lonely self-examination along with his
time-filling stratagems, through Westminster Abbey
('the archdeacon would certainly not come to
morning service at Westminster Abbey, even though
he was in London') and the comically inappropriate
chop-house and cigar-divan, he achieves what is his
peculiar triumph, a sense of heroic action enmeshed
in trivial circumstance. At the climax of the long-
deferred interview the Warden's simple utterance
rises to nobility: 'I cannot boast of my conscience,
when it required the violence of a public newspaper
to awaken it; but, now that it is awake, I must obey
it.' Yet this nobility is accompanied and even
enhanced by the mild absurdity of his 'gesticulations' on the imaginary violoncello, and the 'palpitating heart' with which he returns to face the
archdeacon.

The family relationships of Hardings and Grantlys
complicate the delicate web of loyalties; but the
other characters are more lightly sketched, and the
later Trollope would certainly have made more of
the love interest and the conflict of Eleanor and John
Bold—not necessarily to the improvement of the

novel. In 'low life' he seldom did anything better than the grumpy old bedesmen, whom a lesser novelist would merely have sentimentalized; and the bedroom scene at Plumstead in Chapter II (the publisher's reader cast doubts on its propriety) has a humorous insight reminiscent of Thackeray. Indeed the only passage that seems immature is the account of the Grantly sons, Charles James, Henry, and Samuel, through whom Trollope caricatured three well-known bishops, Blomfield, Philpotts, and Wilberforce. The jokes are now unrecognized, and the passage can only seem baffling to a modern reader, unlike the references to contemporary ecclesiastical controversy in *Barchester Towers*, which are made self-explanatory.

Trollope did not immediately go on to write *Barchester Towers*, but perhaps he had it in mind in the later chapters of *The Warden*. He went out of his way to give a brief sketch of the Reverend Dr Vesey Stanhope of Crabtree Canonicorum, he awakened some interest in poor Mr Quiverful of Puddingdale, and at the end he left the wardenship unfilled. But whether or not he foresaw developments, he must have known that in the two main characters, Mr Harding and Archdeacon Grantly, he had created two potential centres of continuing interest. He was to show them in other crises of church politics—most effectively, in relation to Mrs Proudie and Mr Slope; and in new family relationships—Mr Harding is the perfect grandfather; and even when they are on the periphery of the main situation they often supply a vital commentary. Mr Harding is not again so prominent, but he becomes, as one critic has said, 'a moral touchstone' for the rest; two telling instances are his chance encounter with Adolphus Crosbie, and his conversation with Griselda. In the *Last Chronicle* his slow, gentle

fading from the scene rounds off the whole series.
And the man who pays the most fitting tribute at his
deathbed is the archdeacon himself:

His tenderness has surpassed the tenderness of woman;
and yet, when an occasion came for showing it, he had
all the spirit of a hero.   I shall never forget his resignation of the hospital, and all that I did and said to make
him keep it. . . .   The fact is, he never was wrong.
He couldn't go wrong.   He lacked guile, and he feared
God,—and a man who does both will never go far
astray.   I don't think he ever coveted aught in his life,
—except a new case for his violoncello and somebody
to listen to him while he played it.

KATHLEEN TILLOTSON.

1957.

SELECT BIBLIOGRAPHY

SEPARATE WORKS. *The Macdermots of Ballycloran*, 1847; *The
Kellys and the O'Kellys*, 1848; *La Vendée*, 1850; *The Warden*,
1855; *Barchester Towers*, 1857; *The Three Clerks*, 1858; *Doctor
Thorne*, 1858; *The Bertrams*, 1859; *The West Indies and the
Spanish Main*, 1859; *Castle Richmond*, 1860; *Framley Parsonage*,
1861; *Tales of All Countries*, 1861; *Orley Farm*, 1862; *North
America*, 1862; *The Struggles of Brown, Jones and Robinson*,
U.S. ed., 1862 (English ed., 1870); *Tales of all Countries*, 1863;
Rachel Ray, 1863; *The Small House at Allington*, 1864; *Can You
Forgive Her?*, 1864; *Miss Mackenzie*, 1865; *Hunting Sketches*,
1865; *The Belton Estate*, 1866; *Travelling Sketches*, 1866; *Clergy-
men of the Church of England*, 1866; *Nina Balatka*, 1867; *The
Last Chronicle of Barset*, 1867; *The Claverings*, 1867; *Lotta
Schmidt and Other Stories*, 1867; *Linda Tressel*, 1868; *On Hunting*,
in *British Sports and Pastimes*, 1868; *Phineas Finn, the Irish
Member*, 1869; *He Knew He was Right*, 1869; *Did He Steal It?*,
1869; *The Vicar of Bullhampton*, 1870; *An Editor's Tales*, 1870;
The Commentaries of Caesar, 1870; *Christmas Day at Kirkby
Cottage*, in *Routledge's Christmas Annual*, 1870; *Sir Harry
Hotspur of Humblethwaite*, 1871; *Ralph the Heir*, 1871; *The
Golden Lion of Granpère*, 1872; *The Eustace Diamonds*, 1873;
Australia and New Zealand, 1873; *Phineas Redux*, 1874; *Lady
Anna*, 1874; *Harry Heathcote of Gangoil*, 1874; *The Way We Live
Now*, 1875; *The Prime Minister*, 1876; *The American Senator*,

The Commentaries of Caesar, 1870; *Christmas Day at Kirkby Cottage*, in *Routledge's Christmas Annual*, 1870; *Sir Harry Hotspur of Humblethwaite*, 1871; *Ralph the Heir*, 1871; *The Golden Lion of Granpère*, 1872; *The Eustace Diamonds*, 1873; *Australia and New Zealand*, 1873; *Phineas Redux*, 1874; *Lady Anna*, 1874; *Harry Heathcote of Gangoil*, 1874; *The Way We Live Now*, 1875; *The Prime Minister*, 1876; *The American Senator*, 1877; *Christmas at Thompson Hall*, 1877; *South Africa*, 1878 (abridged and partly rewritten, 1879); *Is He Popenjoy?*, 1878; Iceland, 1878; *How the 'Mastiffs' went to Iceland*, 1878; *The Lady of Launay*, 1878; *Catherine Carmichael or Three Years Running*, in the Christmas number of the *Masonic Magazine*, 1878; *An Eye for an Eye*, 1879; *Thackeray*, 1879; *John Caldigate*, 1879; *Cousin Henry*, 1879; *The Duke's Children*, 1880; *The Life of Cicero*, 1880; *Dr Wortle's School*, 1881; *Whist at our Club*, in *Tales from 'Blackwood,'* vol. xii, 1881; *Ayala's Angel*, 1881; *Why Frau Frohmann raised her Prices, and Other Stories*, 1882; *The Fixed Period*, 1882; *Lord Palmerston*, 1882; *Marion Fay*, 1882; *Kept in the Dark*, 1882; *Two Heroines of Plumpington*, in the Christmas number of *Good Words*, 1882; *Mr Scarborough's Family*, 1883; *The Landleaguers*, 1883; *An Old Man's Love*, 1884; *Thompson Hall*, 1885; *The Noble Jilt*, 1923; *London Tradesmen* (essays from *Pall Mall Gazette*), 1927.

Trollope contributed also to the following periodicals: *Examiner*, *Dublin University Magazine*, *Cornhill*, *St James's Magazine*, *Athenaeum*, *Fortnightly Review*, *Harper's Weekly*, *St Paul's*, *Blackwood*, *The Nineteenth Century*, *North American Review*, *Pall Mall Gazette*, and *Life*, 1849–82.

COLLECTED EDITIONS. *The Barsetshire Novels*, ed. F. Harrison, 8 vols., 1906; *The Barchester Novels*, ed. M. Sadleir, 14 vols., 1929.

BIOGRAPHY AND CRITICISM. *An Autobiography*, 1883; Henry James in *Partial Portraits*, 1888; T. H. S. Escott, *Trollope: His Work, Associates, and Literary Originals*, 1913; Hugh Walpole, *Anthony Trollope* (English Men of Letters), 1928; Michael Sadleir, *Trollope: a commentary*, 1927, 1933; W. G. and J. T. Gerould, *A Guide to Trollope*, 1948; *The Letters of Anthony Trollope*, ed. Bradford A. Booth, 1951; A. O. J. Cockshut, *Anthony Trollope: A Critical Study*, 1955; Bradford A. Booth, *Anthony Trollope*, 1958; Ruth ap Roberts, *Trollope: Artist and Moralist*, 1971.

See also Michael Sadleir, *Trollope: a Bibliography*, 1928.

CONTENTS

THE WARDEN

CHAPTER I

HIRAM'S HOSPITAL

THE Rev. Septimus Harding was, a few years
since, a beneficed clergyman residing in the
cathedral town of —— ; let us call it Barchester.
Were we to name Wells or Salisbury, Exeter,
Hereford, or Gloucester, it might be presumed
that something personal was intended ; and as
this tale will refer mainly to the cathedral
dignitaries of the town in question, we are
anxious that no personality may be suspected.
Let us presume that Barchester is a quiet
town in the West of England, more remark-
able for the beauty of its cathedral and the
antiquity of its monuments, than for any
commercial prosperity ; that the west end of
Barchester is the cathedral close, and that the
aristocracy of Barchester are the bishop, dean,
and canons, with their respective wives and
daughters.

Early in life Mr. Harding found himself
located at Barchester. A fine voice and a
taste for sacred music had decided the position
in which he was to exercise his calling, and

for many years he performed the easy but not highly paid duties of a minor canon. At the age of forty a small living in the close vicinity of the town increased both his work and his income, and at the age of fifty he became precentor of the cathedral.

Mr. Harding had married early in life, and was the father of two daughters. The elder, Susan, was born soon after his marriage; the other, Eleanor, not till ten years later. At the time at which we introduce him to our readers he was living as precentor at Barchester with his younger daughter, then twenty-four years of age; having been many years a widower, and having married his elder daughter to a son of the bishop, a very short time before his installation to the office of precentor.

Scandal at Barchester affirmed that, had it not been for the beauty of his daughter, Mr. Harding would have remained a minor canon; but here probably Scandal lied, as she so often does; for even as a minor canon no one had been more popular among his reverend brethren in the close, than Mr. Harding; and Scandal, before she had reprobated Mr. Harding for being made precentor by his friend the bishop, had loudly blamed the bishop for having so long omitted to do something for his friend Mr. Harding. Be this as it may, Susan Harding, some twelve years since, had married the Rev. Dr. Theophilus Grantly, son of the bishop, archdeacon of Barchester, and rector of Plumstead Episcopi, and her father became, a few months later, precentor of Barchester Cathedral, that office being, as is not usual, in the bishop's gift.

Now there are peculiar circumstances connected with the precentorship which must be explained. In the year 1434 there died at Barchester one John Hiram, who had made money in the town as a woolstapler, and in his will he left the house in which he died and certain meadows and closes near the town, still called Hiram's Butts, and Hiram's Patch, for the support of twelve superannuated woolcarders, all of whom should have been born and bred and spent their days in Barchester; he also appointed that an alms-house should be built for their abode, with a fitting residence for a warden, which warden was also to receive a certain sum annually out of the rents of the said butts and patches. He, moreover, willed, having had a soul alive to harmony, that the precentor of the cathedral should have the option of being also warden of the alms-houses, if the bishop in each case approved.

From that day to this the charity had gone on and prospered—at least, the charity had gone on, and the estates had prospered. Wool carding in Barchester there was no longer any; so the bishop, dean, and warden, who took it in turn to put in the old men, gener-

ally appointed some hangers-on of their own;
worn-out gardeners, decrepit grave-diggers, or
octogenarian sextons, who thankfully received
a comfortable lodging and one shilling and
fourpence a day, such being the stipend to
which, under the will of John Hiram, they
were declared to be entitled. Formerly, indeed,—that is, till within some fifty years of
the 'present time,—they received but sixpence
a day, and their breakfast and dinner were
found them at a common table by the warden,
such an arrangement being in stricter con-
formity with the absolute wording of old
Hiram's will: but this was thought to be
inconvenient, and to suit the tastes of neither
warden nor bedesmen, and the daily one
shilling and fourpence was substituted with
the common consent of all parties, including
the bishop and the corporation of Barchester.

Such was the condition of Hiram's twelve
old men when Mr. Harding was appointed
warden; but if they may be considered as
well-to-do in the world according to their
condition, the happy warden was much more
so. The patches and butts which, in John
Hiram's time, produced hay or fed cows, were
now covered with rows of houses; the value
of the property had gradually increased from
year to year, and century to century, and was
now presumed, by those who knew anything
about it, to bring in a very nice income; and,

by some who knew nothing about it, to have increased to an almost fabulous extent.

The property was farmed by a gentleman in Barchester, who also acted as the bishop's steward—a man whose father and grandfather had been stewards to the bishops of Barchester, and farmers of John Hiram's estate. The Chadwicks had earned a good name in Barchester ; they had lived respected by bishops, deans, canons, and precentors ; they had been buried in the precincts of the cathedral ; they had never been known as griping, hard men, but had always lived comfortably, maintained a good house, and held a high position in Barchester society. The present Mr. Chadwick was a worthy scion of a worthy stock, and the tenants living on the butts and patches, as well as those on the wide episcopal domains of the see, were well pleased to have to do with so worthy and liberal a steward.

For many, many years,—records hardly tell how many, probably from the time when Hiram's wishes had been first fully carried out,—the proceeds of the estate had been paid by the steward or farmer to the warden, and by him divided among the bedesmen ; after which division he paid himself such sums as became his due. Times had been when the poor warden got nothing but his bare house, for the patches had been subject to floods, and the land of Barchester butts was said to be unproductive; and in these hard times the warden was hardly able to make out the daily dole for his twelve dependents. But by degrees things mended; the patches were drained, and cottages began to rise upon the butts, and the wardens, with fairness enough, repaid themselves for the evil days gone by. In bad times the poor men had had their due, and therefore in good times they could expect no more. In this manner the income of the warden had increased; the picturesque house attached to the hospital had been enlarged and adorned, and the office had become one of the most coveted of the snug clerical sinecures attached to our church. It was now wholly in the bishop's gift, and though the dean and chapter, in former days, made a stand on the subject, they had thought it more conducive to their honour to have a rich precentor appointed by the bishop, than a poor one appointed by themselves. The stipend of the precentor of Barchester was eighty pounds a year. The income arising from the warden-ship of the hospital was eight hundred, besides the value of the house.

Murmurs, very slight murmurs, had been heard in Barchester,—few indeed, and far between,—that the proceeds of John Hiram's property had not been fairly divided: but they can hardly be said to have been of such a nature as to have caused uneasiness to any

one: still the thing had been whispered, and
Mr. Harding had heard it. Such was his
character in Barchester, so universal was his
popularity, that the very fact of his appointment would have quieted louder whispers
than those which had been heard; but Mr.
Harding was an open-handed, just-minded
man, and feeling that there might be truth
in what had been said, he had, on his in-
stalment, declared his intention of adding
twopence a day to each man's pittance, making
a sum of sixty-two pounds eleven shillings and
fourpence, which he was to pay out of his
own pocket. In doing so, however, he distinctly and repeatedly observed to the men,
that though he promised for himself, he could
not promise for his successors, and that the
extra twopence could only be looked on as
a gift from himself, and not from the trust.
The bedesmen, however, were most of them
older than Mr. Harding, and were quite
satisfied with the security on which their
extra income was based.

This munificence on the part of Mr. Harding had not been unopposed. Mr. Chadwick
had mildly but seriously dissuaded him from
it; and his strong-minded son-in-law, the
archdeacon, the man of whom alone Mr.
Harding stood in awe, had urgently, nay
vehemently, opposed so impolitic a concession:
but the warden had made known his intention

to the hospital before the archdeacon had been able to interfere, and the deed was done.

Hiram's Hospital, as the retreat is called, is a picturesque building enough, and shows the correct taste with which the ecclesiastical architects of those days were imbued. It stands on the banks of the little river, which flows nearly round the cathedral close, being on the side furthest from the town. The London road crosses the river by a pretty one-arched bridge, and, looking from this bridge, the stranger will see the windows of the old men's rooms, each pair of windows separated by a small buttress. A broad gravel walk runs between the building and the river, which is always trim and cared for ; and at the end of the walk, under the parapet of the approach to the bridge, is a large and well-worn seat, on which, in mild weather, three or four of Hiram's bedesmen are sure to be seen seated. Beyond this row of buttresses, and further from the bridge, and also further from the water which here suddenly bends, are the pretty oriel windows of Mr. Harding's house, and his well-mown lawn. The entrance to the hospital is from the London road, and is made through a ponderous gateway under a heavy stone arch, unnecessary, one would suppose, at any time, for the protection of twelve old men, but greatly conducive to the good appearance of Hiram's charity. On passing through this portal, never closed to any one from six A.M. till ten P.M., and never open afterwards, except on application to a huge, intricately hung, mediæval bell, the handle of which no uninitiated intruder can possibly find, the six doors of the old men's abodes are seen, and beyond them is a slight iron screen, through which the more happy portion of the Barchester *élite* pass into the Elysium of Mr. Harding's dwelling.

Mr. Harding is a small man, now verging on sixty years, but bearing few of the signs of age; his hair is rather grizzled, though not grey, his eye is very mild, but clear and bright, though the double glasses which are held swinging from his hand, unless when fixed upon his nose, show that time has told upon his sight : his hands are delicately white, and both hands and feet are small ; he always wears a black frock coat, black knee-breeches, and black gaiters, and somewhat scandalises some of his more hyper-clerical brethren by a black neck-handkerchief.

Mr. Harding's warmest admirers cannot say that he was ever an industrious man; the circumstances of his life have not called on him to be so ; and yet he can hardly be called an idler. Since his appointment to his pre-centorship, he has published, with all possible additions of vellum, typography, and gilding, a collection of our ancient church music, with some correct dissertations on Purcell, Crotch, and Nares. He has greatly improved the choir of Barchester, which, under his dominion, now rivals that of any cathedral in England. He has taken something more than his fair share in the cathedral services, and has played the violoncello daily to such audiences as he could collect, or, *faute de mieux*, to no audience at all.

We must mention one other peculiarity of Mr. Harding. As we have before stated, he has an income of eight hundred a year, and has no family but his one daughter ; and yet he is never quite at ease in money matters. The vellum and gilding of "Harding's Church Music," cost more than any one knows, except the author, the publisher, and the Rev. Theophilus Grantly, who allows none of his father-in-law's extravagances to escape him. Then he is generous to his daughter, for whose service he keeps a small carriage and pair of ponies. He is, indeed, generous to all, but especially to the twelve old men who are in a peculiar manner under his care. No doubt with such an income Mr. Harding should be above the world, as the saying is ; but at any rate, he is not above Archdeacon Theophilus Grantly, for he is always more or less in debt to his son-in-law, who has, to a certain extent, assumed the arrangement of the precentor's pecuniary affairs.

CHAPTER II

THE BARCHESTER REFORMER

Mr. Harding has been now precentor of Barchester for ten years; and, alas, the murmurs respecting the proceeds of Hiram's estate are again becoming audible. It is not that any one begrudges to Mr. Harding the income which he enjoys, and the comfortable place which so well becomes him; but such matters have begun to be talked of in various parts of England. Eager pushing politicians have asserted in the House of Commons, with very telling indignation, that the grasping priests of the Church of England are gorged with the wealth which the charity of former times has left for the solace of the aged, or the education of the young. The well-known case of the Hospital of St. Cross, has even come before the law courts of the country, and the struggles of Mr. Whiston, at Rochester, have met with sympathy and support. Men are beginning to say that these things must be looked into.

Mr. Harding, whose conscience in the matter is clear, and who has never felt that he had received a pound from Hiram's will to which he was not entitled, has naturally taken the part of the church in talking over these matters with his friend, the bishop, and his son-in-law, the archdeacon. The archdeacon, indeed, Dr. Grantly, has been somewhat loud in the matter: he is a personal friend of the dignitaries of the Rochester Chapter, and has written letters in the public press on the subject of that turbulent Dr. Whiston, which, his admirers think, must well nigh set the question at rest. It is also known at Oxford, that he is the author of the pamphlet signed "Sacerdos" on the subject of the Earl of Guildford and St. Cross, in which it is so clearly argued that the manners of the present times do not admit of a literal adhesion to the very words of the founder's will, but that the interests of the church for which the founder was so deeply concerned, are best consulted in enabling its bishops to reward those shining lights, whose services have been most signally serviceable to Christianity. In answer to this, it is asserted that Henry de Blois, founder of St. Cross, was not greatly interested in the welfare of the reformed church, and that the masters of St. Cross, for many years past, cannot be called shining lights in the service of Christianity; it is, however, stoutly maintained, and no doubt felt, by all the archdeacon's friends, that his logic is conclusive, and has not, in fact, been answered.

With such a tower of strength to back both
his arguments and his conscience, it may be
imagined that Mr. Harding has never felt
any compunction as to receiving his quarterly
sum of two hundred pounds.   Indeed, the
subject has never presented itself to his mind
in that shape.   He has talked not unfre-
quently, and heard very much about the wills
of old founders and the incomes arising from
their estates, during the last year or two ; he
did even, at one moment, feel a doubt (since
expelled by his son-in-law's logic) as to whether
Lord Guildford was clearly entitled to receive
so enormous an income as he does from the
revenues of St. Cross, but that he himself
was overpaid with his modest eight hundred
pounds ;—he who, out of that, voluntarily
gave up sixty-two pounds eleven shillings and
fourpence a year to his twelve old neighbours ;
—he who, for the money, does his precentor's
work as no precentor has done it before, since
Barchester Cathedral was built ;—such an idea
has never sullied his quiet, or disturbed his
conscience.

Nevertheless, Mr. Harding is becoming uneasy at the rumour which he knows to prevail
in Barchester on the subject.   He is aware
that, at any rate, two of his old men have
been heard to say, that if every one had
his own, they might each have their hundred
pounds a year, and live like gentlemen, instead

of a beggarly one shilling and sixpence a day ; and that they had slender cause to be thankful for a miserable dole of twopence, when Mr. Harding and Mr. Chadwick, between them, ran away with thousands of pounds which good old John Hiram never intended for the like of them. It is the ingratitude of this which stings Mr. Harding. One of this discontented pair, Abel Handy, was put into the hospital by himself; he had been a stonemason in Barchester, and had broken his thigh by a fall from a scaffolding, while employed about the cathedral ; and Mr. Harding had given him the first vacancy in the hospital after the occurrence, although Dr. Grantly had been very anxious to put into it an insufferable clerk of his at Plumstead Episcopi, who had lost all his teeth, and whom the archdeacon hardly knew how to get rid of by other means. Dr. Grantly has not forgotten to remind Mr. Harding how well satisfied with his one and sixpence a day old Joe Mutters would have been, and how injudicious it was on the part of Mr. Harding to allow a radical from the town to get into the concern. Probably Dr. Grantly forgot, at the moment, that the charity was intended for broken-down journeymen of Barchester.

There is living at Barchester, a young man, a surgeon, named John Bold, and both

Mr. Harding and Dr. Grantly are well aware
that to him is owing the pestilent rebellious
feeling which has shown itself in the hospital;
yes, and the renewal, too, of that disagreeable
talk about Hiram's estates which is now again
prevalent in Barchester. Nevertheless, Mr.
Harding and Mr. Bold are acquainted with
each other; we may say, are friends, considering the great disparity in their years. Dr.
Grantly, however, has a holy horror of the
impious demagogue, as on one occasion he
called Bold, when speaking of him to the
precentor; and being a more prudent far-
seeing man than Mr. Harding, and possessed
of a stronger head, he already perceives that
this John Bold will work great trouble in
Barchester. He considers that he is to
be regarded as an enemy, and thinks that
he should not be admitted into the camp
on anything like friendly terms. As John
Bold will occupy much of our attention,
we must endeavour to explain who he is,
and why he takes the part of John Hiram's
bedesmen.

John Bold is a young surgeon, who passed
many of his boyish years at Barchester. His
father was a physician in the city of London,
where he made a moderate fortune, which he
invested in houses in that city. The Dragon
of Wantly inn and posting-house, belonged to
him, also four shops in the High Street, and

a moiety of the new row of genteel villas (so called in the advertisement), built outside the town just beyond Hiram's Hospital. To one of these Dr. Bold retired to spend the evening of his life, and to die ; and here his son John spent his holidays, and afterwards his Christmas vacation, when he went from school to study surgery in the London hospitals. Just as John Bold was entitled to write himself surgeon and apothecary, old Dr. Bold died, leaving his Barchester property to his son, and a certain sum in the three per cents. to his daughter Mary, who is some four or five years older than her brother.

John Bold determined to settle himself at Barchester, and look after his own property, as well as the bones and bodies of such of his neighbours as would call upon him for assistance in their troubles. He therefore put up a large brass plate, with " John Bold, Surgeon," on it, to the great disgust of the nine practitioners who were already trying to get a living out of the bishop, dean, and canons ; and began house-keeping with the aid of his sister. At this time he was not more than twenty-four years old ; and though he has now been three years in Barchester, we have not heard that he has done much harm to the nine worthy practitioners. Indeed, their dread of him has died away ; for in three years he has not taken three fees.

Nevertheless, John Bold is a clever man, and would, with practice, be a clever surgeon; but he has got quite into another line of life. Having enough to live on, he has not been forced to work for bread; he has declined to subject himself to what he calls the drudgery of the profession, by which, I believe, he means the general work of a practising surgeon; and has found other employment. He frequently binds up the bruises and sets the limbs of such of the poorer classes as profess his way of thinking—but this he does for love. Now I will not say that the archdeacon is strictly correct in stigmatising John Bold as a demagogue, for I hardly know how extreme must be a man's opinions before he can be justly so called; but Bold is a strong reformer. His passion is the reform of all abuses; state abuses, church abuses, corporation abuses (he has got himself elected a town councillor of Barchester, and has so worried three consecutive mayors, that it became somewhat difficult to find a fourth), abuses in medical practice, and general abuses in the world at large. Bold is thoroughly sincere in his patriotic endeavours to mend mankind, and there is something to be admired in the energy with which he devotes himself to remedying evil and stopping injustice; but I fear that he is too much imbued with the idea that he has a special mission for reforming. It would be well if one so young had a

little more diffidence himself, and more trust
in the honest purposes of others—if he could
be brought to believe that old customs need
not necessarily be evil, and that changes may
possibly be dangerous; but no, Bold has all
the ardour, and all the self-assurance of a
Danton, and hurls his anathemas against time-
honoured practices with the violence of a French
Jacobin.

No wonder that Dr. Grantly should regard
Bold as a firebrand, falling, as he has done,
almost in the centre of the quiet ancient close
of Barchester Cathedral. Dr. Grantly would
have him avoided as the plague; but the old
Doctor and Mr. Harding were fast friends.
Young Johnny Bold used to play as a boy
on Mr. Harding's lawn; he has many a time
won the precentor's heart by listening with
rapt attention to his sacred strains; and since
those days, to tell the truth at once, he has
nearly won another heart within the same walls.

Eleanor Harding has not plighted her troth
to John Bold, nor has she, perhaps, owned to
herself how dear to her the young reformer
is; but she cannot endure that any one
should speak harshly of him. She does not
dare to defend him when her brother-in-law
is so loud against him; for she, like her
father, is somewhat afraid of Dr. Grantly;
but she is beginning greatly to dislike the
archdeacon. She persuades her father that it

would be both unjust and injudicious to banish
his young friend because of his politics; she
cares little to go to houses where she will not
meet him, and, in fact, she is in love.

Nor is there any good reason why Eleanor
Harding should not love John Bold. He has
all those qualities which are likely to touch a
girl's heart. He is brave, eager, and amusing;
well-made and good-looking; young and en-
terprising; his character is in all respects
good; he has sufficient income to support a
wife; he is her father's friend; and, above
all, he is in love with her: then why should
not Eleanor Harding be attached to John
Bold?

Dr. Grantly, who has as many eyes as
Argus, and has long seen how the wind blows
in that direction, thinks there are various strong
reasons why this should not be so. He has not
thought it wise as yet to speak to his father-
in-law on the subject, for he knows how foolishly
indulgent is Mr. Harding in everything that
concerns his daughter; but he has discussed the
matter with his all-trusted help-mate, within
that sacred recess formed by the clerical bed-
curtains at Plumstead Episcopi.

How much sweet solace, how much valued
counsel has our archdeacon received within
that sainted enclosure! 'Tis there alone that
he unbends, and comes down from his high
church pedestal to the level of a mortal man.

In the world Dr. Grantly never lays aside
that demeanour which so well becomes him.
He has all the dignity of an ancient saint with
the sleekness of a modern bishop; he is always
the same; he is always the archdeacon; unlike Homer, he never nods. Even with his
father-in-law, even with the bishop and dean,
he maintains that sonorous tone and lofty deportment which strikes awe into the young
hearts of Barchester, and absolutely cows the
whole parish of Plumstead Episcopi. 'Tis only
when he has exchanged that ever-new shovel
hat for a tasselled nightcap, and those shining
black habiliments for his accustomed *robe de nuit*,
that Dr. Grantly talks, and looks, and thinks
like an ordinary man.

Many of us have often thought how severe
a trial of faith must this be to the wives of
our great church dignitaries. To us these
men are personifications of St. Paul: their
very gait is a speaking sermon; their clean
and sombre apparel exacts from us faith and
submission, and the cardinal virtues seem to
hover round their sacred hats. A dean or
archbishop, in the garb of his order, is sure of
our reverence, and a well-got-up bishop fills
our very souls with awe. But how can this
feeling be perpetuated in the bosoms of those
who see the bishops without their aprons, and
the archdeacons even in a lower state of
dishabille?

Do we not all know some reverend, all but sacred, personage before whom our tongue ceases to be loud, and our step to be elastic? But were we once to see him stretch himself beneath the bed-clothes, yawn widely, and bury his face upon his pillow, we could chatter before him as glibly as before a doctor or a lawyer. From some such cause, doubtless, it arose that our archdeacon listened to the counsels of his wife, though he considered himself entitled to give counsel to every other being whom he met.

"My dear," he said, as he adjusted the copious folds of his nightcap, "there was that John Bold at your father's again to-day. I must say your father is very imprudent."

"He is imprudent—he always was," replied Mrs. Grantly, speaking from under the comfortable bed-clothes. "There's nothing new in that."

"No, my dear, there's nothing new—I know that; but, at the present juncture of affairs, such imprudence is—is—I'll tell you what, my dear, if he does not take care what he's about, John Bold will be off with Eleanor."

"I think he will, whether papa takes care or no; and why not?"

"Why not!" almost screamed the arch-deacon, giving so rough a pull at his nightcap as almost to bring it over his nose; "why not!—that pestilent, interfering upstart, John Bold—the most vulgar young person I ever met! Do you know that he is meddling with your father's affairs in a most uncalled for—most——" And being at a loss for an epithet sufficiently injurious, he finished his expressions of horror by muttering, "Good heavens!" in a manner that had been found very efficacious in clerical meetings of the diocese. He must for the moment have forgotten where he was.

"As to his vulgarity, archdeacon" (Mrs. Grantly had never assumed a more familiar term than this in addressing her husband), "I don't agree with you. Not that I like Mr. Bold—he is a great deal too conceited for me; but then Eleanor does, and it would be the best thing in the world for papa if they were to marry. Bold would never trouble himself about Hiram's Hospital if he were papa's son-in-law." And the lady turned herself round under the bed-clothes, in a manner to which the doctor was well accustomed, and which told him, as plainly as words, that as far as she was concerned the subject was over for that night.

"Good heavens!" murmured the doctor again—he was evidently much put beside himself.

Dr. Grantly is by no means a bad man; he is exactly the man which such an education

as his was most likely to form; his intellect
being sufficient for such a place in the world,
but not sufficient to put him in advance of
it. He performs with a rigid constancy
such of the duties of a parish clergyman as
are, to his thinking, above the sphere of his
curate, but it is as an archdeacon that he
shines.

We believe, as a general rule, that either a
bishop or his archdeacons have sinecures:
where a bishop works, archdeacons have but
little to do, and *vice versâ*. In the diocese of
Barchester the Archdeacon of Barchester does
the work. In that capacity he is diligent,
authoritative, and, as his friends particularly
boast, judicious. His great fault is an overbear-
ing assurance of the virtues and claims of his
order, and his great foible is an equally strong
confidence in the dignity of his own manner
and the eloquence of his own words. He is
a moral man, believing the precepts which he
teaches, and believing also that he acts up to
them ; though we cannot say that he would
give his coat to the man who took his cloak,
or that he is prepared to forgive his brother
even seven times. He is severe enough in
exacting his dues, considering that any laxity
in this respect would endanger the security of
the church ; and, could he have his way, he
would consign to darkness and perdition, not
only every individual reformer, but every

committee and every commission that would
even dare to ask a question respecting the
appropriation of church revenues.

"They are church revenues: the laity
admit it. Surely the church is able to administer her own revenues." 'Twas thus he
was accustomed to argue, when the sacrilegious
doings of Lord John Russell and others were
discussed either at Barchester or at Oxford.

It was no wonder that Dr. Grantly did not
like John Bold, and that his wife's suggestion,
that he should become closely connected with
such a man dismayed him. To give him his
due, the archdeacon never wanted courage;
he was quite willing to meet his enemy on
any field, and with any weapon. He had
that belief in his own arguments that he felt
sure of success, could he only be sure of a
fair fight on the part of his adversary. He
had no idea that John Bold could really prove
that the income of the hospital was mal-
appropriated; why, then, should peace be
sought for on such base terms? What! bribe
an unbelieving enemy of the church with the
sister-in-law of one dignitary, and the daughter
of another—with a young lady whose con-
nections with the diocese and chapter of
Barchester were so close as to give her an
undeniable claim to a husband endowed with
some of its sacred wealth! When Dr. Grantly
talks of unbelieving enemies, he does not mean

to imply want of belief in the doctrines of the church, but an equally dangerous scepticism as to its purity in money matters.

Mrs. Grantly is not usually deaf to the claims of the high order to which she belongs. She and her husband rarely disagree as to the tone with which the church should be defended; how singular, then, that in such a case as this she should be willing to succumb! The archdeacon again murmurs "Good heavens!" as he lays himself beside her, but he does so in a voice audible only to himself, and he repeats it till sleep relieves him from deep thought.

Mr. Harding himself has seen no reason why his daughter should not love John Bold. He has not been unobservant of her feelings, and perhaps his deepest regret at the part which he fears Bold is about to take regarding the hospital, arises from a dread that he may be separated from his daughter, or that she may be separated from the man she loves. He has never spoken to Eleanor about her lover; he is the last man in the world to allude to such a subject unconsulted, even with his own daughter; and had he considered that he had ground to disapprove of Bold, he would have removed her, or forbidden him his house; but he saw no such ground. He would probably have preferred a second clerical son-in-law, for Mr. Harding, also, is attached

to his order; and, failing in that, he would
at any rate have wished that so near a connection should have thought alike with him
on church matters. He would not, however,
reject the man his daughter loved because he
differed on such subjects with himself.

Hitherto Bold had taken no steps in the
matter in any way annoying to Mr. Harding
personally. Some months since, after a severe
battle, which cost him not a little, he gained
a victory over a certain old turnpike woman
in the neighbourhood, of whose charges another
old woman had complained to him. He got
the act of Parliament relating to the trust,
found that his *protégée* had been wrongly taxed,
rode through the gate himself, paying the toll,
then brought an action against the gate-keeper,
and proved that all people coming up a certain
by-lane, and going down a certain other by-
lane, were toll-free. The fame of his success
spread widely abroad, and he began to be
looked on as the upholder of the rights of the
poor of Barchester. Not long after this success, he heard from different quarters that
Hiram's bedesmen were treated as paupers,
whereas the property to which they were, in
effect, heirs, was very large; and he was
instigated by the lawyer whom he had employed in the case of the turnpike, to call upon
Mr. Chadwick for a statement as to the funds
of the estate.

Bold had often expressed his indignation at the malappropriation of church funds in general, in the hearing of his friend the precentor; but the conversation had never referred to anything at Barchester; and when Finney, the attorney, induced him to interfere with the affairs of the hospital, it was against Mr. Chadwick that his efforts were to be directed. Bold soon found that if he interfered with Mr. Chadwick as steward, he must also interfere with Mr. Harding as warden; and though he regretted the situation in which this would place him, he was not the man to flinch from his undertaking from personal motives.

As soon as he had determined to take the matter in hand, he set about his work with his usual energy. He got a copy of John Hiram's will, of the wording of which he made himself perfectly master. He ascertained the extent of the property, and as nearly as he could the value of it; and made out a schedule of what he was informed was the present distribution of its income. Armed with these particulars, he called on Mr. Chadwick, having given that gentleman notice of his visit; and asked him for a statement of the income and expenditure of the hospital for the last twenty-five years.

This was of course refused, Mr. Chadwick alleging that he had no authority for making public the concerns of a property in managing which he was only a paid servant.

"And who is competent to give you that authority, Mr. Chadwick?" asked Bold.

"Only those who employ me, Mr. Bold," said the steward.

"And who are those, Mr. Chadwick?" demanded Bold.

Mr. Chadwick begged to say that if these inquiries were made merely out of curiosity, he must decline answering them: if Mr. Bold had any ulterior proceeding in view, perhaps it would be desirable that any necessary information should be sought for in a professional way by a professional man. Mr. Chadwick's attorneys were Messrs. Cox and Cummins, of Lincoln's Inn. Mr. Bold took down the address of Cox and Cummins, remarked that the weather was cold for the time of the year, and wished Mr. Chadwick good morning. Mr. Chadwick said it was cold for June, and bowed him out.

He at once went to his lawyer, Finney. Now, Bold was not very fond of his attorney, but, as he said, he merely wanted a man who knew the forms of law, and who would do what he was told for his money. He had no idea of putting himself in the hands of a lawyer. He wanted law from a lawyer as he did a coat from a tailor, because he could not make it so well himself; and he thought

Finney the fittest man in Barchester for his
purpose. In one respect, at any rate, he was
right: Finney was humility itself.

Finney advised an instant letter to Cox and
Cummins, mindful of his six-and-eightpence.
"Slap at them at once, Mr. Bold; demand
categorically and explicitly a full statement of
the affairs of the hospital."

"Suppose I were to see Mr. Harding first,"
suggested Bold.

"Yes, yes, by all means," said the acquies-
cing Finney; "though, perhaps, as Mr. Harding is no man of business, it may lead—lead
to some little difficulties; but perhaps you're
right, Mr. Bold—I don't think seeing Mr.
Harding can do any harm." Finney saw
from the expression of his client's face that he
intended to have his own way.

CHAPTER III

THE BISHOP OF BARCHESTER

BOLD at once repaired to the hospital. The day was now far advanced, but he knew that Mr. Harding dined in the summer at four, that Eleanor was accustomed to drive in the evening, and that he might therefore probably find Mr. Harding alone. It was between seven and eight when he reached the slight iron gate leading into the precentor's garden, and though, as Mr. Chadwick observed, the day had been cold for June, the evening was mild, and soft, and sweet. The little gate was open. As he raised the latch he heard the notes of Mr. Harding's violoncello from the far end of the garden, and, advancing before the house and across the lawn, he found him playing: and not without an audience. The musician was seated in a garden-chair just within the summer-house, so as to allow the violoncello which he held between his knees to rest upon the dry stone flooring; before him stood a rough music desk, on which was open a page of that dear sacred book, that much-laboured and much-loved volume of church music, which had cost so many guineas ; and around sat, and lay, and stood, and leaned, ten of the twelve old men who dwelt with him beneath old John Hiram's roof. The two reformers were not there. I will not say that in their hearts they were conscious of any wrong done or to be done to their mild warden, but latterly they had kept aloof from him, and his music was no longer to their taste.

It was amusing to see the positions, and eager listening faces of these well-to-do old men. I will not say that they all appreciated the music which they heard, but they were intent on appearing to do so ; pleased at being where they were, they were determined, as far as in them lay, to give pleasure in return ; and they were not unsuccessful. It gladdened the precentor's heart to think that the old bedesmen whom he loved so well, admired the strains which were to him so full of almost ecstatic joy ; and he used to boast that such was the air of the hospital, as to make it a precinct specially fit for the worship of St. Cecilia.

Immediately before him, on the extreme corner of the bench which ran round the summer-house, sat one old man, with his handkerchief smoothly lain upon his knees, who did enjoy the moment, or acted enjoyment

well.   He was one on whose large frame
many years, for he was over eighty, had made
small havock,—he was still an upright, burly,
handsome figure, with an open, ponderous
brow, round which clung a few, though
very few, thin grey locks. The coarse black
gown of the hospital, the breeches, and
buckled shoes became him well ; and as he
sat with his hands folded on his staff, and his
chin resting on his hands, he was such a
listener as most musicians would be glad to
welcome.

This man was certainly the pride of the
hospital. It had always been the custom that
one should be selected as being to some extent
in authority over the others ; and though Mr.
Bunce, for such was his name, and so he was
always designated by his inferior brethren,
had no greater emoluments than they, he had
assumed, and well knew how to maintain,
the dignity of his elevation. The precentor
delighted to call him his sub-warden, and was
not ashamed, occasionally, when no other
guest was there, to bid him sit down by the
same parlour fire, and drink the full glass of
port which was placed near him. Bunce never
went without the second glass, but no entreaty
ever made him take a third.

" Well, well, Mr. Harding ; you're too good,
much too good," he'd always say, as the second
glass was filled ; but when that was drunk,

and the half hour over, Bunce stood erect, and with a benediction which his patron valued, retired to his own abode. He knew the world too well to risk the comfort of such halcyon moments, by prolonging them till they were disagreeable.

Mr. Bunce, as may be imagined, was most strongly opposed to innovation. Not even Dr. Grantly had a more holy horror of those who would interfere in the affairs of the hospital; he was every inch a churchman, and though he was not very fond of Dr. Grantly personally, that arose from there not being room in the hospital for two people so much alike as the doctor and himself, rather than from any dissimilarity in feeling. Mr. Bunce was inclined to think that the warden and himself could manage the hospital without further assistance; and that, though the bishop was the constitutional visitor, and as such entitled to special reverence from all connected with John Hiram's will, John Hiram never intended that his affairs should be interfered with by an archdeacon.

At the present moment, however, these cares were off his mind, and he was looking at his warden, as though he thought the music heavenly, and the musician hardly less so.

As Bold walked silently over the lawn, Mr. Harding did not at first perceive him, and continued to draw his bow slowly across the plaintive wires; but he soon found from his audience that some stranger was there, and looking up, began to welcome his young friend with frank hospitality.

"Pray, Mr. Harding; pray don't let me disturb you," said Bold; "you know how fond I am of sacred music."

"Oh! it's nothing," said the precentor, shutting up the book and then opening it again as he saw the delightfully imploring look of his old friend Bunce. Oh, Bunce, Bunce, Bunce, I fear that after all thou art but a flatterer. "Well, I'll just finish it then; it's a favourite little bit of Bishop's; and then, Mr. Bold, we'll have a stroll and a chat till Eleanor comes in and gives us tea." And so Bold sat down on the soft turf to listen, or rather to think how, after such sweet harmony, he might best introduce a theme of so much discord, to disturb the peace of him who was so ready to welcome him kindly.

a voice out of nowhere, author's voice

Bold thought that the performance was soon over, for he felt that he had a somewhat difficult task, and he almost regretted the final leave-taking of the last of the old men, slow as they were in going through their adieus.

Bold's heart was in his mouth, as the precentor made some ordinary but kind remark as to the friendliness of the visit.

"One evening call," said he, "is worth ten in the morning. It's all formality in the morning; real social talk never begins till after dinner. That's why I dine early, so as to get as much as I can of it."

"Quite true, Mr. Harding," said the other; "but I fear I've reversed the order of things, and I owe you much apology for troubling you on business at such an hour; but it is on business that I have called just now."

Mr. Harding looked blank and annoyed; there was something in the tone of the young man's voice, which told him that the interview was intended to be disagreeable, and he shrank back at finding his kindly greeting so repulsed.

"I wish to speak to you about the hospital," continued Bold.

"Well, well, anything I can tell you I shall be most happy——"

"It's about the accounts."

"Then, my dear fellow, I can tell you nothing, for I'm as ignorant as a child. All I know is, that they pay me 800*l.* a year. Go to Chadwick, he knows all about the accounts; and now tell me, will poor Mary Jones ever get the use of her limb again?"

"Well, I think she will, if she's careful; but, Mr. Harding, I hope you won't object to discuss with me what I have to say about the hospital."

Mr. Harding gave a deep, long-drawn sigh. He did object, very strongly object, to discuss any such subject with John Bold; but he had not the business tact of Mr. Chadwick, and did not know how to relieve himself from the coming evil; he sighed sadly, but made no answer.

"I have the greatest regard for you, Mr. Harding," continued Bold; "the truest respect, the most sincere——"

"Thank ye, thank ye, Mr. Bold," interjaculated the precentor somewhat impatiently; "I'm much obliged, but never mind that; I'm as likely to be in the wrong as another man—quite as likely."

"But, Mr. Harding, I must express what I feel, lest you should think there is personal enmity in what I'm going to do."

"Personal enmity! Going to do! Why, you're not going to cut my throat, nor put me into the Ecclesiastical Court——"

Bold tried to laugh, but he couldn't. He was quite in earnest, and determined in his course, and couldn't make a joke of it. He walked on awhile in silence before he recommenced his attack, during which Mr. Harding, who had still the bow in his hand, played rapidly on an imaginary violoncello. "I fear there is reason to think that John Hiram's will is not carried out to the letter, Mr. Harding," said the young man at last; "and I have been asked to see into it."

"Very well, I've no objection on earth; and now we need not say another word about it."

"Only one word more, Mr. Harding. Chadwick has referred me to Cox and Cummins, and I think it my duty to apply to them for some statement about the hospital. In what I do I may appear to be interfering with you, and I hope you will forgive me for doing so."

"Mr. Bold," said the other, stopping, and speaking with some solemnity, "if you act justly, say nothing in this matter but the truth, and use no unfair weapons in carrying out your purposes, I shall have nothing to forgive. I presume you think I am not entitled to the income I receive from the hospital, and that others are entitled to it. Whatever some may do, I shall never attribute to you base motives because you hold an opinion opposed to my own, and adverse to my interests : pray do what you consider to be your duty; I can give you no assistance, neither will I offer you any obstacle. Let me, however, suggest to you, that you can in no wise forward your views nor I mine, by any discussion between us. Here comes Eleanor and the ponies, and we'll go in to tea."

Bold, however, felt that he could not sit down at ease with Mr. Harding and his daughter after what had passed, and therefore excused himself with much awkward apology ; and merely raising his hat and bowing as he passed Eleanor and the pony chair, left her in disappointed amazement at his departure.

Mr. Harding's demeanour certainly impressed Bold with a full conviction, that the warden felt that he stood on strong grounds, and almost made him think that he was about to interfere without due warrant in the private affairs of a just and honourable man; but Mr. Harding himself was anything but satisfied with his own view of the case.

In the first place, he wished for Eleanor's sake to think well of Bold and to like him, and yet he could not but feel disgusted at the arrogance of his conduct. What right had he to say that John Hiram's will was not fairly carried out? But then the question would arise within his heart, Was that will fairly acted on? Did John Hiram mean that the warden of his hospital should receive considerably more out of the legacy than all the twelve old men together for whose behoof the hospital was built? Could it be possible that John Bold was right, and that the reverend warden of the hospital had been for the last ten years and more the unjust recipient of an income legally and equitably belonging to others? What if it should be proved before the light of day that he, whose life had been so happy, so quiet, so respected, had absorbed 8000*l.* to which he had no title, and which he could never repay? I do not say that he

feared that such was really the case ; but the
first shade of doubt now fell across his mind,
and from this evening, for many a long, long
day, our good, kind, loving warden was neither
happy nor at ease.

Thoughts of this kind, these first moments
of much misery, oppressed Mr. Harding as he
sat sipping his tea, absent and ill at ease. Poor
Eleanor felt that all was not right, but her
ideas as to the cause of the evening's dis-
comfort did not go beyond her lover, and his
sudden and uncivil departure : she thought
there must have been some quarrel between
Bold and her father, and she was half angry
with both, though she did not attempt to
explain to herself why she was so.

Mr. Harding thought long and deeply over
these things, both before he went to bed, and
after it, as he lay awake, questioning within
himself the validity of his claim to the income
which he enjoyed. It seemed clear at any
rate that, however unfortunate he might be
at having been placed in such a position, no
one could say that he ought either to have
refused the appointment first, or to have
rejected the income afterwards. All the
world—meaning the ecclesiastical world as
confined to the English church—knew that
the wardenship of the Barchester Hospital
was a snug sinecure, but no one had ever
been blamed for accepting it. To how much

blame, however, would he have been open
had he rejected it! How mad would he
have been thought had he declared, when the
situation was vacant and offered to him, that
he had scruples as to receiving 800*l.* a year from
John Hiram's property, and that he had rather
some stranger should possess it! How would
Dr. Grantly have shaken his wise head, and
have consulted with his friends in the close as
to some decent retreat for the coming insanity
of the poor minor canon! If he was right in
accepting the place, it was clear to him also
that he would be wrong in rejecting any part
of the income attached to it. The patronage
was a valuable appanage of the bishopric; and
surely it would not be his duty to lessen the
value of that preferment which had been
bestowed on himself; surely he was bound to
stand by his order.

But somehow these arguments, though they
seemed logical, were not satisfactory. Was
John Hiram's will fairly carried out? that
was the true question; and if not, was
it not his especial duty to see that this was
done,—his especial duty, whatever injury it
might do to his order,—however ill such duty
might be received by his patron and his
friends? At the idea of his friends, his mind
turned unhappily to his son-in-law: he knew
well how strongly he would be supported by
Dr. Grantly, if he could bring himself to put

his case into the archdeacon's hands, and to allow him to fight the battle; but he knew also that he would find no sympathy there for his doubts, no friendly feeling, no inward comfort. Dr. Grantly would be ready enough to take up his cudgel against all comers on behalf of the church militant, but he would do so on the distasteful ground of the church's infallibility. Such a contest would give no comfort to Mr. Harding's doubts; he was not so anxious to prove himself right, as to be so.

I have said before that Dr. Grantly was the working man of the diocese, and that his father the bishop was somewhat inclined to an idle life: so it was; but the bishop, though he had never been an active man, was one whose qualities had rendered him dear to all who knew him. He was the very opposite to his son; he was a bland and a kind old man, opposed by every feeling to authoritative demonstrations and episcopal ostentation. It was perhaps well for him, in his situation, that his son had early in life been able to do that which he could not well do when he was younger, and which he could not have done at all now that he was over seventy. The bishop knew how to entertain the clergy of his diocese, to talk easy small talk with the rectors' wives, and put curates at their ease; but it required the strong hand of

the archdeacon to deal with such as were refractory either in their doctrines or their lives.

The bishop and Mr. Harding loved each
other warmly. They had grown old together,
and had together spent many, many years
in clerical pursuits and clerical conversation.
When one of them was a bishop and the other
only a minor canon they were even then
much together; but since their children had
married, and Mr. Harding had become warden
and precentor, they were all in all to each
other. I will not say that they managed the
diocese between them, but they spent much
time in discussing the man who did, and in
forming little plans to mitigate his wrath
against church delinquents, and soften his
aspirations for church dominion.

Mr. Harding determined to open his mind,
and confess his doubts to his old friend; and
to him he went on the morning after John
Bold's uncourteous visit.

Up to this period no rumour of these cruel
proceedings against the hospital had reached
the bishop's ears. He had doubtless heard
that men existed who questioned his right to
present to a sinecure of 800*l.* a year, as he
had heard from time to time of some special
immorality or disgraceful disturbance in the
usually decent and quiet city of Barchester:
but all he did, and all he was called on to do,
on such occasions, was to shake his head, and

to beg his son, the great dictator, to see that no harm happened to the church.

It was a long story that Mr. Harding had to tell before he made the bishop comprehend his own view of the case; but we need not follow him through the tale. At first the bishop counselled but one step, recommended but one remedy, had but one medicine in his whole pharmacopœia strong enough to touch so grave a disorder—he prescribed the archdeacon. "Refer him to the archdeacon," he repeated, as Mr. Harding spoke of Bold and his visit. "The archdeacon will set you quite right about that," he kindly said, when his friend spoke with hesitation of the justness of his cause. "No man has got up all that so well as the archdeacon"; but the dose, though large, failed to quiet the patient; indeed it almost produced nausea.

"But, bishop," said he, "did you ever read John Hiram's will?"

The bishop thought probably he had, thirty-five years ago, when first instituted to his see, but could not state positively: however, he very well knew that he had the absolute right to present to the wardenship, and that the income of the warden had been regularly settled.

"But, bishop, the question is, who has the power to settle it? If, as this young man says, the will provides that the proceeds of the property are to be divided into shares, who has the power to alter these provisions?" The bishop had an indistinct idea that they altered themselves by the lapse of years : that a kind of ecclesiastical statute of limitation barred the rights of the twelve bedesmen to any increase of income arising from the increased value of property. He said something about tradition ; more of the many learned men who by their practice had confirmed the present arrangement ; then went at some length into the propriety of maintaining the due difference in rank and income between a beneficed clergyman, and certain poor old men who were dependent on charity ; and concluded his argument by another reference to the archdeacon.

The precentor sat thoughtfully gazing at the fire, and listening to the good-natured reasoning of his friend. What the bishop said had a sort of comfort in it, but it was not a sustaining comfort. It made Mr. Harding feel that many others—indeed, all others of his own order—would think him right ; but it failed to prove to him that he truly was so.

" Bishop," said he, at last, after both had sat silent for a while, " I should deceive you and myself too, if I did not tell you that I am very unhappy about this. Suppose that I cannot bring myself to agree with Dr. Grantly !—that I find, after inquiry, that the

young man is right, and that I am wrong—
what then ? "

The two men were sitting near each other
—so near that the bishop was able to lay his
hand upon the other's knee, and he did so
with a gentle pressure. Mr. Harding well
knew what that pressure meant. The bishop
had no further argument to adduce ; he could
not fight for the cause as his son would do ;
he could not prove all the precentor's doubts
to be groundless ; but he could sympathise
with his friend, and he did so ; and Mr. Harding
felt that he had received that for which he
came. There was another period of silence,
after which, the bishop asked with a degree
of irritable energy, very unusual with him,
whether this " pestilent intruder " (meaning John
Bold) had any friends in Barchester.

Mr. Harding had fully made up his mind
to tell the bishop everything ; to speak of his
daughter's love, as well as his own troubles ;
to talk of John Bold in his double capacity
of future son-in-law and present enemy ; and
though he felt it to be sufficiently disagreeable,
now was his time to do it.

" He is very intimate at my own house,
bishop." The bishop stared ; he was not so
far gone in orthodoxy and church-militancy
as his son, but still he could not bring himself
to understand how so declared an enemy of
the establishment could be admitted on terms

of intimacy into the house, not only of so firm a pillar as Mr. Harding, but one so much injured as the warden of the hospital.

"Indeed, I like Mr. Bold much, personally," continued the disinterested victim; "and to tell you the 'truth,'"—he hesitated as he brought out the dreadful tidings,—"I have sometimes thought it not improbable that he would be my second son-in-law." The bishop did not whistle; we believe that they lose the power of doing so on being consecrated; and that in these days one might as easily meet a corrupt judge as a whistling bishop; but he looked as though he would have done so, but for his apron.

What a brother-in-law for the archdeacon! what an alliance for Barchester close! what a connection for even the episcopal palace! The bishop, in his simple mind, felt no doubt that John Bold, had he so much power, would shut up all cathedrals, and probably all parish churches; distribute all tithes among Methodists, Baptists, and other savage tribes; utterly annihilate the sacred bench, and make shovel hats and lawn sleeves as illegal as cowls, sandals, and sackcloth! Here was a nice man to be initiated into the comfortable arcana of ecclesiastical snuggeries; one who doubted the integrity of parsons, and probably disbelieved the Trinity!

Mr. Harding saw what an effect his communication had made, and almost repented the openness of his disclosure ; he, however, did what he could to moderate the grief of his friend and patron. " I did not say that there is any engagement between them. Had there been, Eleanor would have told me : I know her well enough to be assured that she would have done so ; but I see that they are fond of each other ; and as a man and a father, I have had no objection to urge against their intimacy."

" But, Mr. Harding," said the bishop, " how are you to oppose him, if he is your son-in-law ? "

" I don't mean to oppose him ; it is he who opposes me : if anything is to be done in defence, I suppose Chadwick will do it. I suppose——"

" Oh, the archdeacon will see to that : were the young man twice his brother-in-law, the archdeacon will never be deterred from doing what he feels to be right."

Mr. Harding reminded the bishop that the archdeacon and the reformer were not yet brothers, and very probably never would be ; exacted from him a promise that Eleanor's name should not be mentioned in any discussion between the father bishop and son archdeacon respecting the hospital ; and then took his departure, leaving his poor old friend bewildered, amazed, and confounded.

CHAPTER IV

HIRAM'S BEDESMEN

THE parties most interested in the movement which is about to set Barchester by the ears, were not the foremost to discuss the merit of the question, as is often the case; but when the bishop, the archdeacon, the warden, the steward, and Messrs. Cox and Cummins, were all busy with the matter, each in his own way, it is not to be supposed that Hiram's bedesmen themselves were altogether passive spectators. Finney, the attorney, had been among them, asking sly questions, and raising immoderate hopes, creating a party hostile to the warden, and establishing a corps in the enemy's camp, as he figuratively calls it to himself. Poor old men; whoever may be righted or wronged by this inquiry, they at any rate will assuredly be only injured; to them it can only be an unmixed evil. How can their lot be improved? all their wants are supplied; every comfort is administered; they have warm houses, good clothes, plentiful diet, and rest after a life of labour; and above all, that treasure so inestimable in declining years, a true and kind friend to listen to their sorrows, watch over their sickness, and ad-

minister comfort as regards this world, and
the world to come!

John Bold sometimes thinks of this, when he
is talking loudly of the rights of the bedesmen, whom he has taken under his protection ;
but he quiets the suggestion within his breast
with the high-sounding name of justice—" fiat
justitia ruat cœlum." These old men should,
by rights, have one hundred pounds a year
instead of one shilling and sixpence a day,
and the warden should have two hundred
or three hundred pounds instead of eight
hundred pounds. What is unjust must be
wrong; what is wrong should be righted ;
and if he declined the task, who else would
do it?

" Each one of you is clearly entitled to one
hundred pounds a year by common law : " such
had been the important whisper made by
Finney into the ears of Abel Handy, and by
him retailed to his eleven brethren.

Too much must not be expected from the
flesh and blood even of John Hiram's bedesmen, and the positive promise of one hundred
a year to each of the twelve old men, had its
way with most of them. The great Bunce
was not to be wiled away, and was upheld
in his orthodoxy by two adherents. Abel
Handy, who was the leader of the aspirants
after wealth, had, alas, a stronger following.
No less than five of the twelve soon believed

that his views were just, making with their leader a moiety of the hospital. The other three, volatile unstable minds, vacillated between the two chieftains, now led away by the hope of gold, now anxious to propitiate the powers that still existed.

It had been proposed to address a petition to the bishop as visitor, praying his lordship to see justice done to the legal recipients of John Hiram's Charity, and to send copies of this petition and of the reply it would elicit to all the leading London papers, and thereby to obtain notoriety for the subject. This it was thought would pave the way for ulterior legal proceedings. It would have been a great thing to have had the signatures and marks of all the twelve injured legatees ; but this was impossible : Bunce would have cut his hand off sooner than have signed it. It was then suggested by Finney that if even eleven could be induced to sanction the document, the one obstinate recusant might have been represented as unfit to judge on such a question,—in fact, as being *non compos mentis*,—and the petition would have been taken as representing the feeling of the men. But this could not be done : Bunce's friends were as firm as himself, and as yet only six crosses adorned the document. It was the more provoking, as Bunce himself could write his name legibly, and one of those three doubting

souls had for years boasted of like power, and
possessed, indeed, a Bible, in which he was
proud to show his name written by himself
some thirty years ago—"Job Skulpit"; but
it was thought that Job Skulpit, having forgotten his scholarship, on that account recoiled
from the petition, and that the other doubters
would follow as he led them. A petition
signed by half the hospital would have but
a poor effect.

It was in Skulpit's room that the petition
was now lying, waiting such additional signatures as Abel Handy, by his eloquence, could
obtain for it. The six marks it bore were
duly attested, thus :—

his
Abel + Handy,   Greg' + Moody,
mark   mark

his
Mathew + Spriggs,
mark

&c., and places were duly designated in pencil
for those brethren who were now expected to
join : for Skulpit alone was left a spot on which
his genuine signature might be written in
fair clerklike style. Handy had brought in the
document, and spread it out on the small deal
table, and was now standing by it persuasive
and eager. Moody had followed with an
inkhorn, carefully left behind by Finney ; and
Spriggs bore aloft, as though it were a sword,

a well-worn ink-black pen, which from time to time he endeavoured to thrust into Skulpit's unwilling hand.

With the learned man were his two abettors in indecision, William Gazy and Jonathan Crumple. If ever the petition were to be forwarded, now was the time, so said Mr. Finney; and great was the anxiety on the part of those whose one hundred pounds a year, as they believed, mainly depended on the document in question.

"To be kept out of all that money," as the avaricious Moody had muttered to his friend Handy, "by an old fool saying that he can write his own name like his betters."

"Well, Job," said Handy, trying to impart to his own sour, ill-omened visage a smile of approbation, in which he greatly failed; "so you're ready now, Mr. Finney says; here's the place, d'ye see,"—and he put his huge brown finger down on the dirty paper,— "name or mark, it's all one. Come along, old boy; if so be we're to have the spending of this money, why the sooner the better— that's my maxim."

"To be sure," said Moody; "we a'n't none of us so young: we can't stay waiting for old Catgut no longer."

It was thus these miscreants named our excellent friend; the nickname he could easily

have forgiven, but the allusion to the divine
source of all his melodious joy would have
irritated even him. Let us hope he never
knew the insult.

"Only think, old Billy Gazy," said Spriggs,
who rejoiced in greater youth than his brethren,
but having fallen into a fire when drunk,
had had one eye burnt out, one cheek burnt
through, and one arm nearly burnt off, and
who, therefore, in regard to personal appearance, was not the most prepossessing of men;
"a hundred a year, and all to spend: only
think, old Billy Gazy;" and he gave a hideous
grin that showed off his misfortunes to their
full extent.

Old Billy Gazy was not alive to much
enthusiasm—even these golden prospects did
not arouse him to do more than rub his poor
old bleared eyes with the cuff of his bedesman's gown, and gently mutter: "he didn't
know, not he; he didn't know."

"But you'd know, Jonathan," continued
Spriggs, turning to the other friend of Skulpit's, who was sitting on a stool by the table,
gazing vacantly at the petition. Jonathan
Crumple was a meek, mild man, who had
known better days; his means had been
wasted by bad children, who had made his
life wretched till he had been received into
the hospital, of which he had not long been
a member. Since that day he had known

neither sorrow nor trouble, and this attempt to fill him with new hopes was, indeed, a cruelty.

"A hundred a year's a nice thing, for sartain, neighbour Spriggs," said he: "I once had nigh to that myself, but it didn't do me no good." And he gave a low sigh, as he thought of the children of his own loins who had robbed him.

"And shall have again, Joe," said Handy; "and will have some one to keep it right and tight for you this time."

Crumple sighed again—he had learned the impotency of worldly wealth, and would have been satisfied, if left untempted, to have remained happy with one and sixpence a day.

"Come, Skulpit," repeated Handy, getting impatient, "you're not going to go along with old Bunce in helping that parson to rob us all. Take the pen, man, and right yourself. Well," he added, seeing that Skulpit still doubted, "to see a man as is afraid to stand by hisself, is, to my thinking, the meanest thing as is."

"Sink them all for parsons, says I," growled Moody; "hungry beggars, as never thinks their bellies full till they have robbed all and everything."

"Who's to harm you, man?" argued Spriggs: "let them look never so black at you, they can't get you put out when you're once in— no, not old Catgut, with Calves to help him!"

I am sorry to say the archdeacon himself was designated by this scurrilous allusion to his nether person.

"A hundred a year to win, and nothing to lose," continued Handy, "my eyes!—Well, how a man's to doubt about such a bit of cheese as that passes me—but some men is timorous— some men is born with no pluck in them—some men is cowed at the very first sight of a gen'le- man's coat and waistcoat."

Oh, Mr. Harding, if you had but taken the archdeacon's advice in that disputed case, when Joe Mutters was this ungrateful demagogue's rival candidate!

"Afraid of a parson," growled Moody, with a look of ineffable scorn; "I tell ye what I'd be afraid of—I'd be afraid of not getting nothing from 'em but just what I could take by might and right—that's the most I'd be afraid on of any parson of 'em all."

"But," said Skulpit, apologetically, "Mr. Harding's not so bad—he did give us twopence a day, didn't he now?"

"Twopence a day!" exclaimed Spriggs with scorn, opening awfully the red cavern of his lost eye.

"Twopence a day!" muttered Moody with a curse; "sink his twopence!"

"Twopence a day!" exclaimed Handy; "and I'm to go, hat in hand, and thank a chap for twopence a day, when he owes me a hundred

pounds a year: no, thank ye; that may do
for you, but it won't for me. Come, I say,
Skulpit, are you a going to put your mark to
this here paper, or are you not?"

Skulpit looked round in wretched indecision
to his two friends. "What d'ye think, Bill
Gazy?" said he.

But Billy Gazy couldn't think: he made
a noise like the bleating of an old sheep,
which was intended to express the agony of his
doubt, and again muttered that "he didn't
know."

"Take hold, you old cripple," said Handy,
thrusting the pen into poor Billy's hand: "there,
so—ugh! you old fool, you've been and
smeared it all—there—that'll do for you,—
that's as good as the best name as ever was
written:" and a big blotch of ink was presumed
to represent Billy Gazy's acquiescence.

"Now, Jonathan," said Handy, turning to
Crumple.

"A hundred a year's a nice thing, for sartain,"
again argued Crumple. "Well, neighbour
Skulpit, how's it to be?"

"Oh, please yourself," said Skulpit: "please
yourself, and you'll please me."

The pen was thrust into Crumple's hand,
and a faint, wandering, meaningless sign was
made, betokening such sanction and authority
as Jonathan Crumple was able to convey.

"Come, Joe," said Handy, softened by

success, "don't let 'em have to say that old
Bunce has a man like you under his thumb—
a man that always holds his head in the
hospital as high as Bunce himself, though
you're never axed to drink wine, and sneak,
and tell lies about your betters, as he does."

Skulpit held the pen, and made little flourishes
with it in the air, but still hesitated.

"And if you'll be said by me," continued
Handy, "you'll not write your name to it at
all, but just put your mark like the others,"—
the cloud began to clear from Skulpit's brow :—
"we all know you can do it if you like, but
maybe you wouldn't like to seem uppish,
you know."

"Well, the mark would be best," said Skulpit :
"one name and the rest marks, wouldn't look
well, would it ?"

"The worst in the world," said Handy ;
"there—there :" and stooping over the petition,
the learned clerk made a huge cross on the
place left for his signature.

"That's the game," said Handy, triumphantly
pocketing the petition ; "we're all in a boat
now, that is, the nine of us ; and as for old
Bunce, and his cronies, they may——" But
as he was hobbling off to the door, with a
crutch on one side and a stick on the other,
he was met by Bunce himself.

"Well, Handy, and what may old Bunce
do ?" said the grey-haired, upright senior.

Handy muttered something, and was departing; but he was stopped in the doorway by the huge frame of the new comer.

"You've been doing no good here, Abel Handy," said he, "'tis plain to see that; and 'tisn't much good, I'm thinking, you ever do."

"I mind my own business, Master Bunce," muttered the other, "and do you do the same. It a'n't nothing to you what I does—and your spying and poking here won't do no good nor yet no harm."

"I suppose then, Joe," continued Bunce, not noticing his opponent, "if the truth must out, you've stuck your name to that petition of theirs at last."

Skulpit looked as though he were about to sink into nothing with shame.

"What is it to you what he signs?" said Handy. "I suppose if we all wants to ax for our own, we needn't ax leave of you first, Mr. Bunce, big a man as you are: and as to your sneaking in here, into Job's room when he's busy, and where you're not wanted——"

"I've knowed Job Skulpit, man and boy, sixty years," said Bunce, looking at the man of whom he spoke, "and that's ever since the day he was born. I knowed the mother that bore him, when she and I were little wee things, picking daisies together in the close yonder;

and I've lived under the same roof with
him more nor ten years ; and after that I may
come into his room without axing leave, and
yet no sneaking neither."

"So you can, Mr. Bunce," said Skulpit ;
"so you can, any hour, day or night."

"And I'm free also to tell him my mind,"
continued Bunce, looking at the one man and
addressing the other ; "and I'll tell him now
that he's done a foolish and a wrong thing :
he's turned his back upon one who is his best
friend ; and is playing the game of others,
who care nothing for him, whether he be
poor or rich, well or ill, alive or dead. A
hundred a year? Are the lot of you soft
enough to think that if a hundred a year be
to be given, it's the likes of you that will get
it ? "—and he pointed to Billy Gazy, Spriggs,
and Crumple. "Did any of us ever do anything worth half the money? Was it to
make gentlemen of us we were brought in
here, when all the world turned against us,
and we couldn't longer earn our daily bread ?
A'n't you all as rich in your ways as he in
his ? "—and the orator pointed to the side
on which the warden lived. "A'n't you
getting all you hoped for, ay, and more than
you hoped for ? Wouldn't each of you
have given the dearest limb of his body to
secure that which now makes you so un-
thankful ? "

"We wants what John Hiram left us," said Handy; "we wants what's ourn by law; it don't matter what we expected; what's ourn by law should be ourn, and by goles we'll have it."

"Law!" said Bunce, with all the scorn he knew how to command,—"law! Did ye ever know a poor man yet was the better for law, or for a lawyer? Will Mr. Finney ever be as good to you, Job, as that man has been? Will he see to you when you're sick, and comfort you when you're wretched? Will he——"

"No, nor give you port wine, old boy, on cold winter nights! he won't do that, will he?" asked Handy: and laughing at the severity of his own wit, he and his colleagues retired, carrying with them, however, the now powerful petition.

There is no help for spilt milk; and Mr. Bunce could only retire to his own room, disgusted at the frailty of human nature—Job Skulpit scratched his head—Jonathan Crumple again remarked, that, "for sartain, sure a hundred a year was very nice"—and Billy Gazy again rubbed his eyes, and lowly muttered that "he didn't know."

CHAPTER V

DR. GRANTLY VISITS THE HOSPITAL

THOUGH doubt and hesitation disturbed the rest of our poor warden, no such weakness perplexed the nobler breast of his son-in-law. As the indomitable cock preparing for the combat sharpens his spurs, shakes his feathers, and erects his comb, so did the archdeacon arrange his weapons for the coming war, without misgiving and without fear. That he was fully confident of the justice of his cause let no one doubt. Many a man can fight his battle with good courage, but with a doubting conscience; such was not the case with Dr. Grantly. He did not believe in the Gospel with more assurance than he did in the sacred justice of all ecclesiastical revenues. When he put his shoulder to the wheel to defend the income of the present and future precentors of Barchester, he was animated by as strong a sense of a holy cause, as that which gives courage to a missionary in Africa, or enables a sister of mercy to give up the pleasures of the world for the wards of a hospital. He was about to defend the holy of holies from the touch of the profane; to guard the citadel of his church from the most

rampant of its enemies ; to put on his good
armour in the best of fights ; and secure, if
possible, the comforts of his creed for coming
generations of ecclesiastical dignitaries. Such
a work required no ordinary vigour ; and the
archdeacon was, therefore, extraordinarily vig-
orous : it demanded a buoyant courage, and a
heart happy in its toil ; and the archdeacon's
heart was happy, and his courage was buoyant.

He knew that he would not be able to
animate his father-in-law with feelings like
his own, but this did not much disturb him.
He preferred to bear the brunt of the battle
alone, and did not doubt that the warden
would resign himself into his hands with
passive submission.

"Well, Mr. Chadwick," he said, walking
into the steward's office a day or two after
the signing of the petition as commemorated
in the last chapter ; " anything from Cox and
Cummins this morning ? " Mr. Chadwick
handed him a letter ; which he read, stroking
the tight-gaitered calf of his right leg as he
did so. Messrs. Cox and Cummins merely
said that they had as yet received no notice
from their adversaries ; that they could re-
commend no preliminary steps ; but that
should any proceeding really be taken by the
bedesmen, it would be expedient to consult
that very eminent Queen's Counsel, Sir Abraham
Haphazard.

" I quite agree with them," said Dr. Grantly, refolding the letter. " I perfectly agree with them. Haphazard is no doubt the best man ; a thorough churchman, a sound conservative, and in every respect the best man we could get—he's in the house, too, which is a great thing."

Mr. Chadwick quite agreed.

" You remember how completely he put down that scoundrel Horsman about the Bishop of Beverley's income ; how completely he set them all adrift in the earl's case." Since the question of St. Cross had been mooted by the public, one noble lord had become " *the earl*," *par excellence*, in the doctor's estimation. " How he silenced that fellow at Rochester. Of course we must have Haphazard ; and I'll tell you what, Mr. Chadwick, we must take care to be in time, or the other party will forestall us."

With all his admiration for Sir Abraham, the doctor seemed to think it not impossible that that great man might be induced to lend his gigantic powers to the side of the church's enemies.

Having settled this point to his satisfaction, the doctor stepped down to the hospital, to learn how matters were going on there ; and as he walked across the hallowed close, and looked up at the ravens who cawed with a peculiar reverence as he wended his way, he thought with increased acerbity of those whose impiety would venture to disturb the goodly grace of cathedral institutions.

And who has not felt the same? We believe that Mr. Horsman himself would relent, and the spirit of Sir Benjamin Hall give way, were those great reformers to allow themselves to stroll by moonlight round the towers of some of our ancient churches. Who would not feel charity for a prebendary, when walking the quiet length of that long aisle at Winchester, looking at those decent houses, that trim grassplat, and feeling, as one must, the solemn, orderly comfort of the spot! Who could be hard upon a dean while wandering round the sweet close of Hereford, and owning that in that precinct, tone and colour, design and form, solemn tower and storied window, are all in unison, and all perfect! Who could lie basking in the cloisters of Salisbury, and gaze on Jewel's library, and that unequalled spire, without feeling that bishops should some-times be rich!

The tone of our archdeacon's mind must not astonish us; it has been the growth of centuries of church ascendency; and though some fungi now disfigure the tree, though there be much dead wood, for how much good fruit have not we to be thankful? Who, without remorse, can batter down the dead branches of an old oak, now useless, but, ah! still so beautiful, or drag out the fragments of the ancient forest, without feeling that they sheltered the younger plants, to which they are now summoned to give way in a tone so peremptory and so harsh?

The archdeacon, with all his virtues, was not a man of delicate feeling; and after having made his morning salutations in the warden's drawing-room, he did not scruple to commence an attack on "pestilent" John Bold in the presence of Miss Harding, though he rightly guessed that that lady was not indifferent to the name of his enemy.

"Nelly, my dear, fetch me my spectacles from the back room," said her father, anxious to save both her blushes and her feelings.

Eleanor brought the spectacles, while her father was trying, in ambiguous phrases, to explain to her too-practical brother-in-law that it might be as well not to say anything about Bold before her, and then retreated. Nothing had been explained to her about Bold and the hospital; but, with a woman's instinct, she knew that things were going wrong.

"We must soon be doing something," commenced the archdeacon, wiping his brows with a large, bright-coloured handkerchief, for he had felt busy, and had walked quick, and it was a broiling summer's day. "Of course you have heard of the petition?"

Mr. Harding owned, somewhat unwillingly, that he had heard of it.

"Well,"—the archdeacon looked for some expressions of opinion, but none coming, he continued,—"We must be doing something, you know ; we mustn't allow these people to cut the ground from under us while we sit looking on." The archdeacon, who was a practical man, allowed himself the use of every-day expressive modes of speech when among his closest intimates, though no one could soar into a more intricate labyrinth of refined phraseology when the church was the subject and his lower brethren were his auditors.

The warden still looked mutely in his face, making the slightest possible passes with an imaginary fiddle bow, and stopping, as he did so, sundry imaginary strings with the fingers of his other hand. 'Twas his constant consolation in conversational troubles. While these vexed him sorely, the passes would be short and slow, and the upper hand would not be seen to work ; nay the strings on which it operated would sometimes lie concealed in the musician's pocket, and the instrument on which he played would be beneath his chair ; but as his spirit warmed to the subject, —as his trusting heart, looking to the bottom of that which vexed him, would see its clear way out,—he would rise to a higher melody, sweep the unseen strings with a bolder hand,

and swiftly fingering the cords from his neck, down along his waistcoat, and up again to his very ear, create an ecstatic strain of perfect music, audible to himself and to St. Cecilia, and not without effect.

"I quite agree with Cox and Cummins," continued the archdeacon: "they say we must secure Sir Abraham Haphazard. I shall not have the slightest fear in leaving the case in Sir Abraham's hands."

The warden played the slowest and saddest of tunes: it was but a dirge on one string.

"I think Sir Abraham will not be long in letting Master Bold know what he's about. I fancy I hear Sir Abraham cross-questioning him at the Common Pleas."

The warden thought of his income being thus discussed, his modest life, his daily habits, and his easy work; and nothing issued from that single cord, but a low wail of sorrow. "I suppose they've sent this petition up to my father." The warden didn't know; he imagined they would do so this very day.

"What I can't understand is, how you let them do it, with such a command as you have in the place, or should have with such a man as Bunce; I cannot understand why you let them do it."

"Do what?" asked the warden.

"Why, listen to this fellow Bold, and that other low pettifogger, Finney—and get up this petition too: why didn't you tell Bunce to destroy the petition?"

"That would have been hardly wise," said the warden.

"Wise—yes, it would have been very wise if they'd done it among themselves. I must go up to the palace and answer it now, I suppose; it's a very short answer they'll get, I can tell you."

"But why shouldn't they petition, doctor?"

"Why shouldn't they!" responded the archdeacon, in a loud brazen voice, as though all the men in the hospital were expected to hear him through the walls; "why shouldn't they! I'll let them know why they shouldn't: by-the-by, warden, I'd like to say a few words to them all together."

The warden's mind misgave him, and even for a moment he forgot to play. He by no means wished to delegate to his son-in-law his place and authority of warden; he had expressly determined not to interfere in any step which the men might wish to take in the matter under dispute; he was most anxious neither to accuse them nor to defend himself. All these things he was aware the archdeacon would do in his behalf, and that not in the mildest manner; and yet he knew not how to refuse the permission requested.

"I'd so much sooner remain quiet in the matter," said he, in an apologetic voice.

"Quiet!" said the archdeacon, still speaking with his brazen trumpet; "do you wish to be ruined in quiet?"

"Why, if I am to be ruined, certainly."

"Nonsense, warden; I tell you something must be done—we must act; just let me ring the bell, and send the men word that I'll speak to them in the quad."

Mr. Harding knew not how to resist, and the disagreeable order was given. The quad, as it was familiarly called, was a small quadrangle, open on one side to the river, and surrounded on the others by the high wall of Mr. Harding's garden, by one gable end of Mr. Harding's house, and by the end of the row of buildings which formed the residences of the bedesmen. It was flagged all round, and the centre was stoned; small stone gutters ran from the four corners of the square to a grating in the centre; and attached to the end of Mr. Harding's house was a conduit with four cocks covered over from the weather, at which the old men got their water, and very generally performed their morning toilet. It was a quiet, sombre place, shaded over by the trees of the warden's garden. On the side towards the river, there stood a row of stone seats, on which the old men would sit and gaze at the little fish, as they flitted by in the running stream. On the other side of the river was a rich, green meadow, running up to and joining the deanery, and as little open to the public as the garden of the dean itself. Nothing, therefore, could be more private than the quad of the hospital ; and it was there that the archdeacon determined to convey to them his sense of their refractory proceedings.

The servant soon brought in word that the men were assembled in the quad, and the archdeacon, big with his purpose, rose to address them.

" Well, warden, of course you're coming," said he, seeing that Mr. Harding did not prepare to follow him.

" I wish you'd excuse me," said Mr. Harding.

" For heaven's sake, don't let us have division in the camp," replied the archdeacon : " let us have a long pull and a strong pull, but above all a pull altogether ; come, warden, come ; don't be afraid of your duty."

Mr. Harding was afraid ; he was afraid that he was being led to do that which was not his duty : he was not, however, strong enough to resist, so he got up and followed his son-in-law.

The old men were assembled in groups in the quadrangle—eleven of them at least, for poor old Johnny Bell was bed-ridden, and couldn't come ; he had, however, put his mark to the petition, as one of Handy's earliest followers. 'Tis true he could not move from

the bed where he lay; 'tis true he had no
friend on earth, but those whom the hospital
contained; and of those the warden and his
daughter were the most constant and most
appreciated; 'tis true that every thing was
administered to him which his failing body
could require, or which his faint appetite could
enjoy; but still his dull eye had glistened for
a moment at the idea of possessing a hundred
pounds a year " to his own cheek," as Abel
Handy had eloquently expressed it; and poor
old Johnny Bell had greedily put his mark to
the petition.

When the two clergymen appeared, they
all uncovered their heads. Handy was slow
to do it, and hesitated; but the black coat
and waistcoat, of which he had spoken so
irreverently in Skulpit's room, had its effect
even on him, and he too doffed his hat. Bunce,
advancing before the others, bowed lowly to
the archdeacon, and with affectionate reverence expressed his wish, that the warden and
Miss Eleanor were quite well; " and the
doctor's lady," he added, turning to the archdeacon, " and the children at Plumstead, and
my lord;" and having made his speech, he
also retired among the others, and took his
place with the rest upon the stone benches.

As the archdeacon stood up to make his
speech, erect in the middle of that little square,
he looked like an ecclesiastical statue placed

there, as a fitting impersonation of the church militant here on earth ; his shovel hat, large, new, and well-pronounced, a churchman's hat in every inch, declared the profession as plainly as does the Quaker's broad brim ; his heavy eyebrow, large open eyes, and full mouth and chin expressed the solidity of his order ; the broad chest, amply covered with fine cloth, told how well to do was its estate ; one hand ensconced within his pocket, evinced the practical hold which our mother church keeps on her temporal possessions ; and the other, loose for action, was ready to fight if need be in her defence ; and below these the decorous breeches, and neat black gaiters showing so admirably that well-turned leg, betokened the decency, the outward beauty, and grace of our church establishment.

"Now, my men," he began, when he had settled himself well in his position ; " I want to say a few words to you. Your good friend, the warden here, and myself, and my lord the bishop, on whose behalf I wish to speak to you, would all be very sorry, very sorry indeed, that you should have any just ground of complaint. Any just ground of complaint on your part would be removed at once by the warden, or by his lordship, or by me on his behalf, without the necessity of any petition on your part." Here the orator stopped for a moment, expecting that some little murmurs

of applause would show that the weakest of
the men were beginning to give way; but no
such murmurs came. Bunce, himself, even sat
with closed lips, mute and unsatisfactory. "Without the necessity of any petition at all," he
repeated. "I'm told you have addressed a
petition to my lord." He paused for a reply
from the men, and after a while, Handy plucked
up courage, and said, " Yes, we has."

"You have addressed a petition to my lord,
in which, as I am informed, you express an
opinion that you do not receive from Hiram's
estate all that is your due." Here most of
the men expressed their assent. "Now what
is it you ask for? what is it you want that
you hav'n't got here? what is it——"

"A hundred a year," muttered old Moody,
with a voice as if it came out of the ground.

"A hundred a year!" ejaculated the archdeacon militant, defying the impudence of
these claimants with one hand stretched out
and closed, while with the other he tightly
grasped, and secured within his breeches pocket,
that symbol of the church's wealth which his
own loose half-crowns not unaptly represented.
"A hundred a year! Why, my men, you
must be mad ; and you talk about John Hiram's
will! When John Hiram built a hospital for
worn-out old men, worn-out old labouring men,
infirm old men past their work, cripples, blind,
bed-ridden, and such like, do you think he

meant to make gentlemen of them? Do you think John Hiram intended to give a hundred a year to old single men, who earned perhaps two shillings or half-a-crown a day for themselves and families in the best of their time? No, my men, I'll tell you what John Hiram meant; he meant that twelve poor old worn-out labourers, men who could no longer support themselves, who had no friends to support them, who must starve and perish miserably if not protected by the hand of charity; he meant that twelve such men as these should come in here in their poverty and wretchedness, and find within these walls shelter and food before their death, and a little leisure to make their peace with God. That was what John Hiram meant: you have not read John Hiram's will, and I doubt whether those wicked men who are advising you have done so. I have; I know what his will was; and I tell you that that was his will, and that that was his intention."

Not a sound came from the eleven bedes-men, as they sat listening to what, according to the archdeacon, was their intended estate. They grimly stared upon his burly figure, but did not then express, by word or sign, the anger and disgust to which such language was sure to give rise.

"Now let me ask you," he continued, "do you think you are worse off than John Hiram intended to make you? Have you not shelter,

and food, and leisure? Have you not much
more? Have you not every indulgence which
you are capable of enjoying? Have you not
twice better food, twice a better bed, ten
times more money in your pocket than you
were ever able to earn for yourselves before
you were lucky enough to get into this place?
And now you send a petition to the bishop,
asking for a hundred pounds a year! I tell
you what, my friends; you are deluded, and
made fools of by wicked men who are acting
for their own ends. You will never get a
hundred pence a year more than what you
have now: it is very possible that you may
get less; it is very possible that my lord
the bishop, and your warden, may make
changes——"

"No, no, no," interrupted Mr. Harding, who
had been listening with indescribable misery to
the tirade of his son-in-law; "no, my friends.
I want no changes,—at least no changes that
shall make you worse off than you now are, as
long as you and I live together."

"God bless you, Mr. Harding," said Bunce;
and "God bless you, Mr. Harding, God bless
you, sir, we know you was always our friend,"
was exclaimed by enough of the men to make
it appear that the sentiment was general.

The archdeacon had been interrupted in his
speech before he had quite finished it; but he
felt that he could not recommence with dignity

after this little ebullition, and he led the way back into the garden, followed by his father-in-law.

" Well," said he, as soon as he found himself within the cool retreat of the warden's garden ; " I think I spoke to them plainly." And he wiped the perspiration from his brow ; for making a speech under a broiling mid-day sun in summer, in a full suit of thick black cloth, is warm work.

" Yes, you were plain enough," replied the warden, in a tone which did not express approbation.

" And that's everything," said the other, who was clearly well satisfied with himself ; " that's everything : with these sort of people one must be plain, or one will not be understood. Now, I think they did understand me—I think they knew what I meant."

The warden agreed. He certainly thought they had understood to the full what had been said to them.

" They know pretty well what they have to expect from us ; they know how we shall meet any refractory spirit on their part ; they know that we are not afraid of them. And now I'll just step into Chadwick's, and tell him what I've done ; and then I'll go up to the palace, and answer this petition of theirs."

The warden's mind was very full—full nearly to overcharging itself ; and had it done so—

had he allowed himself to speak the thoughts
which were working within him, he would
indeed have astonished the archdeacon by the
reprobation he would have expressed as to the
proceeding of which he had been so unwilling a
witness. But different feelings kept him silent;
he was as yet afraid of differing from his son-in-
law—he was anxious beyond measure to avoid
even a semblance of rupture with any of his
order, and was painfully fearful of having to
come to an open quarrel with any person on
any subject. His life had hitherto been so
quiet, so free from strife ; his little early troubles
had required nothing but passive fortitude;
his subsequent prosperity had never forced
upon him any active cares—had never brought
him into disagreeable contact with any one.
He felt that he would give almost anything—
much more than he knew he ought to do—to
relieve himself from the storm which he feared
was coming. It was so hard that the pleasant
waters of his little stream should be disturbed
and muddied by rough hands ; that his quiet
paths should be made a battle-field ; that the
unobtrusive corner of the world which had been
allotted to him, as though by Providence, should
be invaded and desecrated, and all within it
made miserable and unsound.

Money he had none to give ; the knack of
putting guineas together had never belonged to
him ; but how willingly, with what a foolish

easiness, with what happy alacrity, would he
have abandoned the half of his income for all
time to come, could he by so doing have quietly
dispelled the clouds that were gathering over
him—could he have thus compromised the
matter between the reformer and the conservative, between his possible son-in-law, Bold, and
his positive son-in-law, the archdeacon.

And this compromise would not have been
made from any prudential motive of saving
what would yet remain, for Mr. Harding still
felt little doubt but he should be left for life in
quiet possession of the good things he had, if
he chose to retain them. No; he would have
done so from the sheer love of quiet, and from
a horror of being made the subject of public
talk. He had very often been moved to pity—
to that inward weeping of the heart for others'
woes; but none had he ever pitied more than
that old lord, whose almost fabulous wealth,
drawn from his church preferments, had become
the subject of so much opprobrium, of such public
scorn ; that wretched clerical octogenarian
Crœsus, whom men would not allow to die in
peace—whom all the world united to decry
and to abhor.

Was he to suffer such a fate? Was his
humble name to be bandied in men's mouths,
as the gormandizer of the resources of the
poor, as of one who had filched from the
charity of other ages wealth which had been

intended to relieve the old and the infirm ?
Was he to be gibbeted in the press, to become
a byword for oppression, to be named as an
example of the greed of the English church ?
Should it ever be said that he had robbed
those old men, whom he so truly and so
tenderly loved in his heart of hearts ? As he
slowly paced, hour after hour, under those
noble lime-trees, turning these sad thoughts
within him, he became all but fixed in his
resolve that some great step must be taken to
relieve him from the risk of so terrible a fate.

In the meanwhile, the archdeacon, with
contented mind and unruffled spirit, went
about his business. He said a word or two
to Mr. Chadwick, and then finding, as he
expected, the petition lying in his father's
library, he wrote a short answer to the men,
in which he told them that they had no evils
to redress, but rather great mercies for which
to be thankful ; and having seen the bishop
sign it, he got into his brougham and returned
home to Mrs. Grantly, and Plumstead Episcopi.

CHAPTER VI

THE WARDEN'S TEA PARTY

AFTER much painful doubting, on one thing only could Mr. Harding resolve. He determined that at any rate he would take no offence, and that he would make this question no cause of quarrel either with Bold or with the bedesmen. In furtherance of this resolution, he himself wrote a note to Mr. Bold, the same afternoon, inviting him to meet a few friends and hear some music on an evening named in the next week. Had not this little party been promised to Eleanor, in his present state of mind he would probably have avoided such gaiety; but the promise had been given, the invitations were to be written, and when Eleanor consulted her father on the subject, she was not ill pleased to hear him say, " Oh, I was thinking of Bold, so I took it into my head to write to him myself, but you must write to his sister."

Mary Bold was older than her brother, and, at the time of our story, was just over thirty. She was not an unattractive young woman, though by no means beautiful. Her great merit was the kindliness of her disposition. She was not very clever, nor very animated, nor had she apparently the energy of her brother ; but she was guided by a high principle of right and wrong ; her temper was sweet, and her faults were fewer in number than her virtues. Those who casually met Mary Bold thought little of her ; but those who knew her well loved her well, and the longer they knew her the more they loved her. Among those who were fondest of her was Eleanor Harding, and though Eleanor had never openly talked to her of her brother, each understood the other's feelings about him. The brother and sister were sitting together when the two notes were brought in.

"How odd," said Mary, "that they should send two notes. Well, if Mr. Harding becomes fashionable, the world is going to change."

Her brother understood immediately the nature and intention of the peace-offering ; but it was not so easy for him to behave well in the matter, as it was for Mr Harding. It is much less difficult for the sufferer to be generous than for the oppressor. John Bold felt that he could not go to the warden's party : he never loved Eleanor better than he did now ; he had never so strongly felt how anxious he was to make her his wife as now, when so many obstacles to his doing so appeared in view. Yet here was her father himself, as it were, clearing away those very obstacles, and

still he felt that he could not go to the house
any more as an open friend.

As he sat thinking of these things with the
note in his hand, his sister was waiting for his
decision.

"Well," said she, "I suppose we must
write separate answers, and both say we shall
be very happy."

"You'll go, of course, Mary," said he;
to which she readily assented. "I cannot,"
he continued, looking serious and gloomy;
"I wish I could, with all my heart."

"And why not, John?" said she. She
had as yet heard nothing of the new-found
abuse which her brother was about to reform;
at least nothing which connected it with her
brother's name.

He sat thinking for awhile till he determined
that it would be best to tell her at once what
it was that he was about: it must be done
sooner or later.

"I fear I cannot go to Mr. Harding's
house any more as a friend, just at present."

"Oh, John! Why not? Ah, you've
quarrelled with Eleanor!"

"No, indeed," said he; "I've no quarrel
with her as yet."

"What is it, John?" said she, looking at
him with an anxious, loving face, for she
knew well how much of his heart was there

in that house which he said he could no longer
enter.

"Why," said he at last, "I've taken up the
case of these twelve old men of Hiram's
Hospital, and of course that brings me into
contact with Mr. Harding.   I may have to
oppose him, interfere with him, perhaps injure
him."

Mary looked at him steadily for some time
before she committed herself to reply, and then
merely asked him what he meant to do for
the old men.

"Why, it's a long story, and I don't know
that I can make you understand it.   John
Hiram made a will, and left his property in
charity for certain poor old men, and the proceeds, instead of going to the benefit of these
men, goes chiefly into the pocket of the
warden, and the bishop's steward."

"And you mean to take away from Mr.
Harding his share of it?"

"I don't know what I mean yet.   I mean
to inquire about it.   I mean to see who is
entitled to this property.   I mean to see, if
I can, that justice be done to the poor of the
city of Barchester generally, who are, in fact,
the legatees under the will.   I mean, in short,
to put the matter right, if I can."

"And why are you to do this, John?'

"You might ask the same question of anybody else," said he: "and according to that,

the duty of righting these poor men would belong to nobody. If we are to act on that principle, the weak are never to be protected, injustice is never to be opposed, and no one is to struggle for the poor!" And Bold began to comfort himself in the warmth of his own virtue.

"But is there no one to do this but you, who have known Mr. Harding so long? Surely, John, as a friend, as a young friend, so much younger than Mr. Harding——"

"That's woman's logic, all over, Mary. What has age to do with it? Another man might plead that he was too old; and as to his friendship, if the thing itself be right, private motives should never be allowed to interfere. Because I esteem Mr. Harding, is that a reason that I should neglect a duty which I owe to these old men? or should I give up a work which my conscience tells me is a good one, because I regret the loss of his society?"

"And Eleanor, John?" said the sister, looking timidly into her brother's face.

"Eleanor, that is, Miss Harding, if she thinks fit—that is, if her father—or rather, if she —or, indeed, he,—if they find it necessary— but there is no necessity now to talk about Eleanor Harding; but this I will say, that if she has the kind of spirit for which I give her credit, she will not condemn me for doing what I think to be a duty." And Bold consoled himself with the consolation of a Roman.

Mary sat silent for awhile, till at last her brother reminded her that the notes must be answered, and she got up, and placed her desk before her, took out her pen and paper, wrote on it slowly,—

> " Pakenham Villas, Tuesday morning.

" My dear Eleanor,
        " I —— "

and then stopped, and looked at her brother.

" Well, Mary, why don't you write it ? "

" Oh, John," said she, " dear John, pray think better of this."

" Think better of what ? " said he.

" Of this about the hospital,—of all this about Mr. Harding,—of what you say about those old men. Nothing can call upon you,—no duty can require you to set yourself against your oldest, your best friend. Oh, John, think of Eleanor ; you'll break her heart and your own."

" Nonsense, Mary ; Miss Harding's heart is as safe as yours."

" Pray, pray, for my sake, John, give it up. You know how dearly you love her." And she came and knelt before him on the rug. " Pray give it up. You are going to make yourself, and her, and her father miserable : you are going to make us all miserable. And for what ?

For a dream of justice. You will never make those twelve men happier than they now are."

" You don't understand it, my dear girl," said he, smoothing her hair with his hand.

" I do understand it, John. I understand that this is a chimera—a dream that you have got. I know well that no duty can require you to do this mad—this suicidal thing. I know you love Eleanor Harding with all your heart, and I tell you now that she loves you as well. If there was a plain, a positive duty before you, I would be the last to bid you neglect it for any woman's love; but this—— oh, think again, before you do anything to make it necessary that you and Mr. Harding should be at variance." He did not answer, as she knelt there, leaning on his knees, but by his face she thought that he was inclined to yield. " At any rate let me say that you will go to this party. At any rate do not break with them while your mind is in doubt." And she got up, hoping to conclude her note in the way she desired.

" My mind is not in doubt," at last he said, rising ; " I could never respect myself again, were I to give way now, because Eleanor Harding is beautiful. I do love her : I would give a hand to hear her tell me what you have said, speaking on her behalf ; but I cannot for her sake go back from the task which I have commenced. I hope she may hereafter acknowledge and respect my motives, but I cannot now go as a guest to her father's house." And the Barchester Brutus went out to fortify his own resolution by meditations on his own virtue.

Poor Mary Bold sat down, and sadly finished her note, saying that she would herself attend the party, but that her brother was unavoidably prevented from doing so. I fear that she did not admire as she should have done the self-devotion of his singular virtue.

The party went off as such parties do: there were fat old ladies, in fine silk dresses, and slim young ladies, in gauzy muslin frocks; old gentlemen stood up with their backs to the empty fireplace, looking by no means so comfortable as they would have done in their own armchairs at home; and young gentlemen, rather stiff about the neck, clustered near the door, not as yet sufficiently in courage to attack the muslin frocks, who awaited the battle, drawn up in a semicircular array. The warden endeavoured to induce a charge, but failed signally, not having the tact of a general; his daughter did what she could to comfort the forces under her command, who took in refreshing rations of cake and tea, and patiently looked for the coming engagement: but she herself, Eleanor, had no spirit for the work; the only enemy whose lance she cared to encounter was not there, and she and others were somewhat dull.

Loud above all voices was heard the clear

sonorous tones of the archdeacon as he dilated to brother parsons of the danger of the church, of the fearful rumours of mad reforms even at Oxford, and of the damnable heresies of Dr. Whiston.

Soon, however, sweeter sounds began timidly to make themselves audible. Little movements were made in a quarter notable for round stools and music stands. Wax candles were arranged in sconces, big books were brought from hidden recesses, and the work of the evening commenced.

How often were those pegs twisted and retwisted before our friend found that he had twisted them enough; how many discordant scrapes gave promise of the coming harmony! How much the muslin fluttered and crumpled before Eleanor and another nymph were duly seated at the piano; how closely did that tall Apollo pack himself against the wall, with his flute, long as himself, extending high over the heads of his pretty neighbours; into how small a corner crept that round and florid little minor canon, and there with skill amazing found room to tune his accustomed fiddle!

And now the crash begins: away they go in full flow of harmony together—up hill and down dale—now louder and louder, then lower and lower: now loud, as though stirring the battle; then low, as though mourning the slain. In all, through all, and above all, is heard the

violoncello. Ah, not for nothing were those
pegs so twisted and retwisted—listen, listen!
Now alone that saddest of instruments tells its
touching tale. Silent, and in awe, stand fiddle,
flute, and piano, to hear the sorrows of their
wailing brother. 'Tis but for a moment: before
the melancholy of those low notes has been
fully realised, again comes the full force of
all the band—down go the pedals, away rush
twenty fingers scouring over the bass notes with
all the impetus of passion. Apollo blows till his
stiff neckcloth is no better than a rope, and the
minor canon works both arms till he falls in
a syncope of exhaustion against the wall.

How comes it that now, when all should be
silent, when courtesy, if not taste, should make
men listen,—how is it at this moment the black-
coated corps leave their retreat and begin
skirmishing? One by one they creep forth, and
fire off little guns timidly, and without precision.
Ah, my men, efforts such as these will take
no cities, even though the enemy should be
never so open to assault. At length a more
deadly artillery is brought to bear; slowly, but
with effect, the advance is made; the muslin
ranks are broken, and fall into confusion; the
formidable array of chairs gives way; the battle
is no longer between opposing regiments, but
hand to hand, and foot to foot with single
combatants, as in the glorious days of old, when
fighting was really noble. In corners, and

under the shadow of curtains, behind sofas and half hidden by doors, in retiring windows, and sheltered by hanging tapestry, are blows given and returned, fatal, incurable, dealing death.

Apart from this another combat arises, more sober and more serious. The archdeacon is engaged against two prebendaries, a pursy full-blown rector assisting him, in all the perils and all the enjoyments of short whist. With solemn energy do they watch the shuffled pack, and, all-expectant, eye the coming trump. With what anxious nicety do they arrange their cards, jealous of each other's eyes! Why is that lean doctor so slow—cadaverous man with hollow jaw and sunken eye, ill beseeming the richness of his mother church! Ah, why so slow, thou meagre doctor? See how the archdeacon, speechless in his agony, deposits on the board his cards, and looks to heaven or to the ceiling for support. Hark, how he sighs, as with thumbs in his waistcoat pocket he seems to signify that the end of such torment is not yet even nigh at hand! Vain is the hope, if hope there be, to disturb that meagre doctor. With care precise he places every card, weighs well the value of each mighty ace, each guarded king, and comfort-giving queen ; speculates on knave and ten, counts all his suits, and sets his price upon the whole. At length a card is led, and quick three others fall upon the board. The little doctor leads again, while with lustrous

eye his partner absorbs the trick.   Now thrice
has this been done—thrice has constant fortune
favoured the brace of prebendaries, ere the
archdeacon rouses himself to the battle : but at
the fourth assault he pins to the earth a prostrate
king, laying low his crown and sceptre, bushy
beard, and lowering brow, with a poor deuce.

"As David did Goliath," says the archdeacon,
pushing over the four cards to his partner.   And
then a trump is led, then another trump ; then a
king—and then an ace—and then a long ten,
which brings down from the meagre doctor his
only remaining tower of strength—his cherished
queen of trumps.

"What, no second club?" says the archdeacon
to his partner.

"Only one club," mutters from his inmost
stomach the pursy rector, who sits there red
faced, silent, impervious, careful, a safe but not
a brilliant ally.

But the archdeacon cares not for many clubs,
or for none.   He dashes out his remaining cards
with a speed most annoying to his antagonists,
pushes over to them some four cards as their
allotted portion, shoves the remainder across the
table to the red-faced rector ; calls out "two
by cards and two by honours, and the odd trick
last time," marks a treble under the candle-stick,
and has dealt round the second pack before the
meagre doctor has calculated his losses.

And so went off the warden's party, and men

and women arranging shawls and shoes declared how pleasant it had been ; and Mrs. Good-enough, the red-faced rector's wife, pressing the warden's hand, declared she had never enjoyed herself better ; which showed how little pleasure she allowed herself in this world, as she had sat the whole evening through in the same chair without occupation, not speaking, and unspoken to. And Matilda Johnson, when she allowed young Dickson of the bank to fasten her cloak round her neck, thought that two hundred pounds a year and a little cottage would really do for happiness ; besides, he was sure to be manager some day. And Apollo, folding his flute into his pocket, felt that he had acquitted himself with honour ; and the arch-deacon pleasantly jingled his gains ; but the meagre doctor went off without much audible speech, muttering ever and anon as he went, "three and thirty points !" "three and thirty points !"

And so they all were gone, and Mr. Harding was left alone with his daughter.

What had passed between Eleanor Harding and Mary Bold need not be told. It is indeed a matter of thankfulness that neither the his-torian nor the novelist hears all that is said by their heroes or heroines, or how would three volumes or twenty suffice ! In the present case so little of this sort have I overheard, that I live in hopes of finishing my work within 300 pages, and of completing that pleasant task—a novel in one volume; but something had passed between them, and as the warden blew out the wax candles, and put his instrument into its case, his daughter stood sad and thoughtful by the empty fireplace, determined to speak to her father, but irresolute as to what she would say.

"Well, Eleanor," said he, "are you for bed?"

"Yes," said she, moving, "I suppose so; but papa—— Mr. Bold was not here to-night: do you know why not?"

"He was asked; I wrote to him myself," said the warden.

"But do you know why he did not come, papa?"

"Well, Eleanor, I could guess; but it's no use guessing at such things, my dear. What makes you look so earnest about it?"

"Oh, papa, do tell me," she exclaimed, throwing her arms round him, and looking into his face; "what is it he is going to do? What is it all about? Is there any—any—any—" she didn't well know what word to use—"any danger?"

"Danger, my dear, what sort of danger?"

"Danger to you, danger of trouble, and of loss, and of—— Oh, papa, why hav'n't you told me of all this before?"

Mr. Harding was not the man to judge harshly of any one, much less of the daughter whom he now loved better than any living creature; but still he did judge her wrongly at this moment. He knew that she loved John Bold ; he fully sympathised in her affection ; day after day he thought more of the matter, and, with the tender care of a loving father, tried to arrange in his own mind how matters might be so managed that his daughter's heart should not be made the sacrifice to the dispute which was likely to exist between him and Bold. Now, when she spoke to him for the first time on the subject, it was natural that he should think more of her than of himself, and that he should imagine that her own cares, and not his, were troubling her.

He stood silent before her awhile, as she gazed up into his face, and then kissing her forehead he placed her on the sofa.

" Tell me, Nelly," he said (he only called her Nelly in his kindest, softest, sweestest moods, and yet all his moods were kind and sweet), "tell me, Nelly, do you like Mr. Bold—much ? "

She was quite taken aback by the question. I will not say that she had forgotten herself, and her own love in thinking about John Bold, and while conversing with Mary : she certainly had not done so. She had been sick at heart to think, that a man of whom she could not but own to herself that she loved him, of whose regard she had been so proud, that such a man should turn against her father to ruin him. She had felt her vanity hurt, that his affection for her had not kept him from such a course ; had he really cared for her, he would not have risked her love by such an outrage; but her main fear had been for her father, and when she spoke of danger, it was of danger to him and not to herself.

She was taken aback by the question altogether: " Do I like him, papa?"

" Yes, Nelly, do you like him? Why shouldn't you like him? but that's a poor word—do you love him?" She sat still in his arms without answering him. She certainly had not prepared herself for an avowal of affection, intending, as she had done, to abuse John Bold herself, and to hear her father do so also. "Come, my love," said he, " let us make a clean breast of it: do you tell me what concerns yourself, and I will tell you what concerns me and the hospital."

And then, without waiting for an answer, he described to her, as he best could, the accusation that was made about Hiram's will; the claims which the old men put forward; what he considered the strength and what the weakness of his own position; the course which Bold had taken, and that which he presumed he was about to take; and then by degrees, without further question, he presumed on the fact of Eleanor's love, and spoke of that love as a feeling which he could in no way disapprove: he apologised for Bold, excused what he was doing; nay, praised him for his energy and intentions: made much of his good qualities, and harped on none of his foibles; then, reminding his daughter how late it was, and comforting her with much assurance which he hardly felt himself, he sent her to her room, with flowing eyes and a full heart.

When Mr. Harding met his daughter at breakfast the next morning, there was no further discussion on the matter, nor was the subject mentioned between them for some days. Soon after the party Mary Bold called at the hospital, but there were various persons in the drawing-room at the time, and she therefore said nothing about her brother. On the day following, John Bold met Miss Harding in one of the quiet sombre shaded walks of the close : he was most anxious to see her, but unwilling to call at the warden's house, and had in truth waylaid her in her private haunts.

"My sister tells me," said he, abruptly hurrying on with his premeditated speech, "my sister tells me that you had a delightful party the other evening. I was so sorry I could not be there."

"We were all sorry," said Eleanor, with dignified composure.

"I believe, Miss Harding, you understood why, at this moment——" And Bold hesitated, muttered, stopped, commenced his explanation again, and again broke down.

Eleanor would not help him in the least.

"I think my sister explained to you, Miss Harding ?"

" Pray don't apologise, Mr. Bold ; my father will, I am sure, always be glad to see you, if you like to come to the house now as formerly ; nothing has occurred to alter his feelings ; of your own views you are, of course, the best judge."

" Your father is all that is kind and generous ; he always was so, but you, Miss Harding, your-self—— I hope you will not judge me harshly, because——"

" Mr. Bold," said she, " you may be sure of one thing ; I shall always judge my father to be right, and those who oppose him I shall judge to be wrong. If those who do not know him oppose him, I shall have charity enough to believe that they are wrong, through error of judgment; but should I see him attacked by those who ought to know him, and to love him, and revere him, of such I shall be constrained to form a different opinion." And then curtseying low she sailed on, leaving her lover in anything but a happy state of mind.

CHAPTER VII

THE JUPITER

THOUGH Eleanor Harding rode off from John Bold on a high horse, it must not be supposed that her heart was so elate as her demeanour. In the first place, she had a natural repugnance to losing her lover ; and in the next, she was not quite so sure that she was in the right as she pretended to be. Her father had told her, and that now repeatedly, that Bold was doing nothing unjust or ungenerous, and why then should she rebuke him, and throw him off, when she felt herself so ill able to bear his loss?—but such is human nature, and young-lady-nature especially. As she walked off from him beneath the shady elms of the close, her look, her tone, every motion and gesture of her body, belied her heart ; she would have given the world to have taken him by the hand, to have reasoned with him, persuaded him, cajoled him, coaxed him out of his project ; to have overcome him with all her female artillery, and to have redeemed her father at the cost of herself ; but pride would not let her do this, and she left him without a look or a word of kindness.

Had Bold been judging of another lover and

of another lady he might have understood all this as well as we do ; but in matters of love men do not see clearly in their own affairs. They say that faint heart never won fair lady ; and it is amazing to me how fair ladies are won, so faint are often men's hearts! Were it not for the kindness of their nature, that seeing the weakness of our courage they will occasionally descend from their impregnable fortresses, and themselves aid us in effecting their own defeat, too often would they escape unconquered if not unscathed, and free of body if not of heart.

[margin note: ladies in castle, men trying to break in. Combat metaphor]

Poor Bold crept off quite crest-fallen ; he felt that as regarded Eleanor Harding his fate was sealed, unless he could consent to give up a task to which he had pledged himself, and which indeed it would not be easy for him to give up. Lawyers were engaged, and the question had to a certain extent been taken up by the public ; besides, how could a high-spirited girl like Eleanor Harding really learn to love a man for neglecting a duty which he assumed! Could she allow her affection to be purchased at the cost of his own self-respect ?

As regarded the issue of his attempt at re-formation in the hospital, Bold had no reason hitherto to be discontented with his success. All Barchester was by the ears about it. The bishop, the archdeacon, the warden, the steward, and several other clerical allies, had daily meetings, discussing their tactics, and preparing *not as playful*

metaphor

for the great attack. Sir Abraham Haphazard
had been consulted, but his opinion was not
yet received : copies of Hiram's will, copies
of warden's journals, copies of leases, copies of
accounts, copies of everything that could be
copied, and of some that could not, had been
sent to him ; and the case was assuming most
creditable dimensions. But above all, it had
been mentioned in the daily Jupiter. That
all-powerful organ of the press in one of its
leading thunderbolts launched at St. Cross, had
thus remarked : " Another case, of smaller dimensions indeed, but of similar import, is now
likely to come under public notice. We are
informed that the warden or master of an old
almshouse attached to Barchester Cathedral is in
receipt of twenty-five times the annual income
appointed for him by the will of the founder,
while the sum yearly expended on the absolute
purposes of the charity has always remained
fixed. In other words, the legatees under the
founder's will have received no advantage from
the increase in the value of the property during
the last four centuries, such increase having been
absorbed by the so-called warden. It is impossible to conceive a case of greater injustice.
It is no answer to say that some six or nine
or twelve old men receive as much of the goods
of this world as such old men require. On
what foundation, moral or divine, traditional
or legal, is grounded the warden's claim to

the large income he receives for doing nothing? The contentment of these almsmen, if content they be, can give him no title to this wealth! Does he ever ask himself, when he stretches wide his clerical palm to receive the pay of some dozen of the working clergy, for what service he is so remunerated? Does his conscience ever entertain the question of his right to such subsidies? Or is it possible that the subject never so presents itself to his mind; that he has received for many years, and intends, should God spare him, to receive for years to come, these fruits of the industrious piety of past ages, indifferent as to any right on his own part, or of any injustice to others! We must express an opinion that nowhere but in the Church of England, and only there among its priests, could such a state of moral indifference be found."

I must for the present leave my readers to imagine the state of Mr. Harding's mind after reading the above article. They say that forty thousand copies of the Jupiter were daily sold, and that each copy is read by five persons at the least. Two hundred thousand readers then would hear this accusation against him; two hundred thousand hearts would swell with indignation at the griping injustice, the bare-faced robbery of the warden of Barchester Hospital! And how was he to answer this? How was he to open his inmost heart to this multitude to these thousands, the educated, the polished, the picked men of his own country ; how show them that he was no robber, no avaricious lazy priest scrambling for gold, but a retiring humble-spirited man, who had innocently taken what had innocently been offered to him ?

"Write to the Jupiter," suggested the bishop.

"Yes," said the archdeacon, more worldly wise than his father, "yes, and be smothered with ridicule ; tossed over and over again with scorn ; shaken this way and that, as a rat in the mouth of a practised terrier. You will leave out some word or letter in your answer, and the ignorance of the cathedral clergy will be harped upon ; you will make some small mistake, which will be a falsehood, or some admission, which will be self-condemnation ; you will find yourself to have been vulgar, ill-tempered, irreverend, and illiterate, and the chances are ten to one, but that being a clergy-man you will have been guilty of blasphemy ! A man may have the best of causes, the best of talents, and the best of tempers ; he may write as well as Addison, or as strongly as Junius ; but even with all this he cannot successfully answer, when attacked by the Jupiter. In such matters it is omnipotent. What the Czar is in Russia, or the mob in America, that the Jupiter is in England. Answer such an article ! No, warden ; what-ever you do, don't do that. We were to look

for this sort of thing, you know; but we need
not draw down on our heads more of it than
is necessary."

The article in the Jupiter, while it so greatly
harassed our poor warden, was an immense
triumph to some of the opposite party. Sorry
as Bold was to see Mr. Harding attacked so
personally, it still gave him a feeling of elation
to find his cause taken up by so powerful an
advocate: and as to Finney, the attorney, he
was beside himself. What! to be engaged in
the same cause and on the same side with
the Jupiter; to have the views he had recommended seconded, and furthered, and battled for
by the Jupiter! Perhaps to have his own name
mentioned as that of the learned gentleman
whose efforts had been so successful on behalf
of the poor of Barchester! He might be
examined before committees of the House of
Commons, with heaven knows how much a
day for his personal expenses—he might be
engaged for years on such a suit! There was
no end to the glorious golden dreams which
this leader in the Jupiter produced in the soaring
mind of Finney.

And the old bedesmen, they also heard of
this article, and had a glimmering, indistinct
idea of the marvellous advocate which had now
taken up their cause. Abel Handy limped
hither and thither through the rooms, repeating
all that he understood to have been printed,

with some additions of his own which he thought
should have been added. He told them how
the Jupiter had declared that their warden was
no better than a robber, and that what the
Jupiter said was acknowledged by the world
to be true. How the Jupiter had affirmed
that each one of them—"each one of us,
Jonathan Crumple, think of that,"—had a clear
right to a hundred a year; and that if the
Jupiter had said so, it was better than a
decision of the Lord Chancellor; and then he
carried about the paper, supplied by Mr. Finney,
which, though none of them could read it,
still afforded in its very touch and aspect
positive corroboration of what was told them,
and Jonathan Crumple pondered deeply over
his returning wealth; and Job Skulpit saw how
right he had been in signing the petition, and
said so many scores of times; and Spriggs
leered fearfully with his one eye; and Moody,
as he more nearly approached the coming
golden age, hated more deeply than ever those
who still kept possession of what he so coveted.
Even Billy Gazy and poor bed-ridden Bell
became active and uneasy, and the great Bunce
stood apart with lowering brow, with deep
grief seated in his heart, for he perceived that
evil days were coming.

It had been decided, the archdeacon advising,
that no remonstrance, explanation, or defence
should be addressed from the Barchester con-

clave to the Editor of the Jupiter, but hitherto
that was the only decision to which they had
come.

Sir Abraham Haphazard was deeply engaged
in preparing a bill for the mortification of
papists, to be called the "Convent Custody Bill,"
the purport of which was to enable any Protestant clergyman over fifty years of age to
search any nun whom he suspected of being in
possession of treasonable papers, or jesuitical
symbols : and as there were to be a hundred
and thirty-seven clauses in the bill, each clause
containing a separate thorn for the side of the
papist, and as it was known the bill would be
fought inch by inch, by fifty maddened Irish-
men, the due construction and adequate dove-
tailing of it did consume much of Sir Abraham's
time. The bill had all its desired effect. Of
course it never passed into law ; but it so
completely divided the ranks of the Irish
members, who had bound themselves together to
force on the ministry a bill for compelling all
men to drink Irish whiskey, and all women to
wear Irish poplins, that for the remainder of the
session the Great Poplin and Whiskey League
was utterly harmless.

Thus it happened that Sir Abraham's opinion
was not at once forthcoming, and the un-
certainty, the expectation, and suffering of the
folk of Barchester was maintained at a high
pitch.

CHAPTER VIII

PLUMSTEAD EPISCOPI

THE reader must now be requested to visit the rectory of Plumstead Episcopi ; and as it is as yet still early morning, to ascend again with us into the bed-room of the archdeacon. The mistress of the mansion was at her toilet ; on which we will not dwell with profane eyes, but proceed into a small inner room, where the doctor dressed and kept his boots and sermons ; and here we will take our stand, premising that the door of the room was so open as to admit of a conversation between our reverend Adam and his valued Eve.

" It's all your own fault, archdeacon," said the latter ; " I told you from the beginning how it would end, and papa has no one to thank but you."

" Good gracious, my dear," said the doctor, appearing at the door of his dressing-room, with his face and head enveloped in the rough towel which he was violently using ; " how can you say so ? I am doing my very best."

" I wish you had never done so much," said the lady, interrupting him ; " if you'd just have let John Bold come and go there, as he and papa liked, he and Eleanor would have been married by this time, and we should not have heard one word about all this affair."

"But, my dear——"

"Oh, it's all very well, archdeacon, and of course you're right; I don't for a moment think you'll ever admit that you could be wrong; but the fact is, you've brought this young man down upon papa by huffing him as you have done."

"But, my love——"

"And all because you didn't like John Bold for a brother-in-law. How is she ever to do better? papa hasn't got a shilling; and though Eleanor is well enough, she has not at all a taking style of beauty. I'm sure I don't know how she's to do better than marry John Bold, or as well indeed," added the anxious sister, giving the last twist to her last shoe-string.

Dr. Grantly felt keenly the injustice of this attack; but what could he say? He certainly had huffed John Bold; he certainly had ob- jected to him as a brother-in-law, and a very few months ago the very idea had excited his wrath: but now matters were changed; John Bold had shown his power, and, though he was as odious as ever to the archdeacon, power is always respected, and the reverend dignitary began to think that such an alliance might not have been imprudent. Nevertheless, his motto was still "no surrender;" he would still fight it out; he still believed confidently in Oxford,

in the bench of bishops, in Sir Abraham
Haphazard, and in himself; and it was only
when alone with his wife that doubts of defeat
ever beset him. He once more tried to communicate this confidence to Mrs. Grantly, and
for the twentieth time began to tell her of Sir
Abraham.

"Oh, Sir Abraham!" said she, collecting all
her house keys into her basket before she descended; "Sir Abraham won't get Eleanor a
husband; Sir Abraham won't get papa another
income when he has been worrited out of the
hospital. Mark what I tell you, archdeacon:
while you and Sir Abraham are fighting, papa
will lose his preferment; and what will you do
then with him and Eleanor on your hands?
besides, who's to pay Sir Abraham? I suppose
he won't take the case up for nothing?" And
so the lady descended to family worship among
her children and servants, the pattern of a good
and prudent wife.

Dr. Grantly was blessed with a happy, thriving
family. There were, first, three boys, now at
home from school for the holidays. They
were called, respectively, Charles James, Henry,
and Samuel. The two younger (there were
five in all) were girls; the elder, Florinda, bore the
name of the Archbishop of York's wife, whose
godchild she was: and the younger had been
christened Grizzel, after a sister of the Archbishop of Canterbury. The boys were all clever,

and gave good promise of being well able to meet the cares and trials of the world ; and yet they were not alike in their dispositions, and each had his individual character, and each his separate admirers among the doctor's friends.

Charles James was an exact and careful boy; he never committed himself ; he well knew how much was expected from the eldest son of the Archdeacon of Barchester, and was therefore mindful not to mix too freely with other boys. He had not the great talents of his younger brothers, but he exceeded them in judgment and propriety of demeanour ; his fault, if he had one, was an over-attention to words instead of things ; there was a thought too much *finesse* about him, and, as even his father sometimes told him, he was too fond of a compromise.

The second was the archdeacon's favourite son, and Henry was indeed a brilliant boy. The versatility of his genius was surprising, and the visitors at Plumstead Episcopi were often amazed at the marvellous manner in which he would, when called on, adapt his capacity to apparently most uncongenial pursuits. He appeared once before a large circle as Luther the reformer, and delighted them with the perfect manner in which he assumed the character ; and within three days he again astonished them by acting the part of a Capuchin friar to the very life. For this last exploit his father gave him a golden guinea, and his brothers said the reward had been promised

beforehand in the event of the performance
being successful. He was also sent on a tour
into Devonshire ; a treat which the lad was most
anxious of enjoying. His father's friends there,
however, did not appreciate his talents, and sad
accounts were sent home of the perversity of his
nature. He was a most courageous lad, game
to the backbone.

It was soon known, both at home, where
he lived, and within some miles of Barchester
Cathedral, and also at Westminster, where he
was at school, that young Henry could box well
and would never own himself beat ; other boys
would fight while they had a leg to stand on,
but he would fight with no leg at all. Those
backing him would sometimes think him crushed
by the weight of blows and faint with loss
of blood, and his friends would endeavour to
withdraw him from the contest ; but no, Henry
never gave in, was never weary of the battle
The ring was the only element in which he
seemed to enjoy himself ; and while other boys
were happy in the number of their friends,
he rejoiced most in the multitude of his foes.

His relations could not but admire his pluck,
but they sometimes were forced to regret that
he was inclined to be a bully ; and those not so
partial to him as his father was, observed with
pain that, though he could fawn to the masters
and the archdeacon's friends, he was imperious
and masterful to the servants and the poor.

But perhaps Samuel was the general favourite ;
and dear little Soapy, as he was familiarly
called, was as engaging a child as ever fond
mother petted. He was soft and gentle in his
manners, and attractive in his speech ; the tone
of his voice was melody, and every action was
a grace ; unlike his brothers, he was courteous
to all, he was affable to the lowly, and meek
even to the very scullery maid. He was a boy
of great promise, minding his books and de-
lighting the hearts of his masters. His brothers,
however, were not particularly fond of him ; they
would complain to their mother that Soapy's
civility all meant something ; they thought
that his voice was too often listened to at
Plumstead Episcopi, and evidently feared that,
as he grew up, he would have more weight
in the house than either of them ; there was,
therefore, a sort of agreement among them to
put young Soapy down. This, however, was
not so easy to be done : Samuel, though young,
was sharp ; he could not assume the stiff
decorum of Charles James, nor could he fight
like Henry ; but he was a perfect master of his
own weapons, and contrived, in the teeth of
both of them, to hold the place which he had
assumed. Henry declared that he was a false,
cunning creature ; and Charles James, though
he always spoke of him as his dear brother
Samuel, was not slow to say a word against
him when opportunity offered. To speak the

truth, Samuel was a cunning boy, and those even who loved him best could not but own that for one so young, he was too adroit in choosing his words, and too skilled in modulating his voice.

The two little girls Florinda and Grizzel were nice little girls enough, but they did not possess the strong sterling qualities of their brothers; their voices were not often heard at Plumstead Episcopi; they were bashful and timid by nature, slow to speak before company even when asked to do so; and though they looked very nice in their clean white muslin frocks and pink sashes, they were but little noticed by the archdeacon's visitors.

Whatever of submissive humility may have appeared in the gait and visage of the arch-deacon during his colloquy with his wife in the sanctum of their dressing-rooms, was dispelled as he entered his breakfast-parlour with erect head and powerful step. In the presence of a third person he assumed the lord and master; and that wise and talented lady too well knew the man to whom her lot for life was bound, to stretch her authority beyond the point at which it would be borne. Strangers at Plumstead Episcopi, when they saw the imperious brow with which he commanded silence from the large circle of visitors, children, and servants who came together in the morning to hear him read the word of God, and watched how meekly that

wife seated herself behind her basket of keys
with a little girl on each side, as she caught
that commanding glance; strangers, I say,
seeing this, could little guess that some fifteen
minutes since she had stoutly held her ground
against him, hardly allowing him to open his
mouth in his own defence. But such is the tact
and talent of women!

And now let us observe the well-furnished
breakfast-parlour at Plumstead Episcopi, and
the comfortable air of all the belongings of the
rectory. Comfortable they certainly were, but
neither gorgeous nor even grand; indeed, considering the money that had been spent there,
the eye and taste might have been better
served; there was an air of heaviness about the
rooms which might have been avoided without
any sacrifice of propriety; colours might have
been better chosen and lights more perfectly
diffused: but perhaps in doing so the thorough
clerical aspect of the whole might have been
somewhat marred; at any rate, it was not
without ample consideration that those thick,
dark, costly carpets were put down; those
embossed, but sombre papers hung up; those
heavy curtains draped so as to half-exclude
the light of the sun: nor were these old-
fashioned chairs, bought at a price far exceeding
that now given for more modern goods, without
a purpose. The breakfast-service on the table
was equally costly and equally plain; the

apparent object had been to spend money
without obtaining brilliancy or splendour. The
urn was of thick and solid silver, as were also
the tea-pot, coffee-pot, cream-ewer, and sugar-
bowl ; the cups were old, dim dragon china,
worth about a pound a piece, but very despic-
able in the eyes of the uninitated. The silver
forks were so heavy as to be disagreeable to
the hand, and the bread-basket was of a weight
really formidable to any but robust persons.
The tea consumed was the very best, the
coffee the very blackest, the cream the very
thickest ; there was dry toast and buttered
toast, muffins and crumpets ; hot bread and
cold bread, white bread and brown bread, home-
made bread and bakers' bread, wheaten bread
and oaten bread, and if there be other breads
than these, they were there ; there were eggs
in napkins, and crispy bits of bacon under
silver covers ; and there were little fishes in a
little box, and devilled kidneys frizzling on a
hot-water dish ; which, by-the-by, were placed
closely contiguous to the plate of the worthy
archdeacon himself. Over and above this, on
a snow-white napkin, spread upon the sideboard,
was a huge ham and a huge sirloin ; the
latter having laden the dinner table on the
previous evening. Such was the ordinary fare
at Plumstead Episcopi.

And yet I have never found the rectory a
pleasant house. The fact that man shall not

live by bread alone seemed to be somewhat
forgotten ; and noble as was the appearance
of the host, and sweet and good-natured as
was the face of the hostess, talented as were
the children, and excellent as were the viands
and the wines, in spite of these attractions,
I generally found the rectory somewhat dull.
After breakfast the archdeacon would retire, of
course to his clerical pursuits.   Mrs. Grantly, I
presume, inspected her kitchen, though she had
a first-rate housekeeper, with sixty pounds a
year ; and attended to the lessons of Florinda
and Grizzel, though she had an excellent
governess with thirty pounds a year : but at
any rate she disappeared : and I never could
make companions of the boys.   Charles James,
though he always looked as though there was
something in him, never seemed to have much
to say ; and what he did say he would always
unsay the next minute.   He told me once,
that he considered cricket, on the whole, to
be a gentleman-like game for boys, provided
they would play without running about ; and
that fives, also, was a seemly game, so that
those who played it never heated themselves.
Henry once quarrelled with me for taking his
sister Grizzel's part in a contest between them
as to the best mode of using a watering-pot
for the garden flowers ; and from that day to
this he has not spoken to me, though he speaks
at me often enough.   For half an hour or so

I certainly did like Sammy's gentle speeches; but one gets tired of honey, and I found that he preferred the more admiring listeners whom he met in the kitchen-garden and back precincts of the establishment; besides, I think I once caught Sammy fibbing.

On the whole, therefore, I found the rectory a dull house, though it must be admitted that everything there was of the very best.

After breakfast, on the morning of which we are writing, the archdeacon, as usual, retired to his study, intimating that he was going to be very busy, but that he would see Mr. Chadwick if he called. On entering this sacred room he carefully opened the paper case on which he was wont to compose his favourite sermons, and spread on it a fair sheet of paper, and one partly written on; he then placed his inkstand, looked at his pen, and folded his blotting paper; having done so, he got up again from his seat, stood with his back to the fire-place, and yawned comfortably, stretching out vastly his huge arms, and opening his burly chest. He then walked across the room and locked the door; and having so prepared himself, he threw himself into his easy chair, took from a secret drawer beneath his table a volume of Rabelais, and began to amuse himself with the witty mischief of Panurge; and so passed the archdeacon's morning on that day.

He was left undisturbed at his studies for

an hour or two, when a knock came to the door, and Mr. Chadwick was announced Rabelais retired into the secret drawer, the easy chair seemed knowingly to betake itself off, and when the archdeacon quickly undid his bolt, he was discovered by the steward working, as usual, for that church of which he was so useful a pillar. Mr. Chadwick had just come from London, and was, therefore, known to be the bearer of important news.

" We've got Sir Abraham's opinion at last," said Mr. Chadwick, as he seated himself.

" Well, well, well ! " exclaimed the archdeacon impatiently.

" Oh, it's as long as my arm," said the other ; " it can't be told in a word, but you can read it ; " and he handed him a copy, in heaven knows how many spun-out folios, of the opinion which the attorney-general had managed to cram on the back and sides of the case as originally submitted to him.

" The upshot is," said Chadwick, " that there's a screw loose in their case, and we had better do nothing. They are proceeding against Mr. Harding and myself, and Sir Abraham holds that, under the wording of the will, and subsequent arrangements legally sanctioned, Mr. Harding and I are only paid servants. The defendants should have been either the Corporation of Barchester, or possibly the chapter or your father."

" W—hoo," said the archdeacon ; " so Master Bold is on a wrong scent, is he ? "

" That's Sir Abraham's opinion ; but any scent almost would be a wrong scent. Sir Abraham thinks that if they'd taken the corporation, or the chapter, we could have baffled them. The bishop, he thinks, would be the surest shot ; but even there we could plead that the bishop is only visitor, and that he has never made himself a consenting party to the performance of other duties."

" That's quite clear," said the archdeacon.

" Not quite so clear," said the other. " You see the will says, ' My lord, the bishop, being graciously pleased to see that due justice be done.' Now, it may be a question whether, in accepting and administering the patronage, your father has not accepted also the other duties assigned. It is doubtful, however ; but even if they hit that nail—and they are far off from that yet,—the point is so nice, as Sir Abraham says, that you would force them into fifteen thousand pounds' cost before they could bring it to an issue ! and where's that sum of money to come from ? "

The archdeacon rubbed his hands with delight ; he had never doubted the justice of his case, but he had begun to have some dread of unjust success on the part of his enemies. It was delightful to him thus to hear that their cause was surrounded with such rocks and

shoals ; such causes of shipwreck unseen by the
landsman's eye, but visible enough to the keen
eyes of practical law mariners. How wrong his
wife was to wish that Bold should marry
Eleanor ! Bold ! why, if he should be ass enough
to persevere, he would be a beggar before he
knew whom he was at law with !

" That's excellent, Chadwick—that's excellent !
I told you Sir Abraham was the man for us ; "
and he put down on the table the copy of the
opinion, and patted it fondly.

" Don't you let that be seen, though, archdeacon."

" Who ?—I !—not for worlds," said the doctor.

" People will talk, you know, archdeacon."

" Of course, of course," said the doctor.

" Because, if that gets abroad, it would teach
them how to fight their own battle."

" Quite true," said the doctor.

" No one here in Barchester ought to see that
but you and I, archdeacon."

" No, no, certainly no one else," said the archdeacon, pleased with the closeness of the
confidence ; " no one else shall."

" Mrs. Grantly is very interested in the matter,
I know," said Mr. Chadwick.

Did the archdeacon wink, or did he not ? I
am inclined to think he did not quite wink ; but
that without such, perhaps, unseemly gesture
he communicated to Mr. Chadwick, with the
corner of his eye, intimation that, deep as

was Mrs. Grantly's interest in the matter, it should not procure for her a perusal of that document; and at the same time he partly opened the small drawer, above spoken of, deposited the paper on the volume of Rabelais, and showed to Mr. Chadwick the nature of the key which guarded these hidden treasures. The careful steward then expressed himself contented. Ah! vain man! he could fasten up his Rabelais, and other things secret, with all the skill of Bramah or of Chubb; but where could he fasten up the key which solved these mechanical mysteries? It is probable to us that the contents of no drawer in that house were unknown to its mistress, and we think, moreover, that she was entitled to all such knowledge.

"But," said Mr. Chadwick, "we must, of course, tell your father and Mr. Harding so much of Sir Abraham's opinion as will satisfy them that the matter is doing well."

"Oh, certainly,—yes, of course," said the doctor.

"You had better let them know that Sir Abraham is of opinion that there is no case at any rate against Mr. Harding; and that as the action is worded at present, it must fall to the ground; they must be nonsuited if they carry it on; you had better tell Mr. Harding, that Sir Abraham is clearly of opinion that he is only a servant, and as such, not liable—or if you like it, I'll see Mr. Harding myself."

"Oh, I must see him to-morrow, and my father too, and I'll explain to them exactly so much,—you won't go before lunch, Mr. Chadwick : well, if you will, you must, for I know your time is precious ; " and he shook hands with the diocesan steward, and bowed him out.

And the archdeacon had again recourse to his drawer, and twice read through the essence of Sir Abraham Haphazard's law-enlightened and law-bewildered brains. It was very clear that to Sir Abraham, the justice of the old men's claim or the justice of Mr. Harding's defence were ideas that had never presented themselves. A legal victory over an opposing party was the service for which Sir Abraham was, as he imagined, to be paid ; and that he, according to his lights, had diligently laboured to achieve, and with probable hope of success. Of the intense desire which Mr. Harding felt to be assured on fit authority, that he was wronging no man, that he was entitled in true equity to his income, that he might sleep at night without pangs of conscience, that he was no robber, no spoiler of the poor ; that he and all the world might be openly convinced that he was not the man which the Jupiter had described him to be ; of such longings on the part of Mr. Harding, Sir Abraham was entirely ignorant ; nor, indeed, could it be looked on as part of his business to gratify such desires. Such was not the system on which his battles were fought, and victories gained. Success was his object, and he was generally successful. He conquered his enemies by their weakness rather than by his own strength, and it had been found almost impossible to make up a case, in which Sir Abraham, as an antagonist, would not find a flaw.

The archdeacon was delighted with the closeness of the reasoning. To do him justice, it was not a selfish triumph that he desired ; he would personally lose nothing by defeat, or at least what he might lose did not actuate him ; but neither was it love of justice which made him so anxious, nor even mainly solicitude for his father-in-law. He was fighting a part of a never-ending battle against a never-conquered foe—that of the church against its enemies.

He knew Mr. Harding could not pay all the expense of these doings ; for these long opinions of Sir Abraham's, these causes to be pleaded, these speeches to be made, these various courts through which the case was, he presumed, to be dragged. He knew that he and his father must at least bear the heavier portion of this tremendous cost ; but to do the archdeacon justice, he did not recoil from this. He was a man fond of obtaining money, greedy of a large income, but open-handed enough in expending it, and it was a triumph to him to foresee the success of this measure, although he might be called on to pay so dearly for it himself.

CHAPTER IX

THE CONFERENCE

ON the following morning the archdeacon was with his father betimes, and a note was sent down to the warden begging his attendance at the palace. Dr. Grantly, as he cogitated on the matter, leaning back in his brougham as he journeyed into Barchester, felt that it would be difficult to communicate his own satisfaction either to his father or his father-in-law. He wanted success on his own side and discomfiture on that of his enemies. The bishop wanted peace on the subject; a settled peace if possible, but peace at any rate till the short remainder of his own days had spun itself out; but Mr. Harding required, not only success and peace, but he also demanded that he might stand justified before the world.

The bishop, however, was comparatively easy to deal with; and before the arrival of the other, the dutiful son had persuaded his father that all was going on well, and then the warden arrived.

It was Mr. Harding's wont, whenever he spent a morning at the palace, to seat himself immediately at the bishop's elbow, the bishop occupying a huge arm-chair fitted up with

candlesticks, a reading table, a drawer, and other
paraphernalia, the position of which chair was
never moved, summer or winter ; and when,
as was very usual, the archdeacon was there
also, he confronted the two elders, who thus
were enabled to fight the battle against him
together ; and together submit to defeat, for
such was their constant fate.

Our warden now took his accustomed place,
having greeted his son-in-law as he entered,
and then affectionately inquired after his friend's
health. There was a gentleness about the
bishop to which the soft womanly affection
of Mr. Harding particularly endeared itself,
and it was quaint to see how the two mild
old priests pressed each other's hands, and
smiled and made little signs of love.

" Sir Abraham's opinion has come at last,"
began the archdeacon. Mr. Harding had heard
so much, and was most anxious to know the
result.

" It is quite favourable," said the bishop,
pressing his friend's arm. "I am so glad."

Mr. Harding looked at the mighty bearer of
the important news for confirmation of these
glad tidings.

" Yes," said the archdeacon, " Sir Abraham
has given most minute attention to the case ;
indeed, I knew he would ; most minute attention, and his opinion is—and as to his opinion on
such a subject being correct, no one who knows

Sir Abraham's character, can doubt—his opinion is, that they hav'n't got a leg to stand on."

"But as how, archdeacon?"

"Why, in the first place :—— but you're no lawyer, warden, and I doubt you won't understand it ; the gist of the matter is this : —under Hiram's will two paid guardians have been selected for the hospital ; the law will say two paid servants, and you and I won't quarrel with the name."

"At any rate I will not if I am one of the servants," said Mr. Harding. "A rose, you know——"

"Yes, yes," said the archdeacon, impatient of poetry at such a time. "Well, two paid servants, we'll say ; one to look after the men, and the other to look after the money. You and Chadwick are these two servants, and whether either of you be paid too much, or too little, more or less in fact than the founder willed, it's as clear as daylight that no one can fall foul of either of you for receiving an allotted stipend."

"That does seem clear," said the bishop, who had winced visibly under the words servants and stipend, which, however, appeared to have caused no uneasiness to the archdeacon.

"Quite clear," said he, "and very satisfactory. In point of fact, it being necessary to select such servants for the use of the hospital, the pay to be given to them must depend on the rate of pay for such services, according to their market value at the period in question ; and those who manage the hospital must be the only judges of this."

"And who does manage the hospital ? " asked the warden.

"Oh, let them find that out; that's another question; the action is brought against you and Chadwick, and that's your defence, and a perfect and full defence it is. Now that I think very satisfactory."

"Well," said the bishop, looking inquiringly up into his friend's face, who sat silent awhile, and apparently not so well satisfied.

" And conclusive," continued the archdeacon ; " if they press it to a jury, which they won't do, no twelve men in England will take five minutes to decide against them."

"But according to that," said Mr. Harding, " I might as well have sixteen hundred a year as eight, if the managers choose to allot it to me ; and as I am one of the managers, if not the chief manager, myself, that can hardly be a just arrangement."

" Oh, well, all that's nothing to the question ; the question is, whether this intruding fellow, and a lot of cheating attorneys and pestilent dissenters, are to interfere with an arrange-ment which every one knows is essentially just and serviceable to the church. Pray don't let us be splitting hairs, and that amongst ourselves, or there'll never be an end of the cause or the cost."

Mr. Harding again sat silent for awhile, during which the bishop once and again pressed his arm, and looked in his face to see if he could catch a gleam of a contented and eased mind ; but there was no such gleam, and the poor warden continued playing sad dirges on invisible stringed instruments in all manner of positions : he was ruminating in his mind on this opinion of Sir Abraham, looking to it wearily and earnestly for satisfaction, but finding none. At last he said, "Did you see the opinion, archdeacon ? "

The archdeacon said he had not—that was to say, he had—that was, he had not seen the opinion itself ; he had seen what had been called a copy, but he could not say whether of a whole or part ; nor could he say that what he had seen were the *ipsissima verba* of the great man himself ; but what he had seen contained exactly the decision which he had announced, and which he again declared to be to his mind extremely satisfactory.

"I should like to see the opinion," said the warden ; "that is, a copy of it."

"Well, I suppose you can if you make a point of it ; but I don't see the use myself ; of course it is essential that the purport of it should not be known, and it is therefore unadvisable to multiply copies."

"Why should it not be known?" asked the warden.

"What a question for a man to ask!" said the archdeacon, throwing up his hands in token of his surprise; "but it is like you—a child is not more innocent than you are in matters of business. Can't you see that if we tell them that no action will lie against you, but that one may possibly lie against some other person or persons, that we shall be putting weapons into their hands, and be teaching them how to cut our own throats?"

The warden again sat silent, and the bishop again looked at him wistfully: "The only thing we have now to do," continued the archdeacon, "is to remain quiet, hold our peace, and let them play their own game as they please."

"We are not to make known then," said the warden, "that we have consulted the attorney-general, and that we are advised by him that the founder's will is fully and fairly carried out."

"God bless my soul!" said the archdeacon, "how odd it is that you will not see that all we are to do is to do nothing: why should we say anything about the founder's will? We are in possession; and we know that they are not in a position to put us out: surely that is enough for the present."

Mr. Harding rose from his seat and paced thoughtfully up and down the library, the bishop

the while watching him painfully at every turn,
and the archdeacon continuing to pour forth his
convictions that the affair was in a state to
satisfy any prudent mind.

"And the Jupiter?" said the warden, stopping
suddenly.

"Oh! the Jupiter," answered the other. "The
Jupiter can break no bones. You must bear
with that; there is much of course which it is
our bounden duty to bear; it cannot be all
roses for us here," and the archdeacon looked
exceedingly moral; "besides the matter is too
trivial, of too little general interest to be mentioned again in the Jupiter, unless we stir up
the subject:" and the archdeacon again looked
exceedingly knowing and worldly wise.

The warden continued his walk; the hard
and stinging words of that newspaper article,
each one of which had thrust a thorn as it were
into his inmost soul, were fresh in his memory:
he had read it more than once, word by word,
and what was worse, he fancied it was as well
known to every one as to himself. Was he to
be looked on as the unjust griping priest he had
been there described? Was he to be pointed
at as the consumer of the bread of the poor, and
to be allowed no means of refuting such charges,
of clearing his begrimed name, of standing innocent in the world, as hitherto he had stood?
Was he to bear all this, to receive as usual his
now hated income, and be known as one of

those greedy priests who by their rapacity have
brought disgrace on their church? and why?
Why should he bear all this? why should he
die, for he felt that he could not live, under such
a weight of obloquy? As he paced up and
down the room he resolved in his misery and
enthusiasm that he could with pleasure, if he
were allowed, give up his place, abandon his
pleasant home, leave the hospital, and live poorly,
happily, and with an unsullied name, on the
small remainder of his means.

He was a man somewhat shy of speaking
of himself, even before those who knew him
best, and whom he loved the most; but at
last it burst forth from him, and with a somewhat jerking eloquence he declared that he
could not, would not, bear this misery any
longer.

"If it can be proved," said he at last, "that
I have a just and honest right to this, as God
well knows I always deemed I had; if this
salary or stipend be really my due, I am not
less anxious than another to retain it. I have
the well-being of my child to look to. I am too
old to miss without some pain the comforts to
which I have been used; and I am, as others
are, anxious to prove to the world that I have
been right, and to uphold the place I have held;
but I cannot do it at such a cost as this. I
cannot bear this. Could you tell me to do so?"
and he appealed, almost in tears, to the bishop,

who had left his chair, and was now leaning
on the warden's arm as he stood on the further
side of the table facing the archdeacon. " Could
you tell me to sit there at ease, indifferent, and
satisfied, while such things as these are said
loudly of me in the world ? "

The bishop could feel for him and sympathise
with him, but he could not advise him, he could
only say, " No, no, you shall be asked to do
nothing that is painful ; you shall do just what
your heart tells you to be right ; you shall do
whatever you think best yourself. Theophilus,
don't advise him, pray don't advise the warden
to do anything which is painful."

But the archdeacon, though he could not
sympathise, could advise ; and he saw that the
time had come when it behoved him to do so
in a somewhat peremptory manner.

" Why, my lord," he said, speaking to his
father : and when he called his father " my lord,"
the good old bishop shook in his shoes, for he
knew that an evil time was coming. " Why,
my lord, there are two ways of giving advice ;
there is advice that may be good for the present
day ; and there is advice that may be good for
days to come : now I cannot bring myself to
give the former, if it be incompatible with the
other."

" No, no, no, I suppose not," said the bishop,
reseating himself, and shading his face with
his hands. Mr. Harding sat down with his

back to the further wall, playing to himself some air fitted for so calamitous an occasion, and the archdeacon said out his say standing, with his back to the empty fire-place.

"It is not to be supposed, but that much pain will spring out of this unnecessarily raised question. We must all have foreseen that, and the matter has in no wise gone on worse than we expected ; but it will be weak, yes, and wicked also, to abandon the cause and own ourselves wrong, because the inquiry is painful. It is not only ourselves we have to look to : to a certain extent the interest of the church is in our keeping. Should it be found that one after another of those who hold preferment abandoned it whenever it might be attacked, is it not plain that such attacks would be renewed till nothing was left us ? and, that if so deserted, the Church of England must fall to the ground altogether ? If this be true of many, it is true of one. Were you, accused as you now are, to throw up the wardenship, and to relinquish the preferment which is your property, with the vain object of proving yourself disinterested, you would fail in that object, you would inflict a desperate blow on your brother clergymen, you would encourage every cantankerous dissenter in England to make a similar charge against some source of clerical revenue, and you would do your best to dishearten those who are most anxious to defend you and uphold your position. I can fancy nothing more weak, or more wrong. It is not that you think that there is any justice in these charges, or that you doubt your own right to the wardenship : you are convinced of your own honesty, and yet would yield to them through cowardice."

" Cowardice ! " said the bishop, expostulating. Mr. Harding sat unmoved, gazing on his son-in-law.

" Well, would it not be cowardice ? would he not do so because he is afraid to endure the evil things which will be falsely spoken of him ? Would that not be cowardice? And now let us see the extent of the evil which you dread. The Jupiter publishes an article which a great many, no doubt, will read; but of those who understand the subject how many will believe the Jupiter? Every one knows what its object is ; it has taken up the case against Lord Guildford and against the Dean of Rochester, and that against half a dozen bishops ; and does not every one know that it would take up any case of the kind, right or wrong, false or true, with known justice or known injustice, if by doing so it could further its own views ? Does not all the world know this of the Jupiter ? Who that really knows you will think the worse of you for what the Jupiter says? And why care for those who do not know you? I will say nothing of your own comfort, but I do

say that you could not be justified in throwing
up, in a fit of passion, for such it would be, the
only maintenance that Eleanor has ; and if you
did so, if you really did vacate the wardenship,
and submit to ruin, what would that profit you ?
If you have no future right to the income, you
have had no past right to it ; and the very fact
of your abandoning your position, would create
a demand for repayment of that which you have
already received and spent."

The poor warden groaned as he sat perfectly
still, looking up at the hard-hearted orator who
thus tormented him, and the bishop echoed the
sound faintly from behind his hands; but the
archdeacon cared little for such signs of weakness, and completed his exhortation.

" But let us suppose the office to be left
vacant, and that your own troubles concerning
it were over ; would that satisfy you ? Are
your only aspirations in the matter confined
to yourself and family ? I know they are not.
I know you are as anxious as any of us for
the church to which we belong ; and what a
grievous blow would such an act of apostasy
give her ! You owe it to the church of which
you are a member and a minister, to bear with
this affliction, however severe it may be : you
owe it to my father, who instituted you, to
support his rights : you owe it to those who
preceded you to assert the legality of their
position : you owe it to those who are to come

after you, to maintain uninjured for them that
which you received uninjured from others ; and
you owe to us all the unflinching assistance
of perfect brotherhood in this matter, so that
upholding one another we may support our
great cause without blushing and without disgrace."

And so the archdeacon ceased, and stood
self-satisfied, watching the effect of his spoken
wisdom.

The warden felt himself, to a certain extent,
stifled ; he would have given the world to get
himself out into the open air without speaking
to, or noticing those who were in the room
with him ; but this was impossible. He could
not leave without saying something, and he
felt himself confounded by the archdeacon's
eloquence. There was a heavy, unfeeling,
unanswerable truth in what he had said ; there
was so much practical, but odious common
sense in it, that he neither knew how to assent
or to differ. If it were necessary for him to
suffer, he felt that he could endure without
complaint and without cowardice, providing
that he was self-satisfied of the justice of his
own cause. What he could not endure was,
that he should be accused by others, and not
acquitted by himself. Doubting, as he had
begun to doubt, the justice of his own position
in the hospital, he knew that his own self-
confidence would not be restored because

Mr. Bold had been in error as to some legal form ; nor could he be satisfied to escape, because, through some legal fiction, he who received the greatest benefit from the hospital might be considered only as one of its servants.

The archdeacon's speech had silenced him—stupefied him—annihilated him ; anything but satisfied him. With the bishop it fared not much better. He did not discern clearly how things were, but he saw enough to know that a battle was to be prepared for ; a battle that would destroy his few remaining comforts, and bring him with sorrow to the grave.

The warden still sat, and still looked at the archdeacon, till his thoughts fixed themselves wholly on the means of escape from his present position, and he felt like a bird fascinated by gazing on a snake.

" I hope you agree with me," said the archdeacon at last, breaking the dread silence ; " my lord, I hope *you* agree with me."

Oh what a sigh the bishop gave ! " My lord, I hope you agree with me," again repeated the merciless tyrant.

" Yes, I suppose so," groaned the poor old man, slowly.

" And you, warden ? "

Mr. Harding was now stirred to action—he must speak and move, so he got up and took one turn before he answered.

"Do not press me for an answer just at present; I will do nothing lightly in the matter and of whatever I do I will give you and the bishop notice." And so without another word he took his leave, escaping quickly through the palace hall, and down the lofty steps, nor did he breathe freely till he found himself alone under the huge elms of the silent close. Here he walked long and slowly, thinking on his case with a troubled air, and trying in vain to confute the archdeacon's argument. He then went home, resolved to bear it all—ignominy, suspense, disgrace, self-doubt, and heart-burning—and to do as those would have him, who he still believed were most fit and most able to counsel him aright.

CHAPTER X

TRIBULATION

MR. HARDING was a sadder man than he
had ever yet been when he returned to his own
house. He had been wretched enough on that
well-remembered morning when he was forced
to expose before his son-in-law the publisher's
account for ushering into the world his dear
book of sacred music; when after making
such payments as he could do unassisted, he
found that he was a debtor of more than three
hundred pounds: but his sufferings then were
as nothing to his present misery;—then he
had done wrong, and he knew it, and was
able to resolve that he would not sin in like
manner again; but now he could make no
resolution, and comfort himself by no promises
of firmness. He had been forced to think that
his lot had placed him in a false position, and
he was about to maintain that position against
the opinion of the world and against his own
convictions.

He had read with pity, amounting almost
to horror, the strictures which had appeared
from time to time against the Earl of Guildford as master of St. Cross, and the invectives
that had been heaped on rich diocesan digni-

taries and overgrown sinecure pluralists. In
judging of them, he judged leniently; the
whole bias of his profession had taught him
to think that they were more sinned against
than sinning, and that the animosity with
which they had been pursued was venomous
and unjust; but he had not the less regarded
their plight as most miserable. His hair had
stood on end and his flesh had crept as he
read the things which had been written; he
had wondered how men could live under such
a load of disgrace; how they could face their
fellow-creatures while their names were bandied
about so injuriously and so publicly—and now
this lot was to be his—he, that shy retiring
man, who had so comforted himself in the
hidden obscurity of his lot, who had so enjoyed the unassuming warmth of his own little
corner, he was now to be dragged forth into
the glaring day, and gibbeted before ferocious
multitudes. He entered his own house a crest-
fallen, humiliated man, without a hope of overcoming the wretchedness which affected him.

He wandered into the drawing-room where
was his daughter; but he could not speak to
her now, so he left it, and went into the book-
room. He was not quick enough to escape
Eleanor's glance, or to prevent her from seeing
that he was disturbed; and in a little while
she followed him. She found him seated in
his accustomed chair, with no book open before

him, no pen ready in his hand, no ill-shapen notes of blotted music lying before him as was usual, none of those hospital accounts with which he was so precise and yet so unmethodical : he was doing nothing, thinking of nothing, looking at nothing ; he was merely suffering.

"Leave me, Eleanor, my dear," he said, "leave me, my darling, for a few minutes, for I am busy."

Eleanor saw well how it was, but she did leave him, and glided silently back to her drawing-room. When he had sat awhile, thus alone and unoccupied, he got up to walk again —he could make more of his thoughts walking than sitting, and was creeping out into his garden, when he met Bunce on the threshold.

"Well, Bunce," said he, in a tone that for him was sharp, "what is it ? do you want me ? "

"I was only coming to ask after your reverence," said the old bedesman, touching his hat ; "and to inquire about the news from London," he added after a pause.

The warden winced, and put his hand to his forehead and felt bewildered.

"Attorney Finney has been there this morning," continued Bunce, "and by his looks I guess he is not so well pleased as he once was, and it has got abroad somehow that the archdeacon has had down great news from London, and Handy and Moody are both as black as devils ; and I hope," said the man, trying to assume a cheery tone, "that things are looking up, and that there'll be an end soon to all this stuff which bothers your reverence so sorely."

"Well, I wish there may be, Bunce."

"But about the news, your reverence?" said the old man, almost whispering.

Mr. Harding walked on, and shook his head impatiently. Poor Bunce little knew how he was tormenting his patron.

"If there was anything to cheer you, I should be so glad to know it," said he, with a tone of affection which the warden in all his misery could not resist.

He stopped, and took both the old man's hands in his. "My friend," said he, "my dear old friend, there is nothing: there is no news to cheer me—God's will be done:" and two small hot tears broke away from his eyes and stole down his furrowed cheeks.

"Then God's will be done," said the other solemnly, "but they told me that there was good news from London, and I came to wish your reverence joy; but God's will be done;" and so the warden again walked on, and the bedesman looking wistfully after him, and receiving no encouragement to follow, returned sadly to his own abode.

For a couple of hours the warden remained thus in the garden, now walking, now standing motionless on the turf, and then, as his legs got weary, sitting unconsciously on the garden seats, and then walking again. And Eleanor, hidden behind the muslin curtains of the window, watched him through the trees as he now came in sight, and then again was concealed by the turnings of the walk; and thus the time passed away till five, when the warden crept back to the house and prepared for dinner.

It was but a sorry meal. The demure parlour-maid, as she handed the dishes and changed the plates, saw that all was not right, and was more demure than ever: neither father nor daughter could eat, and the hateful food was soon cleared away, and the bottle of port placed upon the table.

"Would you like Bunce to come in, papa?" said Eleanor, thinking that the company of the old man might lighten his sorrow.

"No, my dear, thank you, not to-day; but are not you going out, Eleanor, this lovely afternoon? don't stay in for me, my dear."

"I thought you seemed so sad, papa."

"Sad," said he, irritated; "well, people must all have their share of sadness here; I am not more exempt than another: but kiss me, dearest, and go now; I will, if possible, be more sociable when you return."

And Eleanor was again banished from her father's sorrow. Ah! her desire now was not to find him happy, but to be allowed to share

his sorrows; not to force him to be sociable,
but to persuade him to be trustful.

She put on her bonnet as desired, and went
up to Mary Bold; this was now her daily
haunt, for John Bold was up in London among
lawyers and church reformers, diving deep into
other questions than that of the wardenship
of Barchester; supplying information to one
member of parliament, and dining with another;
subscribing to funds for the abolition of clerical
incomes, and seconding at that great national
meeting at the Crown and Anchor a resolution
to the effect, that no clergyman of the Church
of England, be he who he might, should have
more than a thousand a year, and none less
than two hundred and fifty. His speech on
this occasion was short, for fifteen had to speak,
and the room was hired for two hours only, at
the expiration of which the Quakers and Mr.
Cobden were to make use of it for an appeal
to the public in aid of the Emperor of Russia;
but it was sharp and effective: at least he was
told so by a companion with whom he now
lived much, and on whom he greatly depended
—one Tom Towers, a very leading genius, and
supposed to have high employment on the staff
of the Jupiter.

So Eleanor, as was now her wont, went up
to Mary Bold, and Mary listened kindly, while
the daughter spoke much of her father, and,
perhaps kinder still, found a listener in Eleanor,

while she spoke about her brother. In the meantime the warden sat alone, leaning on the arm of his chair; he had poured out a glass of wine, but had done so merely from habit, for he left it untouched : there he sat gazing at the open window, and thinking, if he can be said to have thought, of the happiness of his past life. All manner of past delights came before his mind, which at the time he had enjoyed without considering them; his easy days, his absence of all kind of hard work, his pleasant shady home, those twelve old neighbours whose welfare till now had been the source of so much pleasant care, the excellence of his children, the friendship of the dear old bishop, the solemn grandeur of those vaulted aisles, through which he loved to hear his own voice pealing; and then that friend of friends, that choice ally that had never deserted him, that eloquent companion that would always, when asked, discourse such pleasant music, that violoncello of his—ah, how happy he had been ! but it was over now ; his easy days and absence of work had been the crime which brought on him his tribulation ; his shady home was pleasant no longer ; may be it was no longer his ; the old neighbours, whose welfare had been so desired by him, were his enemies ; his daughter was as wretched as himself, and even the bishop was made miserable by his position. He could never again lift up his voice boldly as he had

hitherto done among his brethren, for he felt
that he was disgraced; and he feared even to
touch his bow, for he knew how grievous a
sound of wailing, how piteous a lamentation,
it would produce.

He was still sitting in the same chair and
the same posture, having hardly moved a limb
for two hours, when Eleanor came back to tea,
and succeeded in bringing him with her into
the drawing-room.

The tea seemed as comfortless as the dinner,
though the warden, who had hitherto eaten
nothing all day, devoured the plateful of bread
and butter, unconscious of what he was doing.

Eleanor had made up her mind to force him
to talk to her, but she hardly knew how to commence: she must wait till the urn was gone, till
the servant would no longer be coming in and out.

At last everything was gone, and the drawing-
room door was permanently closed; then
Eleanor, getting up and going round to her
father, put her arm round his neck, and said,
" Papa, won't you tell me what it is ? "

" What what is, my dear ? "

" This new sorrow that torments you; I know
you are unhappy, papa."

" New sorrow ! it's no new sorrow, my dear,
we have all our cares sometimes," and he tried
to smile, but it was a ghastly failure; " but I
shouldn't be so dull a companion; come, we'll
have some music."

"No, papa, not to-night—it would only trouble you to-night;" and she sat upon his knee, as she sometimes would in their gayest moods, and with her arm round his neck, she said, "Papa, I will not leave you till you talk to me; oh, if you only knew how much good it would do to you, to tell me of it all."

The father kissed his daughter, and pressed her to his heart; but still he said nothing; it was so hard to him to speak of his own sorrows; he was so shy a man even with his own child.

"Oh, papa, do tell me what it is; I know it is about the hospital, and what they are doing up in London, and what that cruel newspaper has said; but if there be such cause for sorrow, let us be sorrowful together; we are all in all to each other now: dear, dear papa, do speak to me."

Mr. Harding could not well speak now, for the warm tears were running down his cheeks like rain in May, but he held his child close to his heart, and squeezed her hand as a lover might, and she kissed his forehead and his wet cheeks, and lay upon his bosom, and comforted him as a woman only can do.

"My own child," he said, as soon as his tears would let him speak; "my own, own child, why should you too be unhappy before it is necessary : it may come to that, that we must leave this place, but till that time comes, why should your young days be clouded?"

"And is that all, papa? If that be all, let us

leave it, and have light hearts elsewhere : if that
be all, let us go. Oh, papa, you and I could be
happy if we had only bread to eat, so long as our
hearts were light."

And Eleanor's face was lighted up with enthusiasm as she told her father how he might
banish all his care ; and a gleam of joy shot
across his brow as this idea of escape again
presented itself, and he again fancied for a
moment that he could spurn away from him the
income which the world envied him ; that he
could give the lie to that wielder of the toma-
hawk who had dared to write such things of
him in the Jupiter. That he could leave Sir
Abraham, and the archdeacon, and Bold, and
the rest of them with their lawsuit among them,
and wipe his hands altogether of so sorrow-
stirring a concern. Ah, what happiness might
there be in the distance, with Eleanor and him
in some small cottage, and nothing left of their
former grandeur but their music ! Yes, they
would walk forth with their music books, and
their instruments, and shaking the dust from off
their feet as they went, leave the ungrateful
place. Never did a poor clergyman sigh for a
warm benefice more anxiously than our warden
did now to be rid of his.

"Give it up, papa," she said again, jumping from
his knees and standing on her feet before him,
looking boldly into his face ; "give it up, papa."

Oh, it was sad to see how that momentary

gleam of joy passed away; how the look of
hope was dispersed from that sorrowful face,
as the remembrance of the archdeacon came
back upon our poor warden, and he reflected
that he could not stir from his now hated post.
He was as a man bound with iron, fettered with
adamant : he was in no respect a free agent ;
he had no choice. "Give it up!" oh if he only
could : what an easy way that were out of all
his troubles !

"Papa, don't doubt about it," she continued,
thinking that his hesitation arose from his un-
willingness to abandon so comfortable a home ;
"is it on my account that you would stay here ?
Do you think that I cannot be happy without
a pony-carriage and a fine drawing-room ?
Papa, I never can be happy here, as long as
there is a question as to your honour in staying
here ; but I could be gay as the day is long
in the smallest tiny little cottage, if I could
see you come in and go out with a light
heart. Oh! papa, your face tells so much ;
though you won't speak to me with your voice,
I know how it is with you every time I look
at you."

How he pressed her to his heart again with
almost a spasmodic pressure ! how he kissed
her as the tears fell like rain from his old
eyes ! how he blessed her, and called her by
a hundred soft sweet names which now came
new to his lips ! how he chid himself for ever

having been unhappy with such a treasure in his house, such a jewel on his bosom, with so sweet a flower in the choice garden of his heart! and then the flood-gates of his tongue were loosed, and, at length, with unsparing detail of circumstances, he told her all that he wished, and all that he could not do. He repeated those arguments of the archdeacon, not agreeing in their truth, but explaining his inability to escape from them; how it had been declared to him that he was bound to remain where he was by the interests of his order, by gratitude to the bishop, by the wishes of his friends, by a sense of duty, which, though he could not understand it, he was fain to acknowledge. He told her how he had been accused of cowardice, and though he was not a man to make much of such a charge before the world, now in the full candour of his heart, he explained to her that such an accusation was grievous to him; that he did think it would be unmanly to desert his post, merely to escape his present sufferings, and that, therefore, he must bear as best he might the misery which was prepared for him.

And did she find these details tedious? Oh, no—she encouraged him to dilate on every feeling he expressed, till he laid bare the inmost corners of his heart to her. They spoke together of the archdeacon, as two children might of a stern, unpopular, but still respected school-

master, and of the bishop as a parent kind as
kind could be, but powerless against an omnipotent pedagogue.

And then, when they had discussed all this,
when the father had told all to the child, she
could not be less confiding than he had been;
and as John Bold's name was mentioned between
them, she owned how well she had learned to
love him,—" had loved him once," she said, " but
she would not, could not do so now—no, even
had her troth been plighted to him, she would
have taken it back again—had she sworn to
love him as his wife, she would have discarded
him, and not felt herself forsworn, when he
proved himself the enemy of her father."

But the warden declared that Bold was no
enemy of his, and encouraged her love; and
gently rebuked, as he kissed her, the stern
resolve she had made to cast him off; and then
he spoke to her of happier days when their
trials would all be over; and declared that
her young heart should not be torn asunder
to please either priest or prelate, dean or archdeacon.   No, not if all Oxford were to convocate
together, and agree as to the necessity of the
sacrifice.

And so they greatly comforted each other—
and in what sorrow will not such mutual confidence   give   consolation !—and   with   a   last
expression of tender love they parted, and went
comparatively happy to their rooms.

CHAPTER XI

IPHIGENIA

WHEN Eleanor laid her head on her pillow that night, her mind was anxiously intent on some plan by which she might extricate her father from his misery ; and, in her warm-hearted enthusiasm, self-sacrifice was decided on as the means to be adopted. Was not so good an Agamemnon worthy of an Iphigenia? She would herself personally implore John Bold to desist from his undertaking ; she would explain to him her father's sorrows, the cruel misery of his position ; she would tell him how her father would die if he were thus dragged before the public and exposed to such unmerited ignominy ; she would appeal to his old friendship, to his generosity, to his manliness, to his mercy ; if need were, she would kneel to him for the favour she would ask ; but before she did this, the idea of love must be banished. There must be no bargain in the matter. To his mercy, to his generosity, she could appeal ; but as a pure maiden, hitherto even unsolicited, she could not appeal to his love, nor under such circumstances could she allow him to do so. Of course when so provoked, he would declare his passion ; that was to be expected ;

there had been enough between them to make
such a fact sure; but it was equally certain
that he must be rejected. She could not be
understood as saying, Make my father free
and I am the reward. There would be no
sacrifice in that—not so had Jephthah's daughter
saved her father—not so could she show to that
kindest, dearest of parents how much she was
able to bear for his good. No; to one resolve
must her whole soul be bound; and so resolving,
she felt that she could make her great request
to Bold with as much self-assured confidence
as she could have done to his grandfather.

And now I own I have fears for my heroine:
not as to the upshot of her mission—not in the
least as to that; as to the full success of her
generous scheme, and the ultimate result of
such a project, no one conversant with human
nature and novels can have a doubt; but as to
the amount of sympathy she may receive from
those of her own sex. Girls below twenty
and old ladies above sixty will do her justice;
for in the female heart the soft springs of sweet
romance reopen after many years, and again
gush out with waters pure as in earlier days
and greatly refresh the path that leads down-
wards to the grave. But I fear that the majority
of those between these two eras will not approve
of Eleanor's plan. I fear that unmarried ladies
of thirty-five will declare that there can be no
probability of so absurd a project being carried

through; that young women on their knees
before their lovers are sure to get kissed,
and that they would not put themselves in
such a position did they not expect it ; that
Eleanor is going to Bold, only because circumstances prevent Bold from coming to her ; that
she is certainly a little fool, or a little schemer,
but that in all probability she is thinking a
good deal more about herself than her father.

Dear ladies, you are right as to your appre-
ciation of the circumstances, but very wrong
as to Miss Harding's character. Miss Harding
was much younger than you are, and could
not, therefore, know, as you may do, to what
dangers such an encounter might expose her.
She may get kissed ; I think it very probable
that she will ; but I give my solemn word and
positive assurance, that the remotest idea of
such a catastrophe never occurred to her, as
she made the great resolve now alluded to.

And then she slept ; and then she rose
refreshed, and met her father with her kindest
embrace and most loving smiles ; and on the
whole their breakfast was by no means so
triste as had been their dinner the day before ;
and then, making some excuse to her father
for so soon leaving him, she started on the
commencement of her operations.

She knew that John Bold was in London, and
that, therefore, the scene itself could not be
enacted to-day ; but she also knew that he was

soon to be home, probably on the next day, and it was necessary that some little plan for meeting him should be concerted with his sister Mary. When she got up to the house, she went as usual into the morning sitting-room, and was startled by perceiving, by a stick, a great coat, and sundry parcels which were lying about, that Bold must already have returned.

"John has come back so suddenly," said Mary, coming into the room ; "he has been travelling all night."

"Then I'll come up again some other time," said Eleanor, about to beat a retreat in her sudden dismay.

"He's out now, and will be for the next two hours," said the other ; "he's with that horrid Finney ; he only came to see him, and he returns by the mail train to-night."

Returns by the mail train to-night, thought Eleanor to herself, as she strove to screw up her courage—away again to-night—then it must be now or never ; and she again sat down, having risen to go.

She wished the ordeal could have been postponed : she had fully made up her mind to do the deed, but she had not made up her mind to do it this very day ; and now she felt ill at ease, astray, and in difficulty.

"Mary," she began, " I must see your brother before he goes back."

"Oh yes, of course," said the other ; " I

know he'll be delighted to see you;" and
she tried to treat it as a matter of course, but
she was not the less surprised ; for Mary and
Eleanor had daily talked over John Bold and
his conduct, and his love, and Mary would
insist on calling Eleanor her sister, and would
scold her for not calling Bold by his Christian
name ; and Eleanor would half confess her
love, but like a modest maiden would protest
against such familiarities even with the name
of her lover : and so they talked hour after
hour, and Mary Bold, who was much the elder,
looked forward with happy confidence to the
day when Eleanor would not be ashamed to call
her her sister. She was, however, fully sure that
just at present Eleanor would be much more
likely to avoid her brother than to seek him.

"Mary, I must see your brother, now, to-day,
and beg from him a great favour;" and she
spoke with a solemn air, not at all usual to her ;
and then she went on, and opened to her
friend all her plan, her well-weighed scheme
for saving her father from a sorrow which would,
she said, if it lasted, bring him to his grave.
"But, Mary," she continued, "you must now,
you know, cease any joking about me and
Mr. Bold ; you must now say no more about
that ; I am not ashamed to beg this favour
from your brother, but when I have done so,
there can never be anything further between
us;" and this she said with a staid and solemn

air, quite worthy of Jephthah's daughter or of Iphigenia either.

It was quite clear that Mary Bold did not follow the argument: that Eleanor Harding should appeal, on behalf of her father, to Bold's better feelings, seemed to Mary quite natural; it seemed quite natural that he should relent, overcome by such filial tears, and by so much beauty; but, to her thinking, it was at any rate equally natural, that having relented, John should put his arm round his mistress's waist, and say, "Now having settled that, let us be man and wife, and all will end happily!" Why his good nature should not be rewarded, when such reward would operate to the disadvantage of none, Mary, who had more sense than romance, could not understand; and she said as much.

Eleanor, however, was firm, and made quite an eloquent speech to support her own view of the question: she could not condescend, she said, to ask such a favour on any other terms than those proposed. Mary might, perhaps, think her high-flown, but she had her own ideas, and she could not submit to sacrifice her self-respect.

"But I am sure you love him,—don't you?" pleaded Mary, "and I am sure he loves you better than anything in the world."

Eleanor was going to make another speech, but a tear came to each eye, and she could not; so she pretended to blow her nose, and walked to the window, and made a little inward call on her own courage, and finding herself somewhat sustained, said sententiously,—" Mary, this is nonsense."

" But you do love him," said Mary, who had followed her friend to the window, and now spoke with her arms close wound round the other's waist. "You do love him with all your heart, —you know you do; I defy you to deny it."

" I—" commenced Eleanor, turning sharply round to refute the charge; but the intended falsehood stuck in her throat, and never came to utterance. She could not deny her love, so she took plentifully to tears, and leant upon her friend's bosom and sobbed there, and protested that, love or no love, it would make no difference in her resolve, and called Mary, a thousand times, the most cruel of girls, and swore her to secrecy by a hundred oaths, and ended by declaring that the girl who could betray her friend's love, even to a brother, would be as black a traitor as a soldier in a garrison who should open the city gates to the enemy. While they were yet discussing the matter, Bold returned, and Eleanor was forced into sudden action: she had either to accomplish or abandon her plan; and having slipped into her friend's bed-room, as the gentleman closed the hall door, she washed the marks of tears from her eyes, and resolved within herself to go through with it. "Tell him I am here," said she, "and coming in ; and mind, whatever you do, don't leave us." So Mary informed her brother, with a somewhat sombre air, that Miss Harding was in the next room, and was coming to speak to him.

Eleanor was certainly thinking more of her father than herself, as she arranged her hair before the glass, and removed the traces of sorrow from her face, and yet I should be untrue if I said that she was not anxious to appear well before her lover : why else was she so sedulous with that stubborn curl that would rebel against her hand, and smooth so eagerly her ruffled ribands? why else did she damp her eyes to dispel the redness, and bite her pretty lips to bring back the colour? Of course she was anxious to look her best, for she was but a mortal angel after all. But had she been immortal, had she flitted back to the sitting-room on a cherub's wings, she could not have had a more faithful heart, or a truer wish to save her father at any cost to herself.

John Bold had not met her since the day when she left him in dudgeon in the cathedral close. Since that his whole time had been occupied in promoting the cause against her father, and not unsuccessfully. He had often thought of her, and turned over in his mind a hundred schemes for showing her how disinterested was his love. He would write to her and beseech her not to allow the performance of

a public duty to injure him in her estimation ;
he would write to Mr. Harding, explain all his
views, and boldly claim the warden's daughter,
urging that the untoward circumstances between
them need be no bar to their ancient friendship,
or to a closer tie ; he would throw himself on
his knees before his mistress ; he would wait
and marry the daughter when the father had
lost his home and his income ; he would give up
the lawsuit and go to Australia, with her of
course, leaving the Jupiter and Mr. Finney to
complete the case between them.   Sometimes as
he woke in the morning fevered and impatient,
he would blow out his brains and have done
with all his cares—but this idea was generally
consequent on an imprudent supper enjoyed in
company with Tom Towers.

How beautiful Eleanor appeared to him as
she slowly walked into the room ! Not for
nothing had all those little cares been taken.
Though her sister, the archdeacon's wife, had
spoken slightingly of her charms, Eleanor was
very beautiful when seen aright.   Hers was not
one of those impassive faces, which have the
beauty of a marble bust ; finely chiselled features,
perfect in every line, true to the rules of
symmetry, as lovely to a stranger as to a friend,
unvarying unless in sickness, or as age affects
them.   She had no startling brilliancy of beauty,
no pearly whiteness, no radiant carnation : she
had not the majestic contour that rivets attention,

demands instant wonder, and then disappoints by the coldness of its charms. You might pass Eleanor Harding in the street without notice, but you could hardly pass an evening with her and not lose your heart.

She had never appeared more lovely to her lover than she now did. Her face was animated though it was serious, and her full dark lustrous eyes shone with anxious energy; her hand trembled as she took his, and she could hardly pronounce his name, when she addressed him. Bold wished with all his heart that the Australian scheme was in the act of realisation, and that he and Eleanor were away together, never to hear further of the lawsuit.

He began to talk, asked after her health—said something about London being very stupid, and more about Barchester being very pleasant: declared the weather to be very hot, and then inquired after Mr. Harding.

"My father is not very well," said Eleanor.

John Bold was very sorry, so sorry: he hoped it was nothing serious, and put on the unmeaningly solemn face, which people usually use on such occasions.

"I especially want to speak to you about my father, Mr. Bold; indeed, I am now here on purpose to do so. Papa is very unhappy, very unhappy indeed, about this affair of the hospital: you would pity him, Mr. Bold, if you could see how wretched it has made him."

" Oh, Miss Harding ! "

" Indeed you would,—any one would pity him : but a friend, an old friend as you are— indeed you would. He is an altered man ; his cheerfulness has all gone, and his sweet temper, and his kind happy tone of voice ; you would hardly know him if you saw him, Mr. Bold, he is so much altered ; and—and—if this goes on, he will die." Here Eleanor had recourse to her handkerchief, and so also had her auditors ; but she plucked up her courage, and went on with her tale. " He will break his heart, and die. I am sure, Mr. Bold, it was not you who wrote those cruel things in the newspaper———"

John Bold eagerly protested that it was not, but his heart smote him as to his intimate alliance with Tom Towers.

" No, I am sure it was not ; and papa has not for a moment thought so ; you would not be so cruel—but it has nearly killed him. Papa cannot bear to think that people should so speak of him, and that everybody should hear him so spoken of :—they have called him avaricious, and dishonest, and they say he is robbing the old men, and taking the money of the hospital for nothing."

" I have never said so, Miss Harding. I———"

" No," continued Eleanor, interrupting him, for she was now in the full flood tide of her eloquence ; " no, I am sure you have not, but others have said so ; and if this goes on, if such things are written again, it will kill papa. Oh !

Mr. Bold, if you only knew the state he is in!
Now papa does not care much about money."

Both her auditors, brother and sister, assented
to this, and declared on their own knowledge
that no man lived less addicted to filthy lucre
than the warden.

"Oh! it's so kind of you to say so, Mary, and
of you too, Mr. Bold. I couldn't bear that people
should think unjustly of papa. Do you know he
would give up the hospital altogether, only he
cannot. The archdeacon says it would be
cowardly, and that he would be deserting his
order, and injuring the church. Whatever may
happen, papa will not do that: he would leave
the place to-morrow willingly, and give up his
house, and the income and all, if the archdeacon——" Eleanor was going to say "would
let him," but she stopped herself before she had
compromised her father's dignity; and giving a
long sigh, she added—"Oh, I do so wish he
would."

"No one who knows Mr. Harding personally,
accuses him for a moment," said Bold.

"It is he that has to bear the punishment; it
is he that suffers," said Eleanor; "and what for?
what has he done wrong? how has he deserved
this persecution? he that never had an unkind
thought in his life, he that never said an unkind
word!" and here she broke down, and the
violence of her sobs stopped her utterance.

Bold, for the fifth or sixth time, declared that

neither he nor any of his friends imputed any blame personally to Mr. Harding.

"Then why should he be persecuted?" ejaculated Eleanor through her tears, forgetting in her eagerness that her intention had been to humble herself as a suppliant before John Bold —" why should he be singled out for scorn and disgrace? why should he be made so wretched? Oh! Mr. Bold,"—and she turned towards him as though the kneeling scene were about to be commenced—" oh! Mr. Bold, why did you begin all this? you whom we all so—so—valued!"

To speak the truth, the reformer's punishment was certainly come upon him, for his present plight was not enviable; he had nothing for it but to excuse himself by platitudes about public duty, which it is by no means worth while to repeat, and to reiterate his eulogy on Mr Harding's character. His position was certainly a cruel one: had any gentleman called upon him on behalf of Mr. Harding he could of course have declined to enter upon the subject; but how could he do so with a beautiful girl, with the daughter of the man whom he had injured, with his own love?

In the meantime Eleanor recollected herself, and again summoned up her energies.

"Mr. Bold," said she, "I have come here to implore you to abandon this proceeding."

He stood up from his seat, and looked beyond measure distressed.

"To implore you to abandon it, to implore you to spare my father, to spare either his life or his reason, for one or the other will pay the forfeit if this goes on. I know how much I am asking, and how little right I have to ask anything ; but I think you will listen to me as it is for my father. Oh, Mr. Bold, pray, pray do this for us—pray do not drive to distraction a man who has loved you so well."

She did not absolutely kneel to him, but she followed him as he moved from his chair, and laid her soft hands imploringly upon his arm. Ah ! at any other time how exquisitely valuable would have been that touch ! but now he was distraught, dumb-founded, and unmanned. What could he say to that sweet suppliant ; how explain to her that the matter now was probably beyond his control ; how tell her that he could not quell the storm which he had raised ?

"Surely, surely, John, you cannot refuse her," said his sister.

"I would give her my soul," said he, "if it would serve her."

"Oh, Mr. Bold," said Eleanor, "do not speak so ; I ask nothing for myself; and what I ask for my father, it cannot harm you to grant."

"I would give her my soul, if it would serve her," said Bold, still addressing his sister ; "everything I have is hers, if she will accept it ; my house, my heart, my all ; every hope of my breast is centred in her : her smiles are sweeter to me than the sun, and when I see her in sorrow as she now is, every nerve in my body suffers. No man can love better than I love her."

"No, no, no," ejaculated Eleanor, "there can be no talk of love between us ; will you protect my father from the evil you have brought upon him ?"

"Oh, Eleanor, I will do anything ; let me tell you how I love you !"

"No, no, no," she almost screamed ; "this is unmanly of you, Mr. Bold. Will you, will you, will you leave my father to die in peace in his quiet home?" and seizing him by his arm and hand, she followed him across the room towards the door. "I will not leave you till you promise me ; I'll cling to you in the street ; I'll kneel to you before all the people. You shall promise me this, you shall promise me this, you shall——" And she clung to him with fixed tenacity, and reiterated her resolve with hysterical passion.

"Speak to her, John, answer her," said Mary, bewildered by the unexpected vehemence of Eleanor's manner ; "you cannot have the cruelty to refuse her."

"Promise me, promise me," said Eleanor ; "say that my father is safe—one word will do. I know how true you are ; say one word, and I will let you go."

She still held him, and looked eagerly into his face with her hair dishevelled, and her eyes all bloodshot. She had no thought now of herself, no care now for her appearance, and yet he thought he had never seen her half so lovely ; he was amazed at the intensity of her beauty, and could hardly believe that it was she whom he had dared to love.   " Promise me," said she ; " I will not leave you till you have promised me."

" I will," said he at length, " I do—all I can do, I will do."

" Then may God Almighty bless you for ever and ever !" said Eleanor ; and falling on her knees with her face on Mary's lap, she wept and sobbed like a child : her strength had carried her through her allotted task, but now it was well nigh exhausted.

In a while she was partly recovered, and got up to go, and would have gone, had not Bold made her understand that it was necessary for him to explain to her how far it was in his power to put an end to the proceedings which had been taken against Mr. Harding. Had he spoken on any other subject, she would have vanished, but on that she was bound to hear him ; and now the danger of her position commenced. While she had an active part to play, while she clung to him as a suppliant, it was easy enough for her to reject his proffered love, and cast from her his caressing words ; but now—now that he had yielded, and was talking to her calmly and kindly as to her father's welfare, it was hard enough for her to do so. Then Mary Bold assisted her, but now she was quite on her brother's side. Mary

said but little, but every word she did say gave
some direct and deadly blow. The first thing she
did was to make room for her brother between
herself and Eleanor on the sofa : as the sofa was
full large for three, Eleanor could not resent this,
nor could she show suspicion by taking another
seat ; but she felt it to be a most unkind proceeding. And then Mary would talk as though
they three were joined in some close peculiar
bond together ; as though they were in future
always to wish together, contrive together, and
act together ; and Eleanor could not gainsay
this ; she could not make another speech, and
say, " Mr. Bold and I are mere strangers, Mary,
and are always to remain so ! "

He explained to her that, though undoubtedly
the proceeding against the hospital had commenced solely with himself, many others were
now interested in the matter, some of whom
were much more influential than himself : that
it was to him alone, however, that the lawyers
looked for instruction as to their doings, and,
more important still, for the payment of their
bills ; and he promised that he would at once
give them notice that it was his intention to
abandon the cause. He thought, he said, that
it was not probable that any active steps would
be taken after he had seceded from the matter,
though it was possible that some passing
allusion might still be made to the hospital
in the daily Jupiter. He promised, however,

that he would use his best influence to prevent any further personal allusion being made to Mr. Harding. He then suggested that he would on that afternoon ride over himself to Dr. Grantly, and inform him of his altered intentions on the subject, and with this view, he postponed his immediate return to London.

This was all very pleasant, and Eleanor did enjoy a sort of triumph in the feeling that she had attained the object for which she had sought this interview ; but still the part of Iphigenia was to be played out. The gods had heard her prayer, granted her request, and were they not to have their promised sacrifice ? Eleanor was not a girl to defraud them wilfully ; so, as soon as she decently could, she got up for her bonnet.

"Are you going so soon ? " said Bold, who half an hour since would have given a hundred pounds that he was in London, and she still at Barchester.

"Oh yes ! " said she. "I am so much obliged to you ; papa will feel this to be so kind " (she did not quite appreciate all her father's feelings) ; "of course I must tell him, and I will say that you will see the arch-deacon."

"But may I not say one word for myself ? " said Bold.

"I'll fetch you your bonnet, Eleanor," said Mary, in the act of leaving the room.

"Mary, Mary," said she, getting up and catching her by her dress, "don't go, I'll get my bonnet myself;" but Mary, the traitress, stood fast by the door, and permitted no such retreat. Poor Iphigenia!

And with a volley of impassioned love, John Bold poured forth the feelings of his heart, swearing, as men do, some truths and many falsehoods; and Eleanor repeated with every shade of vehemence the "No, no, no," which had had a short time since so much effect; but now, alas! its strength was gone. Let her be never so vehement, her vehemence was not respected: all her "No, no, no's" were met with counter asseverations, and at last were overpowered. The ground was cut from under her on every side: she was pressed to say whether her father would object; whether she herself had any aversion (aversion! God help her, poor girl! the word nearly made her jump into his arms); any other preference (this she loudly disclaimed); whether it was impossible that she should love him (Eleanor could not say that it was impossible); and so at last, all her defences demolished, all her maiden barriers swept away, she capitulated, or rather marched out with the honours of war, vanquished evidently, palpably vanquished, but still not reduced to the necessity of confessing it.

And so the altar on the shore of the modern Aulis reeked with no sacrifice.

CHAPTER XII

MR. BOLD'S VISIT TO PLUMSTEAD

WHETHER or no the ill-natured prediction made by certain ladies in the beginning of the last chapter, was or was not carried out to the letter, I am not in a position to state; Eleanor, however, certainly did feel herself to have been baffled as she returned home with all her news to her father. Certainly she had been victorious, certainly she had achieved her object, certainly she was not unhappy, and yet she did not feel herself triumphant. Everything would run smooth now. Eleanor was not at all addicted to the Lydian school of romance; she by no means objected to her lover because he came in at the door under the name of Absolute, instead of pulling her out of a window under the name of Beverley; and yet she felt that she had been imposed upon, and could hardly think of Mary Bold with sisterly charity. "I did think I could have trusted Mary," she said to herself over and over again. "Oh that she should have dared to keep me in the room when I tried to get out!" Eleanor, however, felt that the game was up, and that she had now nothing further to do, but to add to the budget of news which was prepared for her father, that John Bold was her accepted lover.

We will, however, now leave her on her way, and go with John Bold to Plumstead Episcopi, merely premising that Eleanor on reaching home will not find things so smooth as she fondly expected; two messengers had come, one to her father, and the other to the archdeacon, and each of them much opposed to her quiet mode of solving all their difficulties; the one in the shape of a number of the Jupiter, and the other in that of a further opinion from Sir Abraham Haphazard.

John Bold got on his horse and rode off to Plumstead Episcopi; not briskly and with eager spur, as men do ride when self-satisfied with their own intentions, but slowly, modestly, thoughtfully, and somewhat in dread of the coming interview. Now and again he would recur to the scene which was just over, support himself by the remembrance of the silence that gives consent, and exult as a happy lover; but even this feeling was not without a shade of remorse. Had he not shown himself childishly weak thus to yield up the resolve of many hours of thought to the tears of a pretty girl? How was he to meet his lawyer? How was he to back out of a matter in which his name was already so publicly concerned? What, oh what! was he to say to Tom Towers? While meditating these painful things he reached the lodge leading up to the archdeacon's glebe, and for the first time in his life found himself within the sacred precincts.

All the doctor's children were together on the slope of the lawn close to the road, as Bold rode up to the hall door. They were there holding high debate on matters evidently of deep interest at Plumstead Episcopi, and the voices of the boys had been heard before the lodge gate was closed.

Florinda and Grizzel, frightened at the sight of so well-known an enemy to the family, fled on the first appearance of the horseman, and ran in terror to their mother's arms; not for them was it, tender branches, to resent injuries, or as members of a church militant to put on armour against its enemies: but the boys stood their ground like heroes, and boldly demanded the business of the intruder.

"Do you want to see anybody here, sir?" said Henry, with a defiant eye and a hostile tone, which plainly said that at any rate no one there wanted to see the person so addressed; and as he spoke he brandished aloft his garden water-pot, holding it by the spout, ready for the braining of any one.

"Henry," said Charles James, slowly, and with a certain dignity of diction, " Mr. Bold of course would not have come without wanting to see some one; if Mr. Bold has a proper ground for wanting to see some person here, of course he has a right to come."

But Samuel stepped lightly up to the horse's head, and offered his services. "Oh, Mr. Bold," said he, "papa, I'm sure, will be glad to see you; I suppose you want to see papa. Shall I hold your horse for you? Oh, what a very pretty horse!" and he turned his head and winked funnily at his brothers; "papa has heard such good news about the old hospital to-day. We know you'll be glad to hear it, because you're such a friend of grandpapa Harding, and so much in love with aunt Nelly!"

"How d'ye do, lads?" said Bold, dismounting; "I want to see your father if he's at home."

"Lads!" said Henry, turning on his heel and addressing himself to his brother, but loud enough to be heard by Bold; "lads, indeed! if we're lads, what does he call himself?"

Charles James condescended to say nothing further, but cocked his hat with much precision, and left the visitor to the care of his youngest brother.

Samuel stayed till the servant came, chatting and patting the horse; but as soon as Bold had disappeared through the front door, he stuck a switch under the animal's tail to make him kick, if possible.

The church reformer soon found himself *tête-à tête* with the archdeacon in that same room, in that sanctum sanctorum of the rectory, to which we have already been introduced. As he entered he heard the click of a certain

patent lock, but it struck him with no surprise:
the worthy clergyman was no doubt hiding from
eyes profane his last much-studied sermon, for
the archdeacon, though he preached but seldom,
was famous for his sermons. No room, Bold
thought, could have been more becoming for a
dignitary of the church; each wall was loaded
with theology; over each separate book-case
was printed in small gold letters the names of
those great divines whose works were ranged
beneath: beginning from the early fathers in due
chronological order, there were to be found the
precious labours of the chosen servants of the
church down to the last pamphlet written in
opposition to the consecration of Dr. Hampden;
and raised above this were to be seen the
busts of the greatest among the great: Chry-
sostom, St. Augustine, Thomas à Becket,
Cardinal Wolsey, Archbishop Laud, and Dr.
Philpotts.

Every appliance that could make study
pleasant and give ease to the over-toiled brain was
there: chairs made to relieve each limb and
muscle; reading-desks and writing-desk to suit
every attitude; lamps and candles mechanically
contrived to throw their light on any favoured
spot, as the student might desire; a shoal of
newspapers to amuse the few leisure moments
which might be stolen from the labours of the
day; and then from the window a view right
through a bosky vista along which ran a broad

green path from the rectory to the church, at the
end of which the tawny-tinted fine old tower
was seen with all its variegated pinnacles and
parapets. Few parish churches in England
are in better repair, or better worth keeping so,
than that at Plumstead Episcopi ; and yet it is
built in a faulty style : the body of the church
is low—so low, that the nearly flat leaden roof
would be visible from the churchyard, were it
not for the carved parapet with which it is
surrounded. It is cruciform, though the tran-
septs are irregular, one being larger than the
other ; and the tower is much too high in pro-
portion to the church : but the colour of the
building is perfect ; it is that rich yellow grey
which one finds nowhere but in the south and
west of England, and which is so strong a
characteristic of most of our old houses of Tudor
architecture. The stone work also is beautiful ;
the mullions of the windows and the thick
tracery of the Gothic workmanship is as rich
as fancy can desire ; and though in gazing on
such a structure, one knows by rule that the
old priests who built it, built it wrong, one
cannot bring oneself to wish that they should
have made it other than it is.

When Bold was ushered into the book-room,
he found its owner standing with his back to
the empty fire-place ready to receive him, and
he could not but perceive that that expansive
brow was elated with triumph, and that those

full heavy lips bore more prominently than usual an appearance of arrogant success.

"Well, Mr. Bold," said he,—"well, what can I do for you? Very happy, I can assure you, to do anything for such a friend of my father-in-law."

"I hope you'll excuse my calling, Dr. Grantly."

"Certainly, certainly," said the archdeacon; "I can assure you, no apology is necessary from Mr. Bold; only let me know what I can do for him."

Dr. Grantly was standing himself, and he did not ask Bold to sit, and therefore he had to tell his tale standing, leaning on the table, with his hat in his hand. He did, however, manage to tell it; and as the archdeacon never once interrupted him, or even encouraged him by a single word, he was not long in coming to the end of it.

"And so, Mr. Bold, I'm to understand, I believe, that you are desirous of abandoning this attack upon Mr. Harding."

"Oh, Dr. Grantly, there has been no attack, I can assure you——"

"Well, well, we won't quarrel about words; I should call it an attack—most men would so call an endeavour to take away from a man every shilling of income that he has to live upon; but it shan't be an attack, if you don't like it; you wish to abandon this—this little game of backgammon you've begun to play."

" I intend to put an end to the legal proceedings which I have commenced."

" I understand," said the archdeacon. " You've already had enough of it; well, I can't say that I am surprised; carrying on a losing lawsuit where one has nothing to gain, but everything to pay, is not pleasant."

Bold turned very red in the face. " You misinterpret my motives," said he; " but, however, that is of little consequence. I did not come to trouble you with my motives, but to tell you a matter of fact. Good morning, Dr. Grantly."

" One moment—one moment," said the other. " I don't exactly appreciate the taste which induced you to make any personal communication to me on the subject; but I dare say I'm wrong, I dare say your judgment is the better of the two; but as you have done me the honour—as you have, as it were, forced me into a certain amount of conversation on a subject which had better, perhaps, have been left to our lawyers, you will excuse me if I ask you to hear my reply to your communication."

" I am in no hurry, Dr. Grantly."

" Well, I am, Mr. Bold; my time is not exactly leisure time, and, therefore, if you please, we'll go to the point at once—you're going to abandon this lawsuit?" and he paused for a reply.

" Yes, Dr. Grantly, I am."

" Having exposed a gentleman who was one of your father's warmest friends, to all the ignominy and insolence which the press could heap upon his name; having somewhat ostentatiously declared that it was your duty as a man of high public virtue to protect those poor old fools whom you have humbugged there at the hospital, you now find that the game costs more than it's worth, and so you make up your mind to have done with it. A prudent resolution, Mr. Bold; but it is a pity you should have been so long coming to it. Has it struck you that we may not now choose to give over? that we may find it necessary to punish the injury you have done to us? Are you aware, sir, that we have gone to enormous expense to resist this iniquitous attempt of yours? "

Bold's face was now furiously red, and he nearly crushed his hat between his hands; but he said nothing.

" We have found it necessary to employ the best advice that money could procure. Are you aware, sir, what may be the probable cost of securing the services of the attorney-general? "

" Not in the least, Dr. Grantly."

" I dare say not, sir. When you recklessly put this affair into the hands of your friend Mr. Finney, whose six and eightpences and thirteen and fourpences may, probably, not amount to a large sum, you were indifferent as to the cost and suffering which such a proceeding might entail on others; but are you aware, sir, that these crushing costs must now come out of your own pocket?"

" Any demand of such a nature which Mr. Harding's lawyer may have to make, will doubtless be made to my lawyer."

" Mr. Harding's lawyer and my lawyer! Did you come here merely to refer me to the lawyers? Upon my word I think the honour of your visit might have been spared! And now, sir, I'll tell what my opinion is—my opinion is, that we shall not allow you to withdraw this matter from the courts."

" You can do as you please, Dr. Grantly; good morning."

" Hear me out, sir," said the archdeacon; " I have here in my hands the last opinion given in this matter by Sir Abraham Haphazard. I dare say you have already heard of this—I dare say it has had something to do with your visit here to-day."

" I know nothing whatever of Sir Abraham Haphazard or his opinion."

" Be that as it may, here it is; he declares most explicitly that under no phasis of the affair whatever have you a leg to stand upon; that Mr. Harding is as safe in his hospital as I am here in my rectory; that a more futile attempt to destroy a man was never made, than this which you have made to ruin Mr. Harding. Here," and he slapped the paper on the table, "I have this opinion from the very first lawyer in the land; and under these circumstances you expect me to make you a low bow for your kind offer to release Mr. Harding from the toils of your net! Sir, your net is not strong enough to hold him; sir, your net has fallen to pieces, and you knew that well enough before I told you— and now, sir, I'll wish you good morning, for I'm busy."

Bold was now choking with passion; he had let the archdeacon run on, because he knew not with what words to interrupt him: but now that he had been so defied and insulted, he could not leave the room without some reply.

"Dr. Grantly," he commenced.

"I have nothing further to say or to hear," said the archdeacon; "I'll do myself the honour to order your horse:" and he rang the bell.

"I came here, Dr. Grantly, with the warmest, kindest feelings——"

"Oh, of course you did; nobody doubts it."

"With the kindest feelings—and they have been most grossly outraged by your treatment."

"Of course they have—I have not chosen to

see my father-in-law ruined ; what an outrage
that has been to your feelings ! "

" The time will come, Dr. Grantly, when
you will understand why I called upon you to-
day."

" No doubt, no doubt. Is Mr. Bold's horse
there ? That's right, open the front door—
good morning, Mr. Bold ; " and the doctor
stalked into his own drawing-room, closing
the door behind him, and making it quite
impossible that John Bold should speak another
word.

As he got on his horse, which he was fain
to do feeling like a dog turned out of a kitchen,
he was again greeted by little Sammy.

" Good bye, Mr. Bold ; I hope we may
have the pleasure of seeing you again before
long ; I am sure papa will always be glad to
see you."

That was certainly the bitterest moment
in John Bold's life ; not even the remembrance
of his successful love could comfort him : nay,
when he thought of Eleanor, he felt that it
was that very love which had brought him to
such a pass. That he should have been so
insulted, and be unable to reply ! That he
should have given up so much to the request
of a girl, and then have had his motives so
misunderstood ! That he should have made
so gross a mistake as this visit of his to the
archdeacon's ! He bit the top of his whip,

till he penetrated the horn of which it was made : he struck the poor animal in his anger, and then was doubly angry with himself at his futile passion. He had been so completely check-mated, so palpably overcome! and what was he to do? He could not continue his action after pledging himself to abandon it; nor was there any revenge in that—it was the very step to which his enemy had endeavoured to goad him!

He threw the reins to the servant who came to take his horse, and rushed upstairs into his drawing-room, where his sister Mary was sitting.

"If there be a devil," said he, "a real devil here on earth, it is Dr. Grantly." He vouchsafed her no further intelligence, but again seizing his hat, he rushed out, and took his departure for London without another word to any one.

CHAPTER XIII

THE WARDEN'S DECISION

THE meeting between Eleanor and her father was not so stormy as that described in the last chapter, but it was hardly more successful. On her return from Bold's house, she found her father in a strange state. He was not sorrowful and silent as he had been on that memorable day when his son-in-law lectured him as to all that he owed to his order; nor was he in his usual quiet mood. When Eleanor reached the hospital, he was walking quickly to and fro upon the lawn, and she soon saw that he was much excited.

"I am going to London, my dear," he said as soon as he saw her.

"London, papa!"

"Yes, my dear, to London; I will have this matter settled some way; there are some things, Eleanor, which I cannot bear."

"Oh, papa, what is it?" said she, leading him by the arm into the house—"I had such good news for you, and now you make me fear I am too late; " and then, before he could let her know what had caused this sudden resolve, or could point to the fatal paper which lay on the table, she told him that the lawsuit

183

was over, that Bold had commissioned her
to assure her father in his name that it would
be abandoned, that there was no further cause
for misery, that the whole matter might be
looked on as though it had never been discussed. She did not tell him with what
determined vehemence she had obtained this
concession in his favour, nor did she mention
the price she was to pay for it.

The warden did not express himself peculiarly
gratified at this intelligence, and Eleanor,
though she had not worked for thanks, and
was by no means disposed to magnify her
own good offices, felt hurt at the manner in
which her news was received.

" Mr. Bold can act as he thinks proper, my
love," said he ; "if Mr. Bold thinks that he
has been wrong, of course he will discontinue
what he is doing ; but that cannot change my
purpose."

" Oh, papa ! " she exclaimed, all but crying
with vexation—" I thought you would have
been so happy—I thought all would have been
right now."

" Mr. Bold," continued he, " has set great
people to work, so great that I doubt they are
now beyond his control. Read that, my dear : "
and the warden, doubling up a number of the
Jupiter, pointed to the peculiar article which
she was to read. It was to the last of the three
leaders, which are generally furnished daily for

the support of the nation, that Mr. Harding
directed her attention. It dealt some heavy
blows on various clerical delinquents ; on families
who had received their tens of thousands yearly
for doing nothing ; on men who, as the article
stated, rolled in wealth which they had neither
earned nor inherited, and which was in fact
stolen from the poorer clergy. It named some
sons of bishops, and grandsons of archbishops ;
men great in their way, who had redeemed
their disgrace in the eyes of many by the
enormity of their plunder ; and then, having
disposed of these leviathans, it descended to
Mr. Harding.

"We alluded some few weeks since to an
instance of similar injustice, though in a more
humble scale, in which the warden of an almshouse at Barchester has become possessed of
the income of the greater part of the whole
institution. Why an almshouse should have a
warden we cannot pretend to explain, nor can
we say what special need twelve old men can
have for the services of a separate clergyman,
seeing that they have twelve reserved seats for
themselves in Barchester Cathedral. But be
this as it may, let the gentleman call himself
warden or precentor, or what he will, let him
be never so scrupulous in exacting religious
duties from his twelve dependants, or never so
negligent as regards the services of the cathedral, it appears palpably clear that he can be

entitled to no portion of the revenue of the
hospital, excepting that which the founder set
apart for him ; and it is equally clear that the
founder did not intend that three-fifths of his
charity should be so consumed.

"The case is certainly a paltry one after the
tens of thousands with which we have been
dealing, for the warden's income is after all but
a poor eight hundred a year : eight hundred a
year is not magnificent preferment of itself, and
the warden may, for anything we know, be
worth much more to the church ; but if so, let
the church pay him out of funds justly at its
own disposal.

"We allude to the question of the Barchester almshouse at the present moment,
because we understand that a plea has been set
up which will be peculiarly revolting to the
minds of English churchmen. An action has
been taken against Mr. Warden Harding, on
behalf of the almsmen, by a gentleman acting
solely on public grounds, and it is to be argued
that Mr. Harding takes nothing but what he
receives as a servant of the hospital, and that
he is not himself responsible for the amount
of stipend given to him for his work. Such a
plea would doubtless be fair, if any one questioned the daily wages of a bricklayer employed
on the building, or the fee of the charwoman
who cleans it ; but we cannot envy the feeling
of a clergyman of the Church of England who

could allow such an argument to be put into his mouth.

"If this plea be put forward, we trust Mr. Harding will be forced as a witness to state the nature of his employment; the amount of work that he does; the income which he receives, and the source from whence he obtained his appointment. We do not think he will receive much public sympathy to atone for the annoyance of such an examination."

As Eleanor read the article her face flushed with indignation, and when she had finished it, she almost feared to look up at her father.

"Well, my dear," said he, "what do you think of that—is it worth while to be a warden at that price?"

"Oh, papa—dear papa!"

"Mr. Bold can't unwrite that, my dear— Mr. Bold can't say that that shan't be read by every clergyman at Oxford; nay, by every gentleman in the land:" and then he walked up and down the room, while Eleanor in mute despair followed him with her eyes—"and I'll tell you what, my dear," he continued, speaking now very calmly, and in a forced manner very unlike himself. "Mr. Bold can't dispute the truth of every word in that article you have just read—nor can I." Eleanor stared at him, as though she scarcely understood the words he was speaking. "Nor can I, Eleanor: that's the worst of all, or would be so if there were no remedy; I have thought much of all this since we were together last night;" and he came and sat beside her, and put his arm round her waist as he had done then. "I have thought much of what the archdeacon has said, and of what this paper says; and I do believe I have no right to be here."

"No right to be warden of the hospital, papa?"

"No right to be warden with eight hundred a year; no right to be warden with such a house as this; no right to spend in luxury money that was intended for charity. Mr. Bold may do as he pleases about his suit, but I hope he will not abandon it for my sake."

Poor Eleanor! this was hard upon her. Was it for this she had made her great resolve? For this that she had laid aside her quiet demeanour, and taken upon her the rants of a tragedy heroine? One may work and not for thanks, but yet feel hurt at not receiving them; and so it was with Eleanor: one may be disinterested in one's good actions, and yet feel discontented that they are not recognised. Charity may be given with the left hand so privily that the right hand does not know it, and yet the left hand may regret to feel that it has no immediate reward. Eleanor had had no wish to burden her father with a weight of obligation, and yet she had looked forward to much delight from the knowledge that she had freed him from his sorrows : now such hopes were entirely over ; all that she had done was of no avail ; she had humbled herself to Bold in vain ; the evil was utterly beyond her power to cure!

She had thought also how gently she would whisper to her father all that her lover had said to her about herself, and how impossible she had found it to reject him : and then she had anticipated her father's kindly kiss and close embrace as he gave his sanction to her love. Alas! she could say nothing of this now. In speaking of Mr. Bold, her father put him aside as one whose thoughts and sayings and acts could be of no moment. Gentle reader, did you ever feel yourself snubbed? Did you ever, when thinking much of your own importance, find yourself suddenly reduced to a nonentity? Such was Eleanor's feeling now.

"They shall not put forward this plea on my behalf," continued the warden. "Whatever may be the truth of the matter, that at any rate is not true ; and the man who wrote that article is right in saying that such a plea is revolting to an honest mind. I will go up to London, my dear, and see these lawyers myself, and if no better excuse can be made for me than that, I and the hospital will part."

"But the archdeacon, papa ?"

"I can't help it, my dear ; there are some things which a man cannot bear,—I cannot bear that"—and he put his hand upon the newspaper.

"But will the archdeacon go with you?"

harmless combat metaphor

To tell the truth, Mr. Harding had made up his mind to steal a march upon the archdeacon. He was aware that he could take no steps without informing his dread son-in-law, but he had resolved that he would send out a note to Plumstead Episcopi detailing his plans, but that the messenger should not leave Barchester till he himself had started for London; so that he might be a day before the doctor, who, he had no doubt, would follow him. In that day, if he had luck, he might arrange it all; he might explain to Sir Abraham that he, as warden, would have nothing further to do with the defence about to be set up; he might send in his official resignation to his friend the bishop, and so make public the whole transaction, that even the doctor would not be able to undo what he had done. He knew too well the doctor's strength and his own weakness to suppose he could do this, if they both reached London together; indeed, he would never be able to get to London, if the doctor knew of his intended journey in time to prevent it.

"No, I think not," said he; "I think I shall start before the archdeacon could be ready—I shall go early to-morrow morning."

"That will be best, papa," said Eleanor, showing that her father's ruse was appreciated.

"Why, yes, my love: the fact is, I wish to do

all this before the archdeacon can—can interfere.   There is a great deal of truth in all he
says—he argues very well, and I can't always
answer him ; but there is an old saying, Nelly,
' every one knows where his own shoe pinches ! '
He'll say that I want moral courage, and strength
of character, and power of endurance, and it's
all true ; but I'm sure I ought not to remain here,
if I have nothing better to put forward than a
quibble : so, Nelly, we shall have to leave this
pretty place."

Eleanor's face brightened up as she assured her
father how cordially she agreed with him.

"True, my love," said he, now again quite
happy and at ease in his manner.   "What good
to us is this place or all the money, if we are to
be ill-spoken of ? "

"Oh, papa, I am so glad ! "

"My darling child.   It did cost me a pang at
first, Nelly, to think that you should lose your
pretty drawing-room, and your ponies, and your
garden : the garden will be the worst of all—but
there is a garden at Crabtree, a very pretty
garden."

Crabtree Parva was the name of the small
living which Mr. Harding had held as a minor
canon, and which still belonged to him.   It was
only worth some eighty pounds a year, and a
small house and glebe, all of which were now
handed over to Mr. Harding's curate ; but it was
to Crabtree glebe that Mr. Harding thought of

retiring. This parish must not be mistaken for that other living, Crabtree Canonicorum, as it is called. Crabtree Canonicorum is a very nice thing ; there are only two hundred parishioners ; there are four hundred acres of glebe ; and the great and small tithes, which both go to the rector, are worth four hundred pounds a year more. Crabtree Canonicorum is in the gift of the dean and chapter, and is at this time possessed by the Honourable and Reverend Dr. Vesey Stanhope, who also fills the prebendal stall of Goosegorge in Barchester Chapter, and holds the united rectory of Eiderdown and Stogpingum, or Stoke Pinquium, as it should be written. This is the same Dr. Vesey Stanhope, whose hospitable villa on the Lake of Como is so well known to the *élite* of English travellers, and whose collection of Lombard butterflies is supposed to be unique.

" Yes," said the warden, musing, " there is a very pretty garden at Crabtree, but I shall be sorry to disturb poor Smith." Smith was the curate of Crabtree, a gentleman who was maintaining a wife and half a dozen children on the income arising from his profession.

Eleanor assured her father that, as far as she was concerned, she could leave her house and her ponies without a single regret : she was only so happy that he was going—going where he would escape all this dreadful turmoil.

" But we will take the music, my dear."

And so they went on planning their future happiness, and plotting how they would arrange it all without the interposition of the archdeacon, and at last they again became confidential, and then the warden did thank her for what she had done, and Eleanor, lying on her father's shoulder, did find an opportunity to tell her secret : and the father gave his blessing to his child, and said that the man whom she loved was honest, good and kindhearted, and right-thinking in the main —one who wanted only a good wife to put him quite upright ;—"a man, my love," he ended by saying, "to whom I firmly believe that I can trust my treasure with safety."

" But what will Dr. Grantly say ?"

" Well, my dear, it can't be helped—we shall be out at Crabtree then."

And Eleanor ran upstairs to prepare her father's clothes for his journey ; and the warden returned to his garden to make his last adieus to every tree, and shrub, and shady nook that he knew so well.

CHAPTER XIV

MOUNT OLYMPUS

WRETCHED in spirit, groaning under the feeling of insult, self-condemning, and ill-satisfied in every way, Bold returned to his London lodgings. Ill as he had fared in his interview with the archdeacon, he was not less under the necessity of carrying out his pledge to Eleanor ; and he went about his ungracious task with a heavy heart.

The attorneys whom he had employed in London received his instructions with surprise and evident misgiving ; however, they could only obey, and mutter something of their sorrow that such heavy costs should only fall upon their own employer,—especially as nothing was wanting but perseverance to throw them on the opposite party. Bold left the office which he had latterly so much frequented, shaking the dust from off his feet ; and before he was down the stairs, an edict had already gone forth for the preparation of the bill.

He next thought of the newspapers. The case had been taken up by more than one ; and he was well aware that the key note had been sounded by the Jupiter. He had been very intimate with Tom Towers, and had

often discussed with him the affairs of the
hospital. Bold could not say that the articles
in that paper had been written at his own
instigation ; he did not even know as a fact
that they had been written by his friend.
Tom Towers had never said that such a view
of the case, or such a side in the dispute,
would be taken by the paper with which he
was connected. Very discreet in such matters
was Tom Towers, and altogether indisposed
to talk loosely of the concerns of that mighty
engine of which it was his high privilege to
move in secret some portion. Nevertheless,
Bold believed that to him were owing those
dreadful words which had caused such panic
at Barchester,—and he conceived himself
bound to prevent their repetition. With this
view he betook himself from the attorney's to
that laboratory where, with amazing chemistry,
Tom Towers compounded thunderbolts for
the destruction of all that is evil, and for the
furtherance of all that is good, in this and other
hemispheres.

Who has not heard of Mount Olympus—that
high abode of all the powers of type, that favoured
seat of the great goddess Pica, that wondrous
habitation of gods and devils, from whence, with
ceaseless hum of steam and never-ending flow
of Castalian ink, issue forth fifty thousand nightly
edicts for the governance of a subject nation ?

Velvet and gilding do not make a throne, nor

gold and jewels a sceptre. It is a throne because the most exalted one sits there—and a sceptre because the most mighty one wields it. So it is with Mount Olympus. Should a stranger make his way thither at dull noonday, or during the sleepy hours of the silent afternoon, he would find no acknowledged temple of power and beauty, no fitting fane for the great Thunderer, no proud façades and pillared roofs to support the dignity of this greatest of earthly potentates. To the outward and uninitiated eye, Mount Olympus is a somewhat humble spot—undistinguished, unadorned,—nay, almost mean. It stands alone, as it were, in a mighty city, close to the densest throng of men, but partaking neither of the noise nor the crowd ; a small secluded, dreary spot, tenanted, one would say, by quiet unambitious people at the easiest rents. " Is this Mount Olympus ? " asks the unbelieving stranger. " Is it from these small, dark, dingy buildings that those infallible laws proceed which cabinets are called upon to obey ; by which bishops are to be guided, lords and commons controlled,—judges instructed in law, generals in strategy, admirals in naval tactics, and orange-women in the management of their barrows ? " " Yes, my friend—from these walls. From here issue the only known infallible bulls for the guidance of British souls and bodies. This little court is the Vatican of England. Here reigns a pope, self-nominated, self-consecrated

—ay, and much stranger too—self-believing !—a pope whom, if you cannot obey him, I would advise you to disobey as silently as possible ; a pope hitherto afraid of no Luther ; a pope who manages his own inquisition, who punishes unbelievers as no most skilful inquisitor of Spain ever dreamt of doing—one who can excommunicate thoroughly, fearfully, radically ; put you beyond the pale of men's charity ; make you odious to your dearest friends, and turn you into a monster to be pointed at by the finger ! "

Oh heavens ! and this is Mount Olympus !

It is a fact amazing to ordinary mortals that the Jupiter is never wrong. With what endless care, with what unsparing labour, do we not strive to get together for our great national council the men most fitting to compose it. And how we fail ! Parliament is always wrong : look at the Jupiter, and see how futile are their meetings, how vain their council, how needless all their trouble ! With what pride do we regard our chief ministers, the great servants of state, the oligarchs of the nation on whose wisdom we lean, to whom we look for guidance in our difficulties ! But what are they to the writers of the Jupiter ? They hold council together and with anxious thought painfully elaborate their country's good ; but when all is done, the Jupiter declares that all is nought. Why should we look to Lord John Russell—why should we regard Palmerston and Gladstone, when Tom Towers without a struggle can put us right? Look at our generals, what faults they make; at our admirals, how inactive they are. What money, honesty, and science can do, is done; and yet how badly are our troops brought together, fed, conveyed, clothed, armed, and managed. The most excellent of our good men do their best to man our ships, with the assistance of all possible external appliances, but in vain. All, all is wrong—alas! alas! Tom Towers, and he alone, knows all about it. Why, oh why, ye earthly ministers, why have ye not followed more closely this heaven-sent messenger that is among us?

Were it not well for us in our ignorance that we confided all things to the Jupiter? Would it not be wise in us to abandon useless talking, idle thinking, and profitless labour? Away with majorities in the House of Commons, with verdicts from judicial bench given after much delay, with doubtful laws, and the fallible attempts of humanity! Does not the Jupiter, coming forth daily with fifty thousand impressions full of unerring decision on every mortal subject, set all matters sufficiently at rest? Is not Tom Towers here, able to guide us and willing.

Yes indeed,—able and willing to guide all men in all things, so long as he is obeyed as autocrat should be obeyed—with undoubting

submission : only let not ungrateful ministers
seek other colleagues than those whom Tom
Towers may approve; let church and state,
law and physic, commerce and agriculture—
the arts of war, and the arts of peace, all listen
and obey, and all will be made perfect. Has
not Tom Towers an all-seeing eye ? From
the diggings of Australia to those of California,
right round the habitable globe, does he not
know, watch, and chronicle the doings of
every one ? From a bishopric in New Zealand
to an unfortunate director of a North-west
passage, is he not the only fit judge of capa-
bility? From the sewers of London to the
Central Railway of India,—from the palaces
of St. Petersburg to the cabins of Connaught,
nothing can escape him. Britons have but to
read, to obey, and be blessed. None but the
fools doubt the wisdom of the Jupiter : none
but the mad dispute its facts.

No established religion has ever been without its unbelievers, even in the country where
it is the most firmly fixed ; no creed has been
without scoffers; no church has so prospered
as to free itself entirely from dissent. There
are those who doubt the Jupiter! They live
and breathe the upper air, walking here unscathed, though scorned—men, born of British
mothers and nursed on English milk, who
scruple not to say that Mount Olympus has its
price, that Tom Towers can be bought for gold !

Such is Mount Olympus, the mouthpiece of all the wisdom of this great country. It may probably be said that no place in this 19th century is more worthy of notice. No treasury mandate armed with the signatures of all the government has half the power of one of those broad sheets, which fly forth from hence so abundantly, armed with no signature at all.

Some great man, some mighty peer—we'll say a noble duke—retires to rest feared and honoured by all his countrymen—fearless himself; if not a good man, at any rate a mighty man—too mighty to care much what men may say about his want of virtue. He rises in the morning degraded, mean, and miserable; an object of men's scorn, anxious only to retire as quickly as may be to some German obscurity, some unseen Italian privacy, or, indeed, anywhere out of sight. What has made this awful change? what has so afflicted him? An article has appeared in the Jupiter; some fifty lines of a narrow column have destroyed all his grace's equanimity, and banished him for ever from the world. No man knows who wrote the bitter words; the clubs talk confusedly of the matter, whispering to each other this and that name; while Tom Towers walks quietly along Pall Mall, with his coat buttoned close against the east wind, as though he were a mortal man

and not a god dispensing thunderbolts from
Mount Olympus.

It was not to Mount Olympus that our friend
Bold betook himself. He had before now
wandered round that lonely spot, thinking
how grand a thing it was to write articles for
the Jupiter ; considering within himself whether
by any stretch of the powers within him he
could ever come to such distinction ; wondering
how Tom Towers would take any little humble
offering of his talents ; calculating that Tom
Towers himself must have once had a beginning,
have once doubted as to his own success.
Towers could not have been born a writer in
the Jupiter. With such ideas, half ambitious
and half awe-struck, had Bold regarded the
silent-looking workshop of the gods ; but he
had never yet by word or sign attempted to
influence the slightest word of his unerring
friend. On such a course was he now intent ;
and not without much inward palpitation did
he betake himself to the quiet abode of wisdom,
where Tom Towers was to be found o' mornings
inhaling ambrosia and sipping nectar in the
shape of toast and tea.

Not far removed from Mount Olympus, but
somewhat nearer to the blessed regions of the
West, is the most favoured abode of Themis.
Washed by the rich tide which now passes
from the towers of Cæsar to Barry's halls of
eloquence ; and again back, with new offerings

of a city's tribute, from the palaces of peers to the mart of merchants, stand those quiet walls which Law has delighted to honour by its presence. What a world within a world is the Temple! how quiet are its "entangled walks," as some one lately has called them, and yet how close to the densest concourse of humanity! how gravely respectable its sober alleys, though removed but by a single step from the profanity of the Strand and the low iniquity of Fleet Street! Old St. Dunstan, with its bell-smiting bludgeoners, has been removed; the ancient shops with their faces full of pleasant history are passing away one by one; the bar itself is to go—its doom has been pronounced by the Jupiter; rumour tells us of some huge building that is to appear in these latitudes dedicated to law, subversive of the courts of Westminster, and antagonistic to the Rolls and Lincoln's Inn; but nothing yet threatens the silent beauty of the Temple: it is the mediæval court of the metropolis.

Here, on the choicest spot of this choice ground, stands a lofty row of chambers, looking obliquely upon the sullied Thames; before the windows, the lawn of the Temple Gardens stretches with that dim yet delicious verdure so refreshing to the eyes of Londoners. If doomed to live within the thickest of London smoke, you would surely say that that would be your chosen spot. Yes, you, you whom

I now address, my dear, middle-aged bachelor
friend, can nowhere be so well domiciled as
here. No one here will ask whether you are
out or at home; alone or with friends: here
no Sabbatarian will investigate your Sundays,
no censorious landlady will scrutinise your empty
bottle, no valetudinarian neighbour will complain of late hours. If you love books, to what
place are books so suitable? The whole
spot is redolent of typography. Would you
worship the Paphian goddess, the groves of
Cyprus are not more taciturn than those of
the Temple. Wit and wine are always here,
and always together; the revels of the Temple
are as those of polished Greece, where the
wildest worshipper of Bacchus never forgot
the dignity of the god whom he adored. Where
can retirement be so completed as here? where
can you be so sure of all the pleasures of society?

It was here that Tom Towers lived, and
cultivated with eminent success the tenth Muse
who now governs the periodical press. But
let it not be supposed that his chambers were
such, or so comfortless, as are frequently the
gaunt abodes of legal aspirants. Four chairs,
a half-filled deal book-case with hangings of
dingy green baize, an old office table covered
with dusty papers, which are not moved once in
six months, and an older Pembroke brother with
rickety legs, for all daily uses—a despatcher
for the preparation of lobsters and coffee, and

an apparatus for the cooking of toast and mutton chops; such utensils and luxuries as these did not suffice for the well-being of Tom Towers. He indulged in four rooms on the first floor, each of which was furnished, if not with the splendour, with probably more than the comfort of Stafford House. Every addition that science and art have lately made to the luxuries of modern life was to be found there. The room in which he usually sat was surrounded by book-shelves carefully filled; nor was there a volume there which was not entitled to its place in such a collection, both by its intrinsic worth and exterior splendour: a pretty portable set of steps in one corner of the room showed that those even on the higher shelves were intended for use. The chamber contained but two works of art—the one, an admirable bust of Sir Robert Peel, by Power, declared the individual politics of our friend; and the other, a singularly long figure of a female devotee, by Millais, told equally plainly the school of art to which he was addicted. This picture was not hung, as pictures usually are, against the wall; there was no inch of wall vacant for such a purpose: it had a stand or desk erected for its own accommodation; and there on her pedestal, framed and glazed, stood the devotional lady looking intently at a lily as no lady ever looked before.

Our modern artists, whom we style Præ-

Raffaellites, have delighted to go back, not
only to the finish and peculiar manner, but
also to the subjects of the early painters. It
is impossible to give them too much praise for
the elaborate perseverance with which they
have equalled the minute perfections of the
masters from whom they take their inspira-
tion : nothing probably can exceed the paint-
ing of some of these latter-day pictures. It
is, however, singular into what faults they fall
as regards their subjects : they are not quite
content to take the old stock groups—a Sebastian with his arrows, a Lucia with her
eyes in a dish, a Lorenzo with a gridiron, or
the Virgin with two children. But they are
anything but happy in their change. As a
rule, no figure should be drawn in a position
which it is impossible to suppose any figure
should maintain. The patient endurance of
St. Sebastian, the wild ecstasy of St. John in
the Wilderness, the maternal love of the
Virgin, are feelings naturally portrayed by a
fixed posture; but the lady with the stiff
back and bent neck, who looks at her flower,
and is still looking from hour to hour, gives
us an idea of pain without grace, and abstraction
without a cause.

It was easy, from his rooms, to see that Tom
Towers was a Sybarite, though by no means
an idle one. He was lingering over his last
cup of tea, surrounded by an ocean of news-

papers, through which he had been swimming,
when John Bold's card was brought in by his
tiger. This tiger never knew that his master
was at home, though he often knew that he
was not, and thus Tom Towers was never
invaded but by his own consent. On this
occasion, after twisting the card twice in his
fingers, he signified to his attendant imp that
he was visible; and the inner door was un-
bolted, and our friend announced.

I have before said that he of the Jupiter
and John Bold were intimate. There was
no very great difference in their ages, for
Towers was still considerably under forty;
and when Bold had been attending the London
hospitals, Towers, who was not then the great
man that he had since become, had been much
with him. Then they had often discussed
together the objects of their ambition and
future prospects; then Tom Towers was
struggling hard to maintain himself, as a
briefless barrister, by short-hand reporting for
any of the papers that would engage him;
then he had not dared to dream of writing
leaders for the Jupiter, or canvassing the
conduct of Cabinet ministers. Things had
altered since that time: the briefless barrister
was still briefless, but he now despised briefs:
could he have been sure of a judge's seat, he
would hardly have left his present career. It
is true he wore no ermine, bore no outward

marks of a world's respect; but with what a
load of inward impotance was he charged! It
is true his name appeared in no large capitals;
on no wall was chalked up "Tom Towers for
ever"—"Freedom of the Press and Tom
Towers:" but what member of Parliament had
half his power? It is true that in far-off
provinces men did not talk daily of Tom Towers,
but they read the Jupiter, and acknowledged
that without the Jupiter life was not worth
having. This kind of hidden but still conscious
glory suited the nature of the man. He loved
to sit silent in a corner of his club and listen
to the loud chattering of politicians, and to
think how they all were in his power—how he
could smite the loudest of them, were it worth
his while to raise his pen for such a purpose.
He loved to watch the great men of whom he
daily wrote, and flatter himself that he was
greater than any of them. Each of them was
responsible to his country, each of them must
answer if inquired into, each of them must
endure abuse with good humour, and insolence
without anger. But to whom was he, Tom
Towers, responsible? No one could insult
him; no one could inquire into him. He
could speak out withering words, and no one
could answer him: ministers courted him,
though perhaps they knew not his name;
bishops feared him; judges doubted their
own verdicts unless he confirmed them; and

generals, in their councils of war, did not consider more deeply what the enemy would do, than what the Jupiter would say. Tom Towers never boasted of the Jupiter; he scarcely ever named the paper even to the most intimate of his friends; he did not even wish to be spoken of as connected with it; but he did not the less value his privileges, or think the less of his own importance. It is probable that Tom Towers considered himself the most powerful man in Europe; and so he walked on from day to day, studiously striving to look a man, but knowing within his breast that he was a god.

CHAPTER XV

"Ah, Bold! how are you? You haven't breakfasted?"

"Oh yes, hours ago. And how are you?"

When one Esquimaux meets another, do the two, as an invariable rule, ask after each other's health? is it inherent in all human nature to make this obliging inquiry? Did any reader of this tale ever meet any friend or acquaintance without asking some such question, and did any one ever listen to the reply? Sometimes a studiously courteous questioner will show so much thought in the matter as to answer it himself, by declaring that had he looked at you he needn't have asked; meaning thereby to signify that you are an absolute personification of health: but such persons are only those who premeditate small effects.

"I suppose you're busy?" inquired Bold.

"Why, yes, rather; or I should say rather not: I have a leisure hour in the day, this is it."

"I want to ask you if you can oblige me in a certain matter."

Towers understood in a moment, from the

tone of his friend's voice, that the certain matter referred to the newspaper. He smiled, and nodded his head, but made no promise.

"You know this lawsuit that I've been engaged in," said Bold.

Tom Towers intimated that he was aware of the action which was pending about the hospital.

"Well, I've abandoned it."

Tom Towers merely raised his eyebrows, thrust his hands into his trousers' pockets, and waited for his friend to proceed.

"Yes, I've given it up. I needn't trouble you with all the history ; but the fact is that the conduct of Mr. Harding—Mr. Harding is the——"

"Oh yes, the master of the place ; the man who takes all the money and does nothing," said Tom Towers, interrupting him.

"Well, I don't know about that ; but his conduct in the matter has been so excellent, so little selfish, so open, that I cannot proceed in the matter to his detriment." Bold's heart misgave him as to Eleanor as he said this ; and yet he felt that what he said was not untrue. "I think nothing should now be done till the wardenship be vacant."

"And be again filled," said Towers, "as it certainly would, before any one heard of the vacancy ; and the same objection would again exist. It's an old story that of the vested rights of the incumbent; but suppose the incumbent has only a vested wrong, and that the poor of the town have a vested right, if they only knew how to get at it: is not that something the case here?"

Bold couldn't deny it, but thought it was one of those cases which required a good deal of management before any real good could be done. It was a pity that he had not considered this before he crept into the lion's mouth, in the shape of an attorney's office.

"It will cost you a good deal, I fear," said Towers.

"A few hundreds," said Bold—"perhaps three hundred; I can't help that, and am prepared for it."

"That's philosophical; it's quite refreshing to hear a man talking of his hundreds in so purely indifferent a manner. But I'm sorry you are giving the matter up; it injures a man to commence a thing of this kind, and not carry it through. Have you seen that?" and he threw a small pamphlet across the table, which was all but damp from the press.

Bold had not seen it nor heard of it; but he was well acquainted with the author of it—a gentleman whose pamphlets, condemnatory of all things in these modern days, had been a good deal talked about of late.

Dr. Pessimist Anticant was a Scotchman, who had passed a great portion of his early days in Germany; he had studied there with much effect, and had learnt to look with German subtilty into the root of things, and to examine for himself their intrinsic worth and worthlessness. No man ever resolved more bravely than he to accept as good nothing that was evil; to banish from him as evil nothing that was good. 'Tis a pity that he should not have recognised the fact, that in this world no good is unalloyed, and that there is but little evil that has not in it some seed of what is goodly.

Returning from Germany, he had astonished the reading public by the vigour of his thoughts, put forth in the quaintest language. He cannot write English, said the critics. No matter, said the public; we can read what he does write, and that without yawning. And so Dr. Pessimist Anticant became popular. Popularity spoilt him for all further real use, as it has done many another. While, with some diffidence, he confined his objurgations to the occasional follies or shortcomings of mankind; while he ridiculed the energy of the squire devoted to the slaughter of partridges, or the mistake of some noble patron who turned a poet into a gauger of beer-barrels, it was all well; we were glad to be told our faults and to look forward to the coming millennium, when all men, having sufficiently studied the works of Dr. Anticant, would become truthful

Dr. Anticant - a sattirical comparison to
    Sir Thomas Carlyle

and energetic. But the doctor mistook the
signs of the times and the minds of men, instituted himself censor of things in general, and
began the great task of reprobating everything
and everybody, without further promise of
any millennium at all. This was not so well;
and, to tell the truth, our author did not
succeed in his undertaking. His theories were
all beautiful, and the code of morals that he
taught us certainly an improvement on the
practices of the age. We all of us could, and
many of us did, learn much from the doctor
while he chose to remain vague, mysterious,
and cloudy; but when he became practical, the
charm was gone.

His allusion to the poet and the partridges
was received very well. "Oh, my poor brother,"
said he, "slaughtered partridges a score of
brace to each gun, and poets gauging ale-
barrels, with sixty pounds a year, at Dumfries,
are not the signs of a great era! perhaps of
the smallest possible era yet written of. Whatever economies we pursue, political or other,
let us see at once that this is the maddest of
the uneconomic; partridges killed by our land
magnates at, shall we say, a guinea a head,
to be retailed in Leadenhall at one shilling
and ninepence, with one poacher in limbo for
every fifty birds! our poet, maker, creator,
gauging ale, and that badly, with no leisure
for making or creating only a little leisure for

drinking, and such like beer-barrel avocations! Truly, a cutting of blocks with fine razors while we scrape our chins so uncomfortably with rusty knives! Oh, my political economist, master of supply and demand, division of labour and high pressure—oh, my loud-speaking friend, tell me, if so much be in you, what is the demand for poets in these kingdoms of Queen Victoria, and what the vouchsafed supply?"

This was all very well; this gave us some hope. We might do better with our next poet, when we got one; and though the partridges might not be abandoned, something could perhaps be done as to the poachers. We were unwilling, however, to take lessons in politics from so misty a professor; and when he came to tell us that the heroes of Westminster were naught, we began to think that he had written enough. His attack upon despatch boxes was not thought to have much in it; but as it is short, the doctor shall again be allowed to speak his sentiments:—

"Could utmost ingenuity in the management of red tape avail anything to men lying gasping —we may say, all but dead; could despatch boxes with never-so-much velvet lining and Chubb's patent, be of comfort to a people *in extremis*, I also, with so many others, would, with parched tongue, call on the name of Lord John Russell; or, my brother, at your advice,

on Lord Aberdeen; or, my cousin, on Lord
Derby, at yours; being, with my parched
tongue, indifferent in such matters. 'Tis all
one. Oh, Derby! Oh, Gladstone! Oh, Palmerston! Oh, Lord John! Each comes running
with serene face and despatch box. Vain physi-
cians! though there were hosts of such, no
despatch box will cure this disorder! What!
are these other doctors' new names, disciples
who have not burdened their souls with tape?
Well, let us call again. Oh, Disraeli, great
oppositionist, man of the bitter brow! or, Oh,
Molesworth, great reformer, thou who promisest
Utopia. They come; each with that serene
face, and each—alas, me! alas, my country!—
each with a despatch box!

" Oh, the serenity of Downing Street!

" My brothers, when hope was over on the
battle field, when no dimmest chance of
victory remained, the ancient Roman could
hide his face within his toga, and die grace-
fully. Can you and I do so now? If so,
'twere best for us; if not, oh my brothers, we
must die disgracefully, for hope of life and
victory I see none left to us in this world
below. I for one cannot trust much to serene
face and despatch box!"

There might be truth in this, there might
be depth of reasoning; but Englishmen did
not see enough in the argument to induce
them to withdraw their confidence from the

present arrangements of the government, and
Dr Anticant's monthly pamphlet on the decay
of the world did not receive so much attention
as his earlier works. He did not confine
himself to politics in these publications, but
roamed at large over all matters of public
interest, and found everything bad. According to him nobody was true, and not only
nobody, but nothing; a man could not take
off his hat to a lady without telling a lie—the
lady would lie again in smiling. The ruffles
of the gentleman's shirt would be fraught with
deceit, and the lady's flounces full of falsehood.
Was ever anything more severe than that
attack of his on chip bonnets, or the anathemas
with which he endeavoured to dust the powder
out of the bishops' wigs?

The pamphlet which Tom Towers now
pushed across the table was entitled " Modern
Charity," and was written with the view of
proving how much in the way of charity was
done by our predecessors—how little by the
present age; and it ended by a comparison
between ancient and modern times, very little
to the credit of the latter.

"Look at this," said Towers, getting up and
turning over the pages of the pamphlet, and
pointing to a passage near the end; "your
friend the warden, who is so little selfish, won't
like that, I fear." Bold read as follows :—

"Heavens, what a sight! Let us with eyes

wide open see the godly man of four centuries
since, the man of the dark ages: let us see how
he does his godlike work, and, again, how the
godly man of these latter days does his.

"Shall we say that the former is one walking painfully through the world, regarding,
as a prudent man, his worldly work, prosper-
ing in it as a diligent man will prosper, but
always with an eye to that better treasure
to which thieves do not creep in? Is there
not much nobility in that old man, as, leaning
on his oaken staff, he walks down the high
street of his native town, and receives from
all courteous salutation and acknowledgment
of his worth?   A noble old man, my august
inhabitants of Belgrave Square and such like
vicinity—a very noble old man, though employed no better than in the wholesale carding
of wool.

"This carding of wool, however, did in those
days bring with it much profit, so that our
ancient friend, when dying, was declared, in
whatever slang then prevailed, to cut up exceeding well. For sons and daughters there was
ample sustenance, with assistance of due industry; for friends and relatives some relief
for grief at this great loss; for aged dependants
comfort in declining years. This was much
for one old man to get done in that dark
fifteenth century. But this was not all: coming
generations of poor wool-carders should bless

the name of this rich one; and a hospital should be founded and endowed with his wealth for the feeding of such of the trade as could not, by diligent carding, any longer duly feed themselves.

" 'Twas thus that an old man in the fifteenth century did his godlike work to the best of his power, and not ignobly, as appears to me.

" We will now take our godly man of latter days. He shall no longer be a wool-carder, for such are not now men of mark. We will suppose him to be one of the best of the good —one who has lacked no opportunities. Our old friend was, after all, but illiterate; our modern friend shall be a man educated in all seemly knowledge; he shall, in short, be that blessed being—a clergyman of the Church of England !

" And now, in what perfectest manner does he in this lower world get his godlike work done and put out of hand ? Heavens ! in the strangest of manners. Oh, my brother ! in a manner not at all to be believed but by the most minute testimony of eyesight. He does it by the magnitude of his appetite—by the power of his gorge ; his only occupation is to swallow the bread prepared with so much anxious care for these impoverished carders of wool—that, and to sing indifferently through his nose once in the week some psalm more or less long—the shorter the better, we should be inclined to say.

"Oh, my civilised friends!—great Britons that never will be slaves, men advanced to infinite state of freedom and knowledge of good and evil—tell me, will you, what becoming monument you will erect to an highly-educated clergyman of the Church of England?"

Bold certainly thought that his friend would not like that: he could not conceive anything that he would like less than this. To what a world of toil and trouble, had he, Bold, given rise by his indiscreet attack upon the hospital!

"You see," said Towers, "that this affair has been much talked of, and the public are with you. I am sorry you should give the matter up. Have you seen the first number of the 'Almshouse'?"

No; Bold had not seen the "Almshouse." He had seen advertisements of Mr. Popular Sentiment's new novel of that name, but had in no way connected it with Barchester Hospital, and had never thought a moment on the subject.

"It's a direct attack on the whole system," said Towers. "It'll go a long way to put down Rochester, and Barchester, and Dulwich, and St. Cross, and all such hotbeds of peculation. It's very clear that Sentiment has been down to Barchester, and got up the whole story there; indeed, I thought he must have had it all from you, it's very well done, as you'll see: his first numbers always are."

Bold declared that Mr. Sentiment had got nothing from him, and that he was deeply grieved to find that the case had become so notorious.

"The fire has gone too far to be quenched," said Towers; "the building must go now; and as the timbers are all rotten, why, I should be inclined to say, the sooner the better. I expected to see you get some *éclat* in the matter."

This was all wormwood to Bold. He had done enough to make his friend the warden miserable for life, and had then backed out just when the success of his project was sufficient to make the question one of real interest. How weakly he had managed his business! he had already done the harm, and then stayed his hand when the good which he had in view was to be commenced. How delightful would it have been to have employed all his energy in such a cause—to have been backed by the Jupiter, and written up to by two of the most popular authors of the day! The idea opened a view into the very world in which he wished to live. To what might it not have given rise? what delightful intimacies—what public praise—to what Athenian banquets and rich flavour of Attic salt?

This, however, was now past hope. He had pledged himself to abandon the cause;

and could he have forgotten the pledge, he had gone too far to retreat. He was now, this moment, sitting in Tom Towers' room with the object of deprecating any further articles in the Jupiter, and, greatly as he disliked the job, his petition to that effect must be made.

" I couldn't continue it," said he, " because I found I was in the wrong."

Tom Towers shrugged his shoulders. How could a successful man be in the wrong! " In that case," said he, " of course you must abandon it."

" And I called this morning to ask you also to abandon it," said Bold.

" To ask me," said Tom Towers, with the most placid of smiles, and a consummate look of gentle surprise, as though Tom Towers was well aware that he of all men was the last to meddle in such matters.

" Yes," said Bold, almost trembling with hesitation. " The Jupiter, you know, has taken the matter up very strongly, Mr. Harding has felt what it has said deeply ; and I thought that if I could explain to you that he personally has not been to blame, these articles might be discontinued."

How calmly impassive was Tom Towers' face, as this innocent little proposition was made ! Had Bold addressed himself to the doorposts in Mount Olympus, they would have shown as much outward sign of assent or dissent. His quiescence was quite admirable ; his discretion certainly more than human.

"My dear fellow," said he, when Bold had quite done speaking, "I really cannot answer for the Jupiter."

"But if you saw that these articles were unjust, I think you would endeavour to put a stop to them : of course nobody doubts that you could, if you chose."

"Nobody and everybody are always very kind, but unfortunately are generally very wrong."

"Come, come, Towers," said Bold, plucking up his courage, and remembering that for Eleanor's sake he was bound to make his best exertion ; "I have no doubt in my own mind but that you wrote the articles yourself; and very well written they were : it will be a great favour if you will in future abstain from any personal allusion to poor Harding."

"My dear Bold," said Tom Towers, "I have a sincere regard for you. I have known you for many years, and value your friendship ; I hope you will let me explain to you, without offence, that none who are connected with the public press can with propriety listen to interference."

"Interference !" said Bold, "I don't want to interfere."

"Ah, but, my dear fellow, you do ; what

else is it? You think that I am able to keep certain remarks out of a newspaper. Your information is probably incorrect, as most public gossip on such subjects is ; but, at any rate, you think I have such power, and you ask me to use it : now that is interference."

" Well, if you choose to call it so."

" And now suppose for a moment that I had this power, and used it as you wish : isn't it clear that it would be a great abuse? Certain men are employed in writing for the public press ; and if they are induced either to write or to abstain from writing by private motives, surely the public press would soon be of little value. Look at the recognised worth of different newspapers, and see if it does not mainly depend on the assurance which the public feel that such a paper is, or is not, independent. You alluded to the Jupiter : surely you cannot but see that the weight of the Jupiter is too great to be moved by any private request, even though it should be made to a much more influential person than myself : you've only to think of this, and you'll see that I am right."

The discretion of Tom Towers was boundless : there was no contradicting what he said, no arguing against such propositions. He took such high ground that there was no getting on it. " The public is defrauded," said he, " whenever private considerations are allowed to have weight." Quite true, thou greatest oracle of the middle of the nineteenth century, thou sententious proclaimer of the purity of the press —the public is defrauded when it is purposely misled. Poor public! how often is it misled! against what a world of fraud has it to contend!

Bold took his leave, and got out of the room as quickly as he could, inwardly denouncing his friend Tom Towers as a prig and a humbug. "I know he wrote those articles," said Bold to himself; "I know he got his information from me. He was ready enough to take my word for gospel when it suited his own views, and to set Mr. Harding up before the public as an impostor on no other testimony than my chance conversation; but when I offer him real evidence opposed to his own views, he tells me that private motives are detrimental to public justice! Confound his arrogance! What is any public question but a conglomeration of private interests? What is any newspaper article but an expression of the views taken by one side? Truth! it takes an age to ascertain the truth of any question! The idea of Tom Towers talking of public motives and purity of purpose! Why, it wouldn't give him a moment's uneasiness to change his politics to-morrow, if the paper required it."

Such were John Bold's inward exclamations as he made his way out of the quiet labyrinth of the Temple; and yet there was no position of worldly power so coveted in Bold's ambition as that held by the man of whom he was thinking. It was the impregnability of the place which made Bold so angry with the possessor of it, and it was the same quality which made it appear so desirable.

Passing into the Strand, he saw in a bookseller's window an announcement of the first number of the "Almshouse;" so he purchased a copy, and hurrying back to his lodgings, proceeded to ascertain what Mr. Popular Sentiment had to say to the public on the subject which had lately occupied so much of his own attention.

In former times great objects were attained by great work. When evils were to be reformed, reformers set about their heavy task with grave decorum and laborious argument. An age was occupied in proving a grievance, and philosophical researches were printed in folio pages, which it took a life to write, and an eternity to read. We get on now with a lighter step, and quicker : ridicule is found to be more convincing than argument, imaginary agonies touch more than true sorrows, and monthly novels convince, when learned quartos fail to do so. If the world is to be set right, the work will be done by shilling numbers.

Of all such reformers Mr. Sentiment is the most powerful. It is incredible the number of evil practices he has put down : it is to be feared he will soon lack subjects, and that

when he has made the working classes comfortable, and got bitter beer put into proper-
sized pint bottles, there will be nothing further
for him left to do. Mr. Sentiment is certainly
a very powerful man, and perhaps not the less
so that his good poor people are so very good ;
his hard rich people so very hard ; and the
genuinely honest so very honest. Namby-
pamby in these days is not thrown away if
it be introduced in the proper quarters.
Divine peeresses are no longer interesting,
though possessed of every virtue ; but a pattern
peasant or an immaculate manufacturing hero
may talk as much twaddle as one of Mrs.
Radcliffe's heroines, and still be listened to.
Perhaps, however, Mr. Sentiment's great attraction is in his second-rate characters. If
his heroes and heroines walk upon stilts, as
heroes and heroines, I fear, ever must, their
attendant satellites are as natural as though
one met them in the street : they walk and
talk like men and women, and live among
our friends a rattling, lively life ; yes, live,
and will live till the names of their calling
shall be forgotten in their own, and Buckett
and Mrs. Gamp will be the only words left
to us to signify a detective police officer or a
monthly nurse.

"The Almshouse" opened with a scene in
a clergyman's house. Every luxury to be
purchased by wealth was described as being

there: all the appearances of household indulgence generally found amongst the most
self-indulgent of the rich were crowded into
this abode. Here the reader was introduced
to the demon of the book, the Mephistopheles
of the drama. What story was ever written
without a demon? what novel, what history,
what work of any sort, what world, would
be perfect without existing principles both of
good and evil? The demon of the "Almshouse" was the clerical owner of this comfortable abode. He was a man well stricken
in years, but still strong to do evil: he was
one who looked cruelly out of a hot, passion-
ate, bloodshot eye ; who had a huge red nose
with a carbuncle, thick lips, and a great double,
flabby chin, which swelled out into solid
substance, like a turkey cock's comb, when
sudden anger inspired him: he had a hot,
furrowed, low brow, from which a few grizzled
hairs were not yet rubbed off by the friction
of his handkerchief: he wore a loose unstarched
white handkerchief, black loose ill-made clothes,
and huge loose shoes, adapted to many corns
and various bunions : his husky voice told tales
of much daily port wine, and his language was
not so decorous as became a clergyman. Such
was the master of Mr. Sentiment's "Almshouse." He was a widower, but at present
accompanied by two daughters, and a thin
and somewhat insipid curate. One of the

young ladies was devoted to her father and
the fashionable world, and she of course was
the favourite; the other was equally addicted
to Puseyism and the curate.

The second chapter of course introduced
the reader to the more especial inmates of
the hospital. Here were discovered eight old
men; and it was given to be understood that
four vacancies remained unfilled, through the
perverse ill-nature of the clerical gentleman
with the double chin. The state of these eight
paupers was touchingly dreadful: sixpence-
farthing a-day had been sufficient for their
diet when the almshouse was founded; and
on sixpence-farthing a-day were they still
doomed to starve, though food was four times
as dear, and money four times as plentiful. It
was shocking to find how the conversation of
these eight starved old men in their dormitory
shamed that of the clergyman's family in his
rich drawing-room. The absolute words they
uttered were not perhaps spoken in the purest
English, and it might be difficult to distinguish
from their dialect to what part of the country
they belonged; the beauty of the sentiment,
however, amply atoned for the imperfection
of the language; and it was really a pity that
these eight old men could not be sent through
the country as moral missionaries, instead of
being immured and starved in that wretched
almshouse.

Bold finished the number; and as he threw it aside, he thought that that at least had no direct appliance to Mr. Harding, and that the absurdly strong colouring of the picture would disenable the work from doing either good or harm. He was wrong. The artist who paints for the million must use glaring colours, as no one knew better than Mr. Sentiment when he described the inhabitants of his alms-house ; and the radical reform which has now swept over such establishments has owed more to the twenty numbers of Mr. Sentiment's novel, than to all the true complaints which have escaped from the public for the last half century.

CHAPTER XVI

A LONG DAY IN LONDON

THE warden had to make use of all his very moderate powers of intrigue to give his son-in-law the slip, and get out of Barchester without being stopped on his road. No schoolboy ever ran away from school with more precaution and more dread of detection ; no convict, slipping down from a prison wall, ever feared to see the gaoler more entirely than Mr. Harding did to see his son-in-law, as he drove up in the pony carriage to the railway station, on the morning of his escape to London.

The evening before he went, he wrote a note to the archdeacon, explaining that he should start on the morrow on his journey ; that it was his intention to see the attorney-general if possible, and to decide on his future plans in accordance with what he heard from that gentleman ; he excused himself for giving Dr. Grantly no earlier notice, by stating that his resolve was very sudden ; and having entrusted this note to Eleanor, with the perfect, though not expressed, understanding that it was to be sent over to Plumstead Episcopi without haste, he took his departure.

He also prepared and carried with him a note

for Sir Abraham Haphazard, in which he stated
his name, explaining that he was the defendant
in the case of " The Queen on behalf of the Wool-
carders of Barchester *v.* Trustees under the will
of the late John Hiram," for so was the suit de-
nominated, and begged the illustrious and learned
gentleman to vouchsafe to him ten minutes'
audience at any hour on the next day. Mr.
Harding calculated that for that one day he was
safe ; his son-in-law, he had no doubt, would
arrive in town by an early train, but not early
enough to reach the truant till he should have
escaped from his hotel after breakfast ; and could
he thus manage to see the lawyer on that very
day, the deed might be done before the archdeacon could interfere.

On his arrival in town the warden drove, as
was his wont, to the Chapter Hotel and Coffee
House, near St. Paul's. His visits to London of
late had not been frequent ; but in those happy
days when Harding's church music was going
through the press, he had been often there ; and
as the publisher's house was in Paternoster Row,
and the printer's press in Fleet Street, the
Chapter Hotel and Coffee House had been
convenient. It was a quiet, sombre, clerical
house, beseeming such a man as the warden, and
thus he afterwards frequented it. Had he dared,
he would on this occasion have gone elsewhere
to throw the archdeacon further off the scent ; but
he did not know what violent steps his son-in-law

might take for his recovery if he were not found at his usual haunt, and he deemed it not prudent to make himself the object of a hunt through London.

Arrived at his inn, he ordered dinner, and went forth to the attorney-general's chambers. There he learnt that Sir Abraham was in Court, and would not probably return that day. He would go direct from Court to the House ; all appointments were, as a rule, made at the chambers ; the clerk could by no means promise an interview for the next day ; was able, on the other hand, to say that such interview was, he thought, impossible ; but that Sir Abraham would certainly be at the House in the course of the night, when an answer from himself might possibly be elicited.

To the House Mr. Harding went, and left his note, not finding Sir Abraham there. He added a most piteous entreaty that he might be favoured with an answer that evening, for which he would return. He then journeyed back sadly to the Chapter Coffee House, digesting his great thoughts, as best he might, in a clattering omnibus, wedged in between a wet old lady and a journeyman glazier, returning from his work with his tools in his lap. In melancholy solitude he discussed his mutton chop and pint of port. What is there in this world more melancholy than such a dinner ? A dinner, though alone, in a country hotel

may be worthy of some energy; the waiter,
if you are known, will make much of you;
the landlord will make you a bow, and perhaps
put the fish on the table; if you ring you are
attended to, and there is some life about it.
A dinner at a London eatinghouse is also
lively enough, if it have no other attraction.
There is plenty of noise and stir about it, and
the rapid whirl of voices and rattle of dishes
disperses sadness.   But a solitary dinner in
an old, respectable, sombre, solid London inn,
where nothing makes any noise but the old
waiter's creaking shoes; where one plate slowly
goes and another slowly comes without a sound;
where the two or three guests would as soon
think of knocking each other down as of
speaking; where the servants whisper, and
the whole household is disturbed if an order
be given above the voice—what can be more
melancholy than a mutton chop and a pint
of port in such a place?

Having gone through this, Mr. Harding
got into another omnibus, and again returned
to the House. Yes, Sir Abraham was there,
and was that moment on his legs, fighting
eagerly for the hundred and seventh clause
of the Convent Custody Bill. Mr. Harding's
note had been delivered to him; and if Mr.
Harding would wait some two or three hours,
Sir Abraham could be asked whether there was
any answer. The House was not full, and

perhaps Mr. Harding might get admittance into the Strangers' Gallery, which admission, with the help of five shillings, Mr. Harding was able to effect.

This bill of Sir Abraham's had been read a second time and passed into committee. A hundred and six clauses had already been discussed, and had occupied only four mornings and five evening sittings : nine of the hundred and six clauses were passed, fifty-five were withdrawn by consent, fourteen had been altered so as to mean the reverse of the original proposition, eleven had been postponed for further consideration, and seventeen had been directly negatived. The hundred and seventh ordered the bodily searching of nuns for Jesuitical symbols by aged clergymen, and was considered to be the real mainstay of the whole bill. No intention had ever existed to pass such a law as that proposed, but the government did not intend to abandon it till their object was fully attained by the discussion of this clause. It was known that it would be insisted on with terrible vehemence by Protestant Irish members, and as vehemently denounced by the Roman Catholic; and it was justly considered that no further union between the parties would be possible after such a battle. The innocent Irish fell into the trap as they always do, and whisky and poplins became a drug in the market.

A florid-faced gentleman with a nice head of

hair, from the south of Ireland, had succeeded in catching the speaker's eye by the time that Mr. Harding had got into the gallery, and was denouncing the proposed sacrilege, his whole face glowing with a fine theatrical frenzy.

" And is this a Christian country ? " said he. (Loud cheers ; counter cheers from the ministerial benches. " Some doubt as to that," from a voice below the gangway.) " No, it can be no Christian country, in which the head of the bar, the lagal adviser (loud laughter and cheers)—yes, I say the lagal adviser of the crown (great cheers and laughter)—can stand up in his seat in this house (prolonged cheers and laughter), and attempt to lagalise indacent assaults on the bodies of religious ladies." (Deafening cheers and laughter, which were prolonged till the honourable member resumed his seat.)

When Mr. Harding had listened to this and much more of the same kind for about three hours, he returned to the door of the house, and received back from the messenger his own note, with the following words scrawled in pencil on the back of it :—" To-morrow, 10 P.M.—my chambers. Λ. H."

He was so far successful,—but 10 P.M. : what an hour Sir Abraham had named for a legal interview ! Mr. Harding felt perfectly sure that long before that Dr. Grantly would be in London. Dr. Grantly could not, however, know that this interview had been arranged, nor could he learn it unless he managed to get hold of Sir Abraham before that hour; and as this was very improbable, Mr. Harding determined to start from his hotel early, merely leaving word that he should dine out, and unless luck were much against him, he might still escape the archdeacon till his return from the attorney-general's chambers.

He was at breakfast at nine, and for the twentieth time consulted his "Bradshaw," to see at what earliest hour Dr. Grantly could arrive from Barchester. As he examined the columns, he was nearly petrified by the reflection that perhaps the archdeacon might come up by the night mail-train! His heart sank within him at the horrid idea, and for a moment he felt himself dragged back to Barchester without accomplishing any portion of his object. Then he remembered that had Dr. Grantly done so, he would have been in the hotel, looking for him long since.

" Waiter," said he, timidly.

The waiter approached, creaking in his shoes, but voiceless.

" Did any gentleman—a clergyman, arrive here by the night mail-train ? "

" No, sir, not one," whispered the waiter, putting his mouth nearly close to the warden's ear.

Mr. Harding was reassured.

" Waiter," said he again, and the waiter again creaked up. " If any one calls for me, I am

going to dine out, and shall return about eleven
o'clock."

The waiter nodded, but did not this time
vouchsafe any reply ; and Mr. Harding, taking
up his hat, proceeded out to pass a long day in
the best way he could, somewhere out of sight
of the archdeacon.

"Bradshaw" had told him twenty times that
Dr. Grantly could not be at Paddington station
till 2 P.M., and our poor friend might therefore
have trusted to the shelter of the hotel for some
hours longer with perfect safety ; but he was
nervous. There was no knowing what steps the
archdeacon might take for his apprehension : a
message by electric telegraph might desire the
landlord of the hotel to set a watch upon him ;
some letter might come which he might find
himself unable to disobey ; at any rate, he could
not feel himself secure in any place at which
the archdeacon could expect to find him ; and at
10 A.M. he started forth to spend twelve hours in
London.

Mr. Harding had friends in town, had he chosen
to seek them ; but he felt that he was in no
humour for ordinary calls, and he did not now
wish to consult with any one as to the great step
which he had determined to take. As he had
said to his daughter, no one knows where the
shoe pinches but the wearer. There are some
points on which no man can be contented to
follow the advice of another—some subjects on

which a man can consult his own conscience only·
Our warden had made up his mind that it was
good for him at any cost to get rid of this
grievance; his daughter was the only person
whose concurrence appeared necessary to him,
and she did concur with him most heartily.
Under such circumstances he would not, if he
could help it, consult any one further, till advice
would be useless. Should the archdeacon catch
him, indeed, there would be much advice, and
much consultiaton of a kind not to be avoided ;
but he hoped better things ; and as he felt that
he could not now converse on indifferent subjects,
he resolved to see no one till after his interview
with the attorney-general.

He determined to take sanctuary in Westminster Abbey, so he again went thither in an
omnibus, and finding that the doors were not open
for morning service, he paid his twopence, and
went in as a sight-seer. It occurred to him that
he had no definite place of rest for the day, and
that he should be absolutely worn out before his
interview if he attempted to walk about from 10
A.M. to 10 P.M., so he sat himself down on a
stone step, and gazed up at the figure of William
Pitt, who looks as though he had just entered the
church for the first time in his life, and was anything but pleased at finding himself there.

He had been sitting unmolested about twenty
minutes, when the verger asked him whether he
wouldn't like to walk round. Mr. Harding

didn't want to walk anywhere, and declined, merely observing that he was waiting for the morning service.   The verger seeing that he was a clergyman, told him that the doors of the choir were now open, and showed him into a seat. This was a great point gained; the archdeacon would certainly not come to morning service at Westminster Abbey, even though he were in London; and here the warden could rest quietly, and, when the time came, duly say his prayers.

He longed to get up from his seat, and examine the music-books of the choristers, and the copy of the litany from which the service was chanted, to see how far the little details at Westminster corresponded with those at Barchester, and whether he thought his own voice would fill the church well from the Westminster precentor's seat.   There would, however be impropriety in such meddling, and he sat perfectly still, looking up at the noble roof, and guarded against the coming fatigues of the day.

By degrees two or three people entered: the very same damp old woman who had nearly obliterated him in the omnibus, or some other just like her; a couple of young ladies with their veils down, and gilt crosses conspicuous on their prayer-books; an old man on crutches; a party who were seeing the abbey, and thought they might as well hear the service for their twopence, as opportunity served; and a young woman with her prayer-book done up in her handkerchief, who rushed in late, and, in her hurried entry, tumbled over one of the forms, and made such a noise that every one, even the officiating minor canon, was startled, and she herself was so frightened by the echo of her own catastrophe, that she was nearly thrown into fits by the panic.

Mr. Harding was not much edified by the manner of the service. The minor canon in question hurried in, somewhat late, in a surplice not in the neatest order, and was followed by a dozen choristers, who were also not as trim as they might have been: they all jostled into their places with a quick hurried step, and the service was soon commenced. Soon commenced and soon over, for there was no music, and time was not unnecessarily lost in the chanting. On the whole, Mr. Harding was of the opinion that things were managed better at Barchester, though even there he knew that there was room for improvement.

It appears to us a question whether any clergyman can go through our church service with decorum, morning after morning, in an immense building, surrounded by not more than a dozen listeners. The best actors cannot act well before empty benches, and though there is, of course, a higher motive in one case than the other, still even the best of clergymen cannot but be influenced by their audience; and to expect that a duty should be well done under

such circumstances, would be to require from
human nature more than human power.

When the two ladies with the gilt crosses,
the old man with his crutch, and the still
palpitating housemaid were going, Mr. Harding
found himself obliged to go too.   The verger
stood in his way, and looked at him and looked
at the door, and so he went.   But he returned
again in a few minutes, and re-entered with
another twopence.   There was no other sanctuary so good for him.

As he walked slowly down the nave, and
then up one aisle, and then again down the
nave and up the other aisle, he tried to think
gravely of the step he was about to take.   He
was going to give up eight hundred a year
voluntarily ; and doom himself to live for the
rest of his life on about a hundred and fifty.
He knew that he had hitherto failed to realise
this fact as he ought to do.   Could he maintain
his own independence and support his daughter
on a hundred and fifty pounds a year without
being a burden on any one?   His son-in-law
was rich, but nothing could induce him to lean
on his son-in-law after acting, as he intended
to do, in most direct opposition to his counsel.
The bishop was rich, but he was about to throw
away the bishop's best gift, and that in a manner
to injure materially the patronage of the giver :
he could neither expect nor accept anything
further from the bishop.   There would be not

only no merit, but positive disgrace, in giving up his wardenship, if he were not prepared to meet the world without it. Yes, he must from this time forward bound all his human wishes for himself and his daughter to the poor extent of so limited an income. He knew he had not thought sufficiently of this, that he had been carried away by enthusiasm, and had hitherto not brought home to himself the full reality of his position.

He thought most about his daughter, naturally. It was true that she was engaged, and he knew enough of his proposed son-in-law to be sure that his own altered circumstances would make no obstacle to such a marriage ; nay, he was sure that the very fact of his poverty would induce Bold more anxiously to press the matter ; but he disliked counting on Bold in this emergency, brought on, as it had been, by his doing. He did not like saying to himself, Bold has turned me out of my house and income, and, therefore, he must relieve me of my daughter ; he preferred reckoning on Eleanor as the companion of his poverty and exile,—as the sharer of his small income.

Some modest provision for his daughter had been long since made. His life was insured for three thousand pounds, and this sum was to go to Eleanor. The archdeacon, for some years past, had paid the premium, and had secured himself by the immediate possession

of a small property which was to have gone
to Mrs. Grantly after her father's death. This
matter, therefore, had been out of the warden's
hands long since, as, indeed, had all the business
transactions of his family, and his anxiety
was, therefore, confined to his own life income.

Yes. A hundred and fifty per annum was
very small, but still it might suffice; but how
was he to chant the litany at the cathedral on
Sunday mornings, and get the service done at
Crabtree Parva? True, Crabtree Church was
not quite a mile and a half from the cathedral;
but he could not be in two places at once!
Crabtree was a small village, and afternoon
service might suffice, but still this went against
his conscience, it was not right that his parishioners should be robbed of any of their privileges
on account of his poverty. He might, to be
sure, make some arrangement for doing week-
day service at the cathedral, but he had chanted
the litany at Barchester so long, and had a
conscious feeling that he did it so well, that he
was unwilling to give up the duty.

Thinking of such things, turning over in his
own mind together small desires and grave
duties, but never hesitating for a moment as
to the necessity of leaving the hospital, Mr.
Harding walked up and down the abbey, or sat
still meditating on the same stone step, hour
after hour. One verger went and another came,
but they did not disturb him; every now and

then they crept up and looked at him, but they did so with a reverential stare, and, on the whole, Mr. Harding found his retreat well chosen. About four o'clock his comfort was disturbed by an enemy in the shape of hunger; it was necessary that he should dine, and it was clear that he could not dine in the abbey; so he left his sanctuary not willingly, and betook himself to the neighbourhood of the Strand to look for food.

His eyes had become so accustomed to the gloom of the church, that they were dazed when he got out into the full light of day, and he felt confused and ashamed of himself, as though people were staring at him. He hurried along, still in dread of the archdeacon, till he came to Charing Cross, and then re-membered that in one of his passages through the Strand he had seen the words " Chops and Steaks" on a placard in a shop window. He remembered the shop distinctly; it was next door to a trunk-seller's, and there was a cigar shop on the other side. He couldn't go to his hotel for dinner, which to him hitherto was the only known mode of dining in London at his own expense; and, therefore, he would get a steak at the shop in the Strand. Arch-deacon Grantly would certainly not come to such a place for his dinner.

He found the house easily—just as he had observed it, between the trunks and the cigars.

He was rather daunted by the huge quantity of fish which he saw in the window. There were barrels of oysters, hecatombs of lobsters, a few tremendous-looking crabs, and a tub full of pickled salmon ; not, however, being aware of any connection between shell-fish and iniquity, he entered, and modestly asked a slatternly woman, who was picking oysters out of a great watery reservoir, whether he could have a mutton chop and a potato.

The woman looked somewhat surprised, but answered in the affirmative, and a slipshod girl ushered him into a long back room, filled with boxes for the accommodation of parties, in one of which he took his seat. In a more miserably forlorn place he could not have found himself : the room smelt of fish, and sawdust, and stale tobacco smoke, with a slight taint of escaped gas ; everything was rough, and dirty, and disreputable ; the cloth which they put before him was abominable ; the knives and forks were bruised, and hacked, and filthy ; and everything was impregnated with fish. He had one comfort, however : he was quite alone ; there was no one there to look on his dismay ; nor was it probable that any one would come to do so. It was a London supper-house. About one o'clock at night the place would be lively enough, but at the present time his seclusion was as deep as it had been in the abbey.

In about half an hour the untidy girl, not yet dressed for her evening labours, brought him his chop and potatoes, and Mr. Harding begged for a pint of sherry. He was impressed with an idea, which was generally prevalent a few years since, and is not yet wholly removed from the minds of men, that to order a dinner at any kind of inn, without also ordering a pint of wine for the benefit of the landlord, was a kind of fraud; not punishable, indeed, by law, but not the less abominable on that account. Mr. Harding remembered his coming poverty, and would willingly have saved his half-crown, but he thought he had no alternative; and he was soon put in possession of some horrid mixture procured from the neighbouring public-house.

His chop and potatoes, however, were eatable, and having got over as best he might the disgust created by the knives and forks, he contrived to swallow his dinner. He was not much disturbed: one young man, with pale face and watery fish-like eyes, wearing his hat ominously on one side, did come in and stare at him, and ask the girl audibly enough, "Who that old cock was;" but the annoyance went no further, and the warden was left seated on his wooden bench in peace, endeavouring to distinguish the different scents arising from lobsters, oysters, and salmon.

Unknowing as Mr. Harding was in the ways

of London, he felt that he had somehow selected
an ineligible dining-house, and that he had
better leave it. It was hardly five o'clock—
how was he to pass the time till ten? Five
miserable hours! He was already tired, and it
was impossible that he should continue walking
so long. He thought of getting into an omnibus,
and going out to Fulham for the sake of coming
back in another: this, however, would be weary
work, and as he paid his bill to the woman in
the shop, he asked her if there were any place
near where he could get a cup of coffee.
Though she did keep a shell-fish supper-house,
she was very civil, and directed him to the
cigar divan on the other side of the street.

Mr. Harding had not a much correcter notion
of a cigar divan than he had of a London
dinner-house, but he was desperately in want
of rest, and went as he was directed. He
thought he must have made some mistake when
he found himself in a cigar shop, but the man
behind the counter saw immediately that he
was a stranger, and understood what he wanted.
" One shilling, sir—thank ye, sir—cigar, sir?—
ticket for coffee, sir—you'll only have to call
the waiter. Up those stairs, if you please, sir.
Better take the cigar, sir— you can always give
it to a friend you know. Well, sir, thank ye,
sir—as you are so good, I'll smoke it myself."
And so Mr. Harding ascended to the divan,
with his ticket for coffee, but minus the cigar.

The place seemed much more suitable to his
requirements than the room in which he had
dined : there was, to be sure, a strong smell
of tobacco, to which he was not accustomed;
but after the shell-fish, the tobacco did not seem
disagreeable. There were quantities of books,
and long rows of sofas. What on earth could
be more luxurious than a sofa, a book, and a
cup of coffee? An old waiter came up to him,
with a couple of magazines and an evening
paper. Was ever anything so civil? Would he
have a cup of coffee, or would he prefer sherbet?
Sherbet! Was he absolutely in an Eastern
divan, with the slight addition of all the London
periodicals? He had, however, an idea that
sherbet should be drunk sitting cross-legged,
and as he was not quite up to this, he ordered
the coffee.

The coffee came, and was unexceptionable.
Why, this divan was a paradise! The civil old
waiter suggested to him a game of chess : though
a chess player he was not equal to this, so he
declined, and, putting up his weary legs on the
sofa, leisurely sipped his coffee, and turned over
the pages of his Blackwood. He might have
been so engaged for about an hour, for the
old waiter enticed him to a second cup of coffee,
when a musical clock began to play. Mr.
Harding then closed his magazine, keeping his
place with his finger, and lay, listening with
closed eyes to the clock. Soon the clock

seemed to turn into a violoncello, with piano
accompaniments, and Mr. Harding began to
fancy the old waiter was the Bishop of Barchester ; he was inexpressibly shocked that
the bishop should have brought him his coffee
with his own hands ; then Dr. Grantly came
in, with a basket full of lobsters, which he
would not be induced to leave downstairs in
the kitchen ; and then the warden couldn't quite
understand why so many people would smoke
in the bishop's drawing-room ; and so he fell
fast asleep, and his dreams wandered away to
his accustomed stall in Barchester Cathedral,
and the twelve old men he was so soon about
to leave for ever.

He was fatigued, and slept soundly for some
time.   Some sudden stop in the musical clock
woke him at length, and he jumped up with
a start, surprised to find the room quite full ;
it had been nearly empty when his nap began.
With nervous anxiety he pulled out his watch,
and found that it was half-past nine.   He seized
his hat, and, hurrying down stairs, started at
a rapid pace for Lincoln's Inn.

It still wanted twenty minutes to ten when
the warden found himself at the bottom of Sir
Abraham's stairs, so he walked leisurely up and
down the quiet inn to cool himself.   It was
a beautiful evening at the end of August.   He
had recovered from his fatigue ; his sleep and
the coffee had refreshed him, and he was

surprised to find that he was absolutely enjoying himself, when the inn clock struck ten.
The sound was hardly over before he knocked
at Sir Abraham's door, and was informed by
the clerk who received him that the great man
would be with him immediately.

CHAPTER XVII

SIR ABRAHAM HAPHAZARD

MR. HARDING was shown into a comfortable inner sitting-room, looking more like a gentleman's book-room than a lawyer's chambers, and there waited for Sir Abraham. Nor was he kept waiting long: in ten or fifteen minutes he heard a clatter of voices speaking quickly in the passage, and then the attorney-general entered.

"Very sorry to keep you waiting, Mr. Warden," said Sir Abraham, shaking hands with him; "and sorry, too, to name so disagreeable an hour; but your notice was short, and as you said to-day, I named the very earliest hour that was not disposed of."

Mr. Harding assured him that he was aware that it was he that should apologise.

Sir Abraham was a tall thin man, with hair prematurely grey, but bearing no other sign of age; he had a slight stoop, in his neck rather than his back, acquired by his constant habit of leaning forward as he addressed his various audiences. He might be fifty years old, and would have looked young for his age, had not constant work hardened his features, and given him the appearance of a machine with a mind.

His face was full of intellect, but devoid of
natural expression. You would say he was a
man to use, and then have done with ; a man
to be sought for on great emergencies, but ill
adapted for ordinary services ; a man whom you
would ask to defend your property, but to whom
you would be sorry to confide your love. He
was bright as a diamond, and as cutting, and
also as unimpressionable. He knew every one
whom to know was an honour, but he was
without a friend ; he wanted none, however, and
knew not the meaning of the word in other than
its parliamentary sense. A friend ! Had he
not always been sufficient to himself, and now,
at fifty, was it likely that he should trust
another ? He was married, indeed, and had
children, but what time had he for the soft
idleness of conjugal felicity ? His working days
or term times were occupied from his time of
rising to the late hour at which he went to rest,
and even his vacations were more full of labour
than the busiest days of other men. He
never quarrelled with his wife, but he never talked
to her,—he never had time to talk, he was so
taken up with speaking. She, poor lady, was
not unhappy ; she had all that money could give
her, she would probably live to be a peeress, and
she really thought Sir Abraham the best of
husbands.

Sir Abraham was a man of wit, and sparkled
among the brightest at the dinner-tables of

political grandees : indeed, he always sparkled ;
whether in society, in the House of Commons, or
the courts of law, coruscations flew from him ;
glittering sparkles, as from hot steel, but no
heat; no cold heart was ever cheered by warmth
from him, no unhappy soul ever dropped a portion
of its burden at his door.

With him success alone was praiseworthy, and
he knew none so successful as himself. No one
had thrust him forward ; no powerful friends had
pushed him along on his road to power.   No, he
was attorney-general, and would, in all human
probability, be lord chancellor by sheer dint of
his own industry and his own talent.   Who else
in all the world rose so high with so little help ?
A premier, indeed !   Who had ever been premier
without mighty friends ?   An archbishop !   Yes,
the son or grandson of a great noble, or else,
probably, his tutor.   But he, Sir Abraham, had
had no mighty lord at his back ; his father
had been a country apothecary, his mother a
farmer's daughter.   Why should he respect any
but himself ?   And so he glitters along through
the world, the brightest among the bright ; and
when his glitter is gone, and he is gathered to
his fathers, no eye will be dim with a tear, no
heart will mourn for its lost friend.

" And so, Mr. Warden," said Sir Abraham,
" all our trouble about this lawsuit is at an end."

Mr. Harding said he hoped so, but he didn't
at all understand what Sir Abraham meant.

Sir Abraham, with all his sharpness, could not have looked into his heart and read his intentions.

"All over. You need trouble yourself no further about it ; of course they must pay the costs, and the absolute expense to you and Dr. Grantly will be trifling—that is, compared with what it might have been if it had been continued."

"I fear I don't quite understand you, Sir Abraham."

"Don't you know that their attorneys have noticed us that they have withdrawn the suit ? "

Mr. Harding explained to the lawyer that he knew nothing of this, although he had heard in a round-about way that such an intention had been talked of ; and he also at length succeeded in making Sir Abraham understand that even this did not satisfy him. The attorney-general stood up, put his hands into his breeches' pockets, and raised his eyebrows, as Mr. Harding proceeded to detail the grievance from which he now wished to rid himself.

"I know I have no right to trouble you personally with this matter, but as it is of most vital importance to me, as all my happiness is concerned in it, I thought I might venture to seek your own advice."

Sir Abraham bowed, and declared his clients were entitled to the best advice he could give them ; particularly a client so respectable in every way as the Warden of Barchester Hospital.

"A spoken word, Sir Abraham, is often of more value than volumes of written advice. The truth is, I am ill satisfied with this matter as it stands at present. I do see—I cannot help seeing, that the affairs of the hospital are not arranged according to the will of the founder."

"None of such institutions are, Mr. Harding, nor can they be; the altered circumstances in which we live do not admit of it."

"Quite true—that is quite true; but I can't see that those altered circumstances give me a right to eight hundred a year. I don't know whether I ever read John Hiram's will, but were I to read it now I could not understand it. What I want you, Sir Abraham, to tell me, is this—am I, as warden, legally and distinctly entitled to the proceeds of the property, after the due maintenance of the twelve bedesmen?"

Sir Abraham declared that he couldn't exactly say in so many words that Mr. Harding was legally entitled to, &c., &c., &c., and ended in expressing a strong opinion that it would be madness to raise any further question on the matter, as the suit was to be,—nay, was, abandoned.

Mr. Harding, seated in his chair, began to play a slow tune on an imaginary violoncello.

"Nay, my dear sir," continued the attorney-general, "there is no further ground for any question ; I don't see that you have the power of raising it."

"I can resign," said Mr. Harding, slowly playing away with his right hand, as though the bow were beneath the chair in which he was sitting.

"What! throw it up altogether?" said the attorney-general, gazing with utter astonishment at his client.

"Did you see those articles in the Jupiter?" said Mr. Harding, piteously, appealing to the sympathy of the lawyer.

Sir Abraham said he had seen them. This poor little clergyman, cowed into such an act of extreme weakness by a newspaper article, was to Sir Abraham so contemptible an object, that he hardly knew how to talk to him as to a rational being.

"Hadn't you better wait," said he, "till Dr. Grantly is in town with you? Wouldn't it be better to postpone any serious step till you can consult with him?"

Mr. Harding declared vehemently that he could not wait, and Sir Abraham began seriously to doubt his sanity.

"Of course," said the latter, "if you have private means sufficient for your wants, and if this——"

"I haven't a sixpence, Sir Abraham," said the warden.

"God bless me! Why, Mr. Harding, how do you mean to live?"

Mr. Harding proceeded to explain to the man of law that he meant to keep his precentorship,—that was eighty pounds a year; and, also, that he meant to fall back upon his own little living of Crabtree, which was another eighty pounds. That, to be sure, the duties of the two were hardly compatible; but perhaps he might effect an exchange. And then, recollecting that the attorney-general would hardly care to hear how the service of a cathedral church is divided among the minor canons, stopped short in his explanations.

Sir Abraham listened in pitying wonder. "I really think, Mr. Harding, you had better wait for the archdeacon. This is a most serious step: one for which, in my opinion, there is not the slightest necessity; and, as you have done me the honour of asking my advice, I must implore you to do nothing without the approval of your friends. A man is never the best judge of his own position."

"A man is the best judge of what he feels himself. I'd sooner beg my bread till my death, than read such another article as those two that have appeared, and feel, as I do, that the writer has truth on his side."

"Have you not a daughter, Mr. Harding— an unmarried daughter?"

"I have," said he, now standing also, but still

playing away on his fiddle with his hand behind his back. "I have, Sir Abraham; and she and I are completely agreed on this subject."

"Pray excuse me, Mr. Harding, if what I say seems impertinent : but surely it is you that should be prudent on her behalf. She is young, and does not know the meaning of living on an income of a hundred and fifty pounds a year. On her account give up this idea. Believe me, it is sheer Quixotism."

The warden walked away to the window, and then back to his chair; and then, irresolute what to say, took another turn to the window. The attorney-general was really extremely patient, but he was beginning to think that the interview had been long enough.

"But if this income be not justly mine, what if she and I have both to beg?" said the warden at last, sharply, and in a voice so different from that he had hitherto used, that Sir Abraham was startled. "If so, it would be better to beg."

"My dear sir, nobody now questions its justness."

"Yes, Sir Abraham, one does question it,— the most important of all witnesses against me, —I question it myself. My God knows whether or no I love my daughter; but I would sooner that she and I should both beg, than that she should live in comfort on money which is truly the property of the poor. It may seem strange

to you, Sir Abraham, it is strange to myself
that I should have been ten years in that happy
home, and not have thought of these things,
till they were so roughly dinned into my ears.
I cannot boast of my conscience, when it
required the violence of a public newspaper to
awaken it ; but, now that it is awake, I must
obey it. When I came here I did not know
that the suit was withdrawn by Mr. Bold, and
my object was to beg you to abandon my
defence. As there is no action, there can be
no defence ; but it is, at any rate, as well that
you should know that from to-morrow I shall
cease to be the warden of the hospital. My
friends and I differ on this subject, Sir Abraham,
and that adds much to my sorrow : but it cannot
be helped." And, as he finished what he had
to say, he played up such a tune as never
before had graced the chambers of any attorney-
general. He was standing up, gallantly fronting
Sir Abraham, and his right arm passed with
bold and rapid sweeps before him, as though
he were embracing some huge instrument, which
allowed him to stand thus erect ; and with the
fingers of his left hand he stopped, with pre-
ternatural velocity, a multitude of strings, which
ranged from the top of his collar to the bottom
of the lappet of his coat. Sir Abraham listened
and looked in wonder. As he had never before
seen Mr. Harding, the meaning of these wild
gesticulations was lost upon him ; but he per-

ceived that the gentleman who had a few
minutes since been so subdued as to be unable
to speak without hesitation, was now impassioned
—nay, almost violent.

"You'll sleep on this, Mr. Harding, and to-
morrow——"

"I have done more than sleep upon it," said
the warden ; "I have laid awake upon it, and
that night after night. I found I could not
sleep upon it ; now I hope to do so."

The attorney-general had no answer to make
to this ; so he expressed a quiet hope that
whatever settlement was finally made would
be satisfactory ; and Mr. Harding withdrew,
thanking the great man for his kind attention.

Mr. Harding was sufficiently satisfied with
the interview to feel a glow of comfort as he
descended into the small old square of Lincoln's
Inn. It was a calm, bright, beautiful night, and
by the light of the moon, even the chapel of
Lincoln's Inn, and the sombre row of chambers,
which surround the quadrangle, looked well.
He stood still a moment to collect his thoughts,
and reflect on what he had done, and was about
to do. He knew that the attorney-general
regarded him as little better than a fool, but
that he did not mind ; he and the attorney-
general had not much in common between
them ; he knew also that others, whom he did
care about, would think so too ; but Eleanor,
he was sure, would exult in what he had done,

and the bishop, he trusted, would sympathise with him.

In the meantime he had to meet the archdeacon, and so he walked slowly down Chancery Lane and along Fleet Street, feeling sure that his work for the night was not yet over.   When he reached the hotel he rang the bell quietly, and with a palpitating heart ; he almost longed to escape round the corner, and delay the coming storm by a further walk round St. Paul's Churchyard, but he heard the slow creaking shoes of the old waiter approaching, and he stood his ground manfully.

CHAPTER XVIII

THE WARDEN IS VERY OBSTINATE

"Dr. Grantly is here, sir," greeted his ears before the door was well open, "and Mrs. Grantly; they have a sitting-room above, and are waiting up for you."

There was something in the tone of the man's voice which seemed to indicate that even he looked upon the warden as a runaway schoolboy, just recaptured by his guardian, and that he pitied the culprit, though he could not but be horrified at the crime.

The warden endeavoured to appear unconcerned, as he said, "Oh, indeed! I'll go upstairs at once;" but he failed signally: there was, perhaps, a ray of comfort in the presence of his married daughter; that is to say, of comparative comfort, seeing that his son-in-law was there: but how much would he have preferred that they should both have been safe at Plumstead Episcopi! However, upstairs he went, the waiter slowly preceding him; and on the door being opened the archdeacon was discovered standing in the middle of the room, erect, indeed, as usual, but oh! how sorrowful! and on a dingy sofa behind him reclined his patient wife.

"Papa, I thought you were never coming back," said the lady; "it's twelve o'clock."

"Yes, my dear," said the warden. "The attorney-general named ten for my meeting; to be sure ten is late, but what could I do, you know? Great men will have their own way."

And he gave his daughter a kiss, and shook hands with the doctor, and again tried to look unconcerned.

"And you have absolutely been with the attorney-general?" asked the archdeacon.

Mr. Harding signified that he had.

"Good heavens, how unfortunate!" And the archdeacon raised his huge hands in the manner in which his friends are so accustomed to see him express disapprobation and astonishment. "What will Sir Abraham think of it? Did you not know that it is not customary for clients to go direct to their counsel?"

"Isn't it?" asked the warden, innocently. "Well, at any rate, I've done it now. Sir Abraham didn't seem to think it so very strange."

The archdeacon gave a sigh that would have moved a man-of-war.

"But, papa, what did you say to Sir Abraham?" asked the lady.

"I asked him, my dear, to explain John Hiram's will to me. He couldn't explain it in the only way which would have satisfied me, and so I resigned the wardenship."

"Resigned it!" said the archdeacon, in a solemn voice, sad and low, but yet sufficiently audible; a sort of whisper that Macready would have envied, and the galleries have applauded with a couple of rounds. "Resigned it! Good heavens!" and the dignitary of the church sank back horrified into a horsehair armchair.

"At least I told Sir Abraham that I would resign; and of course I must now do so."

"Not at all," said the archdeacon, catching a ray of hope. "Nothing that you say in such a way to your own counsel can be in any way binding on you; of course you were there to ask his advice. I'm sure, Sir Abraham did not advise any such step."

Mr. Harding could not say that he had.

"I am sure he disadvised you from it," continued the reverend cross-examiner.

Mr. Harding could not deny this.

"I'm sure Sir Abraham must have advised you to consult your friends."

To this proposition also Mr. Harding was obliged to assent.

"Then your threat of resignation amounts to nothing, and we are just where we were before."

Mr. Harding was now standing on the rug, moving uneasily from one foot to the other. He made no distinct answer to the archdeacon's last proposition, for his mind was chiefly engaged on thinking how he could escape to bed. That his resignation was a thing finally fixed on, a fact all but completed, was not in his mind a matter of any doubt ; he knew his own weakness ; he knew how prone he was to be led ; but he was not weak enough to give way now, to go back from the position to which his conscience had driven him, after having purposely come to London to declare his determination : he did not in the least doubt his resolution, but he greatly doubted his power of defending it against his son-in-law.

"You must be very tired, Susan," said he : "wouldn't you like to go to bed ? "

But Susan didn't want to go till her husband went—she had an idea that her papa might be bullied if she were away : she wasn't tired at all, or at least she said so.

The archdeacon was pacing the room, expressing, by certain noddles of his head, his opinion of the utter fatuity of his father-in-law.

"Why," at last he said,—and angels might have blushed at the rebuke expressed in his tone and emphasis—"Why did you go off from Barchester so suddenly ?   Why did you take such a step without giving us notice, after what had passed at the palace ? "

The warden hung his head, and made no reply ; he could not condescend to say that he had not intended to give his son-in-law the slip ; and as he had not the courage to avow it, he said nothing.

"Papa has been too much for you," said the lady.

The archdeacon took another turn, and again ejaculated, " Good heavens ! " this time in a very low whisper, but still audible.

" I think I'll go to bed," said the warden, taking up a side candle.

" At any rate, you'll promise me to take no further step without consultation," said the archdeacon. Mr. Harding made no answer, but slowly proceeded to light his candle. " Of course," continued the other, " such a declaration as that you made to Sir Abraham means nothing. Come, warden, promise me this. The whole affair, you see, is already settled, and that with very little trouble or expense. Bold has been compelled to abandon his action, and all you have to do is to remain quiet at the hospital." Mr. Harding still made no reply, but looked meekly into his son-in-law's face. The archdeacon thought he knew his father-in-law, but he was mistaken ; he thought that he had already talked over a vacillating man to resign his promise. " Come," said he, " promise Susan to give up this idea of resigning the wardenship."

The warden looked at his daughter, thinking probably at the moment that if Eleanor were contented with him, he need not so much regard his other child, and said, " I am sure Susan will not ask me to break my word, or to do what I know to be wrong."

" Papa," said she, "it would be madness in you

to throw up your preferment. What are you to live on?"

"God, that feeds the young ravens, will take care of me also," said Mr. Harding, with a smile, as though afraid of giving offence by making his reference to scripture too solemn.

"Pish!" said the archdeacon, turning away rapidly; "if the ravens persisted in refusing the food prepared for them, they wouldn't be fed." A clergyman generally dislikes to be met in argument by any scriptural quotation; he feels as affronted as a doctor does, when recommended by an old woman to take some favourite dose, or as a lawyer when an unprofessional man attempts to put him down by a quibble.

"I shall have the living of Crabtree," modestly suggested the warden.

"Eighty pounds a year!" sneered the archdeacon.

"And the precentorship," said the father-in-law.

"It goes with the wardenship," said the son-in-law. Mr. Harding was prepared to argue this point, and began to do so, but Dr. Grantly stopped him. "My dear warden," said he, "this is all nonsense. Eighty pounds or a hundred and sixty makes very little difference. You can't live on it—you can't ruin Eleanor's prospects for ever. In point of fact, you can't resign; the bishop wouldn't accept it; the whole thing is settled. What I now want to do is to prevent any inconvenient tittle tattle,—any more newspaper articles."

" That's what I want, too," said the warden.

" And to prevent that," continued the other, " we mustn't let any talk of resignation get abroad."

" But I shall resign," said the warden, very, very, meekly.

" Good heavens! Susan, my dear, what can I say to him ? "

" But, papa," said Mrs. Grantly, getting up, and putting her arm through that of her father, " what is Eleanor to do if you throw away your income ? "

A hot tear stood in each of the warden's eyes as he looked round upon his married daughter. Why should one sister who was so rich predict poverty for another ? some such idea as this was on his mind, but he gave no utterance to it. Then he thought of the pelican feeding its young with blood from its own breast, but he gave no utterance to that either ; and then of Eleanor waiting for him at home, waiting to congratulate him on the end of all his trouble.

" Think of Eleanor, papa," said Mrs. Grantly.

" I do think of her," said her father.

" And you will not do this rash thing ? " The lady was really moved beyond her usual calm composure.

" It can never be rash to do right," said he.
" I shall certainly resign this wardenship.'

" Then, Mr. Harding, there is nothing before
you but ruin," said the archdeacon, now moved
beyond all endurance.   " Ruin both for you and
Eleanor.   How do you mean to pay the
monstrous expenses of this action ? "

Mrs. Grantly suggested that, as the action
was abandoned, the costs would not be heavy.

" Indeed they will, my dear," continued he.
" One cannot have the attorney-general up at
twelve o'clock at night for nothing ;—but of
course your father has not thought of this."

" I will sell my furniture," said the warden.

" Furniture ! " ejaculated the other, with a
most powerful sneer.

" Come, archdeacon," said the lady, " we
needn't mind that at present.   You know you
never expected papa to pay the costs."

" Such absurdity is enough to provoke Job,"
said the archdeacon, marching quickly up and
down the room.   " Your father is like a child.
Eight hundred pounds a-year !—eight hundred
and eighty with the house—with nothing to
do.   The very place for him.   And to throw
that up because some scoundrel writes an article
in a newspaper !   Well—I have done my duty.
If he chooses to ruin his child I cannot help
it ; " and he stood still at the fireplace, and
looked at himself in a dingy mirror which stood
on the chimney-piece.

There was a pause for about a minute, and then the warden, finding that nothing else was coming, lighted his candle, and quietly said, " Good night."

" Good night, papa," said the lady.

And so the warden retired : but, as he closed the door behind him, he heard the well-known ejaculation—slower, lower, more solemn, more ponderous than ever—" Good heavens ! "

CHAPTER XIX

THE WARDEN RESIGNS

THE party met the next morning at breakfast; and a very sombre affair it was—very unlike the breakfasts at Plumstead Episcopi.

There were three thin, small, dry bits of bacon, each an inch long, served up under a huge old plated cover; there were four three-cornered bits of toast, and four square bits of buttered toast; there was a loaf of bread, and some oily-looking butter; and on the side-board there were the remains of a cold shoulder of mutton. The archdeacon, however, had not come up from his rectory to St. Paul's Churchyard to enjoy himself and therefore nothing was said of the scanty fare.

The guests were as sorry as the viands—hardly anything was said over the breakfast-table. The archdeacon munched his toast in ominous silence, turning over bitter thoughts in his deep mind. The warden tried to talk to his daughter, and she tried to answer him; but they both failed. There were no feelings at present in common between them. The warden was thinking only of getting back to Barchester, and calculating whether the archdeacon would expect him to wait for him; and Mrs. Grantly was preparing herself for a grand attack which she was to make on her father, as agreed upon between herself and her husband during their curtain confabulation of that morning.

When the waiter had creaked out of the room with the last of the teacups, the archdeacon got up and went to the window, as though to admire the view. The room looked out on a narrow passage which runs from St. Paul's Churchyard to Paternoster Row; and Dr. Grantly patiently perused the names of the three shopkeepers whose doors were in view. The warden still kept his seat at the table, and examined the pattern of the table-cloth; and Mrs. Grantly, seating herself on the sofa, began to knit.

After awhile the warden pulled his Bradshaw out of his pocket, and began laboriously to consult it. There was a train for Barchester at 10 A.M. That was out of the question, for it was nearly ten already. Another at 3 P.M.; another, the night-mail train, at 9 P.M. The three o'clock train would take him home to tea, and would suit very well.

" My dear," said he, " I think I shall go back home at three o'clock to-day. I shall get home at half-past eight. I don't think there's anything to keep me in London."

" The archdeacon and I return by the early train to-morrow, papa ; won't you wait and go back with us ? "

" Why, Eleanor will expect me to-night ; and I've so much to do ; and—— "

" Much to do ! " said the archdeacon *sotto voce ;*
but the warden heard him.

" You'd better wait for us, papa."

" Thank ye, my dear !   I think I'll go this
afternoon."   The tamest animal will turn when
driven too hard, and even Mr. Harding was
beginning to fight for his own way.

" I suppose you won't be back before three? "
said the lady, addressing her husband.

" I must leave this at two," said the warden.

" Quite out of the question," said the archdeacon, answering his wife, and still reading
the shopkeepers' names; " I don't suppose I
shall be back till five."

There was another long pause, during which
Mr. Harding continued to study his " Bradshaw."

" I must go to Cox and Cumming," said the
archdeacon at last.

" Oh, to Cox and Cumming," said the warden.
It was quite a matter of indifference to him
where his son-in-law went.

The names of Cox and Cumming had now no
interest in his ears.   What had he to do with
Cox and Cumming further, having already had
his suit finally adjudicated upon in a court of
conscience, a judgment without power of appeal
fully registered, and the matter settled so that
all the lawyers in London could not disturb it.
The archdeacon could go to Cox and Cumming,
could remain there all day in anxious discussion ;

but what might be said there was no longer
matter of interest to him, who was so soon to
lay aside the name of warden of Barchester
Hospital.

The archdeacon took up his shining new
clerical hat, and put on his black new clerical
gloves, and looked heavy, respectable, decorous,
and opulent, a decided clergyman of the Church
of England, every inch of him. " I suppose I
shall see you at Barchester the day after to-
morrow," said he.

The warden supposed he would.

" I must once more beseech you to take no
further steps till you see my father ; if you owe
me nothing," and the archdeacon looked as
though he thought a great deal were due to
him, " at least you owe so much to my father ; "
and, without waiting for a reply, Dr. Grantly
wended his way to Cox and Cumming.

Mrs. Grantly waited till the last fall of her
husband's foot was heard, as he turned out of
the court into St. Paul's Churchyard, and then
commenced her task of talking her father over.

" Papa," she began, " this is a most serious
business."

" Indeed it is," said the warden, ringing the
bell.

" I greatly feel the distress of mind you must
have endured."

" I am sure you do, my dear ; " and he ordered
the waiter to bring him pen, ink, and paper.

" Are you going to write, papa ? "

" Yes, my dear—I am going to write my resignation to the bishop."

" Pray, pray, papa, put it off till our return, —pray put it off till you have seen the bishop, —dear papa ! for my sake, for Eleanor's !——"

" It is for your sake and Eleanor's that I do this. I hope, at least, that my children may never have to be ashamed of their father."

" How can you talk about shame, papa ? " and she stopped while the waiter creaked in with the paper, and then slowly creaked out again ; " how can you talk about shame ? you know what all your friends think about this question."

The warden spread his paper on the table, placing it on the meagre blotting-book, which the hotel afforded, and sat himself down to write.

" You won't refuse me one request, papa ? " continued his daughter ; " you won't refuse to delay your letter for two short days ?—two days can make no possible difference."

" My dear," said he naïvely, " if I waited till I got to Barchester, I might, perhaps, be prevented."

" But surely you would not wish to offend the bishop ? " said she.

" God forbid ! The bishop is not apt to take offence, and knows me too well to take in bad part anything that I may be called on to do."

" But, papa——"

" Susan," said he, " my mind on this subject is made up ; it is not without much repugnance that I act in opposition to the advice of such men as Sir Abraham Haphazard and the arch-deacon ; but in this matter I can take no advice, I cannot alter the resolution to which I have come."

" But two days, papa——"

" No,—nor can I delay it. You may add to my present unhappiness by pressing me, but you cannot change my purpose ; it will be a comfort to me if you will let the matter rest : " and, dipping his pen into the inkstand, he fixed his eyes intently on the paper.

There was something in his manner which taught his daughter to perceive that he was in earnest ; she had at one time ruled supreme in her father's house, but she knew that there were moments when, mild and meek as he was, he would have his way, and the present was an occasion of the sort. She returned, therefore, to her knitting, and very shortly after left the room.

The warden was now at liberty to compose his letter, and, as it was characteristic of the man, it shall be given at full length. The official letter, which, when written, seemed to him to be too formally cold to be sent alone to so dear a friend, was accompanied by a private note : and both are here inserted.

The letter of resignation ran as follows :—

"CHAPTER HOTEL, ST. PAUL'S,
"LONDON, — August, 18—.

"My Lord Bishop,

"It is with the greatest pain that I feel myself constrained to resign into your Lordship's hands the wardenship of the hospital at Barchester, which you so kindly conferred upon me, now nearly twelve years since.

"I need not explain the circumstances which have made this step appear necessary to me. You are aware that a question has arisen as to the right of the warden to the income which has been allotted to the wardenship ; it has seemed to me that this right is not well made out, and I hesitate to incur the risk of taking an income to which my legal claim appears doubtful.

"The office of precentor of the cathedral is, as your Lordship is aware, joined to that of the warden ; that is to say, the precentor has for many years been the warden of the hospital ; there is, however, nothing to make the junction of the two offices necessary, and, unless you or the dean and chapter object to such an arrangement, I would wish to keep the precentorship. The income of this office will now be necessary to me ; indeed, I do not know why I should be ashamed to say that I should have difficulty in supporting myself without it.

" Your Lordship, and such others as you may please to consult on the matter, will at once see that my resignation of the wardenship need offer not the slightest bar to its occupation by another person. I am thought in the wrong by all those whom I have consulted in the matter ; I have very little but an inward and an unguided conviction of my own to bring me to this step, and I shall, indeed, be hurt to find that any slur is thrown on the preferment which your kindness bestowed on me, by my resignation of it. I, at any rate for one, shall look on any successor whom you may appoint as enjoying a clerical situation of the highest respectability, and one to which your Lordship's nomination gives an indefeasible right.

" I cannot finish this official letter without again thanking your Lordship for all your great kindness, and I beg to subscribe myself

" Your Lordship's most obedient servant,
                    "SEPTIMUS HARDING,

"Warden of Barchester Hospital
"and Precentor of the cathedral."

He then wrote the following private note :—

" My dear Bishop,
        " I cannot send you the accompanying official letter without a warmer expression of thanks for all your kindness than wonld befit a document which may to a certain degree be

made public.   You, I know, will understand
the feeling, and, perhaps, pity the weakness
which makes me resign the hospital.   I am not
made of calibre strong enough to withstand
public attack. Were I convinced that I stood
on ground perfectly firm, that I was certainly
justified in taking eight hundred a year under
Hiram's will, I should feel bound by duty to
retain the position, however unendurable might
be the nature of the assault; but, as I do not
feel this conviction, I cannot believe that you
will think me wrong in what I am doing.

" I had at one time an idea of keeping only
some moderate portion of the income, perhaps
three hundred a year, and of remitting the
remainder to the trustees; but it occurred to
me, and I think with reason, that by so doing
I should place my successors in an invidious
position, and greatly damage your patronage.

" My dear friend, let me have a line from
you to say that you do not blame me for what
I am doing, and that the officiating vicar of
Crabtree Parva will be the same to you as the
warden of the hospital.

" I am very anxious about the precentorship;
the archdeacon thinks it must go with the
wardenship; I think not, and that, having it,
I cannot be ousted.   I will, however, be guided
by you and the dean.   No other duty will suit
me so well, or come so much within my power
of adequate performance.

"I thank you from my heart for the preferment which I am now giving up, and for all your kindness, and am, dear bishop, now as always,

"Yours most sincerely,

"SEPTIMUS HARDING.

"LONDON, — *August*, 18—."

Having written these letters and made a copy of the former one for the benefit of the archdeacon, Mr. Harding, whom we must now cease to call the warden, he having designated himself so for the last time, found that it was nearly two o'clock, and that he must prepare for his journey. Yes, from this time he never again admitted the name by which he had been so familiarly known, and in which, to tell the truth, he had rejoiced. The love of titles is common to all men, and a vicar or fellow is as pleased at becoming Mr. Archdeacon or Mr. Provost, as a lieutenant at getting his captaincy, or a city tallow-chandler in becoming Sir John on the occasion of a Queen's visit to a new bridge. But warden he was no longer, and the name of precentor, though the office was to him so dear, confers in itself no sufficient distinction ; our friend, therefore, again became Mr. Harding.

Mrs. Grantly had gone out ; he had, therefore, no one to delay him by further entreaties to postpone his journey ; he had soon arranged his bag, and paid his bill, and, leaving a note for his daughter, in which he put the copy of his official letter, he got into a cab and drove away to the station with something of triumph in his heart.

Had he not cause for triumph? Had he not been supremely successful? Had he not for the first time in his life held his own purpose against that of his son-in-law, and manfully combated against great odds,—against the archdeacon's wife as well as the archdeacon? Had he not gained a great victory, and was it not fit that he should step into his cab with triumph?

He had not told Eleanor when he would return, but she was on the look out for him by every train by which he could arrive, and the pony-carriage was at the Barchester station when the train drew up at the platform.

" My dear," said he, sitting beside her, as she steered her little vessel to one side of the road to make room for the clattering omnibus as they passed from the station into the town ; " I hope you'll be able to feel a proper degree of respect for the vicar of Crabtree."

" Dear papa," said she, " I am so glad."

There was great comfort in returning home to that pleasant house, though he was to leave it so soon, and in discussing with his daughter all that he had done, and all that he had to do. It must take some time to get out of one house into another ; the curate at Crabtree could not be abolished under six months, that is, unless

other provision could be made for him; and
then the furniture—the most of that must be
sold to pay Sir Abraham Haphazard for sitting
up till twelve at night.   Mr. Harding was
strangely ignorant as to lawyers' bills; he had
no idea, from twenty pounds to two thousand,
as to the sum in which he was indebted for
legal assistance.   True, he had called in no
lawyer himself; truly, he had been no consenting
party to the employment of either Cox and
Cumming, or Sir Abraham; he had never been
consulted on such matters;—the archdeacon
had managed all this himself, never for a
moment suspecting that Mr. Harding would
take upon him to end the matter in a way of
his own.   Had the lawyers' bills been ten
thousand pounds, Mr. Harding could not have
helped it; but he was not on that account
disposed to dispute his own liability.   The
question never occurred to him; but it did
occur to him that he had very little money at
his banker's, that he could receive nothing further
from the hospital, and that the sale of the
furniture was his only resource.

"Not all, papa," said Eleanor, pleadingly.

"Not quite all, my dear," said he; "that is,
if we can help it.   We must have a little at
Crabtree—but it can only be a little; we must
put a bold front on it, Nelly; it isn't easy to
come down from affluence to poverty."

And so they planned their future mode of

life ; the father taking comfort from the reflection
that his daughter would soon be freed from it,
and she resolving that her father would soon
have in her own house a ready means of
escape from the solitude of the Crabtree
vicarage.

When the archdeacon left his wife and father-
in-law at the Chapter Coffee House to go to
Messrs. Cox and Cumming, he had no very de-
fined idea of what he had to do when he got
there. Gentlemen when at law, or in any way
engaged in matters requiring legal assistance,
are very apt to go to their lawyers without
much absolute necessity ;— gentlemen when
doing so, are apt to describe such attendance
as quite compulsory, and very disagreeable.
The lawyers, on the other hand, do not at all
see the necessity, though they quite agree as to
the disagreeable nature of the visit ;—gentlemen
when so engaged are usually somewhat gravelled
at finding nothing to say to their learned friends ;
they generally talk a little politics, a little
weather, ask some few foolish questions about
their suit, and then withdraw, having passed
half an hour in a small, dingy waiting-room, in
company with some junior assistant-clerk, and
ten minutes with the members of the firm ; the
business is then over for which the gentleman
has come up to London, probably a distance of
a hundred and fifty miles.   To be sure he goes
to the play, and dines at his friend's club, and

has a bachelor's liberty and bachelor's recreation for three or four days; and he could not probably plead the desire of such gratifications as a reason to his wife for a trip to London.

Married ladies, when your husbands find they are positively obliged to attend their legal advisers, the nature of the duty to be performed is generally of this description.

The archdeacon would not have dreamt of leaving London without going to Cox and Cumming; and yet he had nothing to say to them. The game was up; he plainly saw that Mr. Harding in this matter was not to be moved; his only remaining business on this head was to pay the bill and have done with it: and I think it may be taken for granted, that whatever the cause may be that takes a gentleman to a lawyer's chambers, he never goes there to pay his bill.

Dr. Grantly, however, in the eyes of Messrs. Cox and Cumming, represented the spiritualities of the diocese of Barchester, as Mr. Chadwick did the temporalities, and was, therefore, too great a man to undergo the half-hour in the clerk's room. It will not be necessary that we should listen to the notes of sorrow in which the archdeacon bewailed to Mr. Cox the weakness of his father-in-law, and the end of all their hopes of triumph; nor need we repeat the various exclamations of surprise with which the mournful intelligence was received. No

tragedy occurred, though Mr. Cox, a short and
somewhat bull-necked man, was very near
a fit of apoplexy when he first attempted to
ejaculate that fatal word—resign !

Over and over again did Mr. Cox attempt
to enforce on the archdeacon the propriety of
urging on Mr. Warden the madness of the
deed he was about to do.

" Eight hundred a year !" said Mr. Cox.

" And nothing whatever to do !" said Mr.
Cumming, who had joined the conference.

" No private fortune, I believe," said Mr. Cox.

" Not a shilling," said Mr. Cumming, in a
very low voice, shaking his head.

" I never heard of such a case in all my
experience," said Mr. Cox.

" Eight hundred a year, and as nice a house
as any gentleman could wish to hang up his
hat in," said Mr. Cumming.

" And an unmarried daughter, I believe," said
Mr. Cox, with much moral seriousness in his
tone. The archdeacon only sighed as each
separate wail was uttered, and shook his head,
signifying that the fatuity of some people was
past belief.

" I'll tell you what he might do," said Mr.
Cumming, brightening up. " I'll tell you how
you might save it—let him exchange."

" Exchange where ? " said the archdeacon.

" Exchange for a living. There's Quiverful,
of Puddingdale ; he has twelve children, and

would be delighted to get the hospital. To
be sure Puddingdale is only four hundred, but
that would be saving something out of the
fire: Mr. Harding would have a curate, and
still keep three hundred or three hundred and
fifty."

The archdeacon opened his ears and listened;
he really thought the scheme might do.

"The newspapers," continued Mr. Cumming,
"might hammer away at Quiverful every day
for the next six months without his minding
them."

The archdeacon took up his hat, and returned
to his hotel, thinking the matter over deeply;
at any rate he would sound Quiverful: a man
with twelve children would do much to double
his income.

CHAPTER XX

FAREWELL

ON the morning after Mr. Harding's return home, he received a note from the bishop full of affection, condolence, and praise. "Pray come to me at once," wrote the bishop, "that we may see what had better be done; as to the hospital, I will not say a word to dissuade you; but I don't like your going to Crabtree: at any rate, come to me at once."

Mr. Harding did go to him at once; and long and confidential was the consultation between the two old friends. There they sat together the whole long day, plotting to get the better of the archdeacon, and to carry out little schemes of their own, which they knew would be opposed by the whole weight of his authority.

The bishop's first idea was, that Mr. Harding, if left to himself, would certainly starve—not in the figurative sense in which so many of our ladies and gentlemen do starve on incomes from one to five hundred a year; not that he would be starved as regarded dress coats, port wine, and pocket-money; but that he would positively perish of inanition for want of bread.

"How is a man to live, when he gives up all his income?" said the bishop to himself. And

then the good-natured little man began to consider how his friend might be best rescued from
a death so horrid and painful.

His first proposition to Mr. Harding was,
that they should live together at the palace.
He, the bishop, positively assured Mr. Harding
that he wanted another resident chaplain : not
a young, working chaplain, but a steady,
middle-aged chaplain ; one who would dine
and drink a glass of wine with him, talk about
the archdeacon, and poke the fire. The bishop
did not positively name all these duties, but
he gave Mr. Harding to understand that such
would be the nature of the service required.

It was not without much difficulty that Mr.
Harding made his friend see that this would
not suit him ; that he could not throw up the
bishop's preferment, and then come and hang
on at the bishop's table ; that he could not
allow people to say of him that it was an easy
matter to abandon his own income, as he was
able to sponge on that of another person. He
succeeded, however, in explaining that the plan
would not do, and then the bishop brought
forward another which he had in his sleeve. He,
the bishop, had in his will left certain moneys to
Mr. Harding's two daughters, imagining that
Mr. Harding would himself want no such assistance during his own lifetime. This legacy
amounted to three thousand pounds each, duty
free ; and he now pressed it as a gift on his friend.

" The girls, you know," said he, " will have
it just the same when you're gone—and they
won't want it sooner—and as for the interest
during my lifetime, it isn't worth talking about.
I have more than enough."

With much difficulty and heartfelt sorrow,
Mr. Harding refused also this offer. No ; his
wish was to support himself, however poorly,
—not to be supported on the charity of any
one. It was hard to make the bishop understand this ; it was hard to make him comprehend that the only real favour he could confer
was the continuation of his independent friendship ; but at last even this was done. At any
rate, thought the bishop, he will come and dine
with me from time to time, and if he be
absolutely starving I shall see it.

Touching the precentorship, the bishop was
clearly of opinion that it could be held without
the other situation—an opinion from which no
one differed ; and it was therefore soon settled
among all the parties concerned, that Mr.
Harding should still be the precentor of the
cathedral.

On the day following Mr. Harding's return,
the archdeacon reached Plumstead full of Mr.
Cumming's scheme regarding Puddingdale and
Mr. Quiverful. On the very next morning he
drove over to Puddingdale, and obtained the
full consent of the wretched clerical Priam, who
was endeavouring to feed his poor Hecuba and

a dozen of Hectors on the small proceeds of his ecclesiastical kingdom. Mr. Quiverful had no doubts as to the legal rights of the warden; his conscience would be quite clear as to accepting the income; and as to the Jupiter, he begged to assure the archdeacon that he was quite indifferent to any emanations from the profane portion of the periodical press.

Having so far succeeded, he next sounded the bishop; but here he was astonished by most unexpected resistance. The bishop did not think it would do. "Not do, why not?" and seeing that his father was not shaken, he repeated the question in a severer form: "Why not do, my lord?"

His lordship looked very unhappy, and shuffled about in his chair, but still didn't give way; he thought Puddingdale wouldn't do for Mr. Harding; it was too far from Barchester.

"Oh! of course he'll have a curate."

The bishop also thought that Mr. Quiverful wouldn't do for the hospital; such an exchange wouldn't look well at such a time; and, when pressed harder, he declared he didn't think Mr. Harding would accept of Puddingdale under any circumstances.

"How is he to live?" demanded the archdeacon.

The bishop, with tears in his eyes, declared that he had not the slightest conception how life was to be sustained within him at all.

The archdeacon then left his father, and went
down to the hospital ; but Mr. Harding wouldn't
listen at all to the Puddingdale scheme. To
his eyes it had no attraction ; it savoured of
simony, and was likely to bring down upon him
harder and more deserved strictures than any
he had yet received : he positively declined to
become vicar of Puddingdale under any circumstances.

The archdeacon waxed wroth, talked big,
and looked bigger ; he said something about
dependence and beggary, spoke of the duty
every man was under to earn his bread, made
passing allusions to the follies of youth and
waywardness of age, as though Mr. Harding
were afflicted by both, and ended by declaring
that he had done. He felt that he had left
no stone unturned to arrange matters on the
best and easiest footing ; that he had, in fact,
so arranged them, that he had so managed that
there was no further need of any anxiety in the
matter. And how had he been paid ? His
advice had been systematically rejected ; he had
been not only slighted, but distrusted and
avoided ; he and his measures had been utterly
thrown over, as had been Sir Abraham, who,
he had reason to know, was much pained at
what had occurred. He now found it was useless
to interfere any further, and he should retire.
If any further assistance were required from
him, he would probably be called on, and should

be again happy to come forward. And so he left the hospital, and has not since entered it from that day to this.

And here we must take leave of Archdeacon Grantly. We fear that he is represented in these pages as being worse than he is ; but we have had to do with his foibles, and not with his virtues. We have seen only the weak side of the man, and have lacked the opportunity of bringing him forward on his strong ground. That he is a man somewhat too fond of his own way, and not sufficiently scrupulous in his manner of achieving it, his best friends cannot deny. That he is bigoted in favour, not so much of his doctrines as of his cloth, is also true: and it is true that the possession of a large income is a desire that sits near his heart. Nevertheless, the archdeacon is a gentleman and a man of conscience ; he spends his money liberally, and does the work he has to do with the best of his ability ; he improves the tone of society of those among whom he lives. His aspirations are of a healthy, if not of the highest, kind. Though never an austere man, he up-holds propriety of conduct both by example and precept. He is generous to the poor, and hospitable to the rich ; in matters of religion he is sincere, and yet no Pharisee ; he is in earnest, and yet no fanatic. On the whole, the Archdeacon of Barchester is a man doing more good than harm,—a man to be furthered and

supported, though perhaps also to be controlled;
and it is matter of regret to us that the course
of our narrative has required that we should
see more of his weakness than his strength.

Mr. Harding allowed himself no rest till
everything was prepared for his departure from
the hospital. It may be as well to mention
that he was not driven to the stern necessity
of selling all his furniture: he had been quite
in earnest in his intention to do so, but it was
soon made known to him that the claims of
Messrs. Cox and Cumming made no such step
obligatory. The archdeacon had thought it
wise to make use of the threat of the lawyer's
bill, to frighten his father-in-law into compliance;
but he had no intention to saddle Mr. Harding
with costs, which had been incurred by no
means exclusively for his benefit. The amount
of the bill was added to the diocesan account,
and was, in fact, paid out of the bishop's pocket,
without any consciousness on the part of his
lordship. A great part of his furniture he did
resolve to sell, having no other means to dispose
of it; and the ponies and carriages were trans-
ferred, by private contract, to the use of an
old maiden lady in the city.

For his present use Mr. Harding took a
lodging in Barchester, and thither were conveyed such articles as he wanted for daily use
—his music, books, and instruments, his own
armchair, and Eleanor's pet sofa; her teapoy

and his cellaret, and also the slender but still
sufficient contents of his wine-cellar. Mrs.
Grantly had much wished that her sister would
reside at Plumstead, till her father's house at
Crabtree should be ready for her ; but Eleanor
herself strongly resisted this proposal. It was
in vain urged upon her, that a lady in lodgings
cost more than a gentleman ; and that, under
her father's present circumstances, such an
expense should be avoided. Eleanor had not
pressed her father to give up the hospital,
in order that she might live at Plumstead
Rectory, and he alone in his Barchester
lodgings ; nor did Eleanor think that she would
be treating a certain gentleman very fairly,
if she betook herself to the house which he
would be the least desirous of entering of any
in the county. So she got a little bed-room
for herself behind the sitting-room, and just
over the little back parlour of the chemist,
with whom they were to lodge. There was
somewhat of a savour of senna softened by
peppermint about the place ; but, on the whole,
the lodgings were clean and comfortable.

The day had been fixed for the migration
of the ex-warden, and all Barchester were in
a state of excitement on the subject. Opinion
was much divided as to the propriety of Mr.
Harding's conduct. The mercantile part of the
community, the mayor and corporation, and
council, also most of the ladies, were loud in

his praise. Nothing could be more noble,
nothing more generous, nothing more upright.
But the gentry were of a different way of
thinking,—especially the lawyers and the clergymen. They said such conduct was very weak
and undignified ; that Mr. Harding evinced a
lamentable want of *esprit de corps*, as well as
courage ; and that such an abdication must do
much harm, and could do but little good.

On the evening before he left, he summoned
all the bedesmen into his parlour to wish them
good-bye. With Bunce he had been in frequent
communication since his return from London,
and had been at much pains to explain to the
old man the cause of his resignation, without
in any way prejudicing the position of his
successor. The others, also, he had seen more
or less frequently ; and had heard from most
of them separately some expression of regret
at his departure ; but he had postponed his
farewell till the last evening.

He now bade the maid put wine and glasses
on the table ; and had the chairs arranged
around the room ; and sent Bunce to each of
the men to request they would come and say
farewell to their late warden. Soon the noise
of aged scuffling feet was heard upon the gravel
and in the little hall, and the eleven men
who were enabled to leave their rooms were
assembled.

"Come in, my friends, come in," said the

warden—he was still warden then. "Come in, and sit down;" and he took the hand of Abel Handy, who was the nearest to him, and led the limping grumbler to a chair. The others followed slowly and bashfully: the infirm, the lame, and the blind; poor wretches! who had been so happy, had they but known it! Now their aged faces were covered with shame, and every kind word from their master was a coal of fire burning on their heads.

When first the news had reached them that Mr. Harding was going to leave the hospital, it had been received with a kind of triumph; —his departure was, as it were, a prelude to success. He had admitted his want of right to the money about which they were disputing; and as it did not belong to him, of course it did to them. The one hundred a year to each of them was actually becoming a reality; and Abel Handy was a hero, and Bunce a faint-hearted sycophant, worthy neither honour nor fellowship. But other tidings soon made their way into the old men's rooms. It was first notified to them that the income abandoned by Mr. Harding would not come to them; and these accounts were confirmed by attorney Finney. They were then informed that Mr. Harding's place would be at once filled by another. That the new warden could not be a kinder man they all knew; that he would be a less friendly one most suspected; and then came the bitter information that, from the moment of Mr. Harding's departure, the twopence a day, his own peculiar gift, must of necessity be withdrawn.

And this was to be the end of all their mighty struggle—of their fight for their rights— of their petition, and their debates and their hopes! They were to change the best of masters for a possible bad one, and to lose twopence a day each man! No; unfortunate as this was, it was not the worst, or nearly the worst, as will just now be seen.

" Sit down, sit down, my friends," said the warden ; " I want to say a word to you, and to drink your healths, before I leave you. Come up here, Moody, here is a chair for you ; come, Jonathan Crumple—" and by degrees he got the men to be seated. It was not surprising that they should hang back with faint hearts, having returned so much kindness with such deep ingratitude. Last of all of them came Bunce, and with sorrowful mien and slow step got into his accustomed seat near the fire-place.

When they were all in their places, Mr. Harding rose to address them ; and then finding himself not quite at home on his legs, he sat down again. " My dear old friends," said he, "you all know that I am going to leave you."

There was a sort of murmur ran round the

room, intended, perhaps, to express regret at his departure ; but it was but a murmur, and might have meant that or anything else.

"There has been lately some misunderstanding between us. You have thought, I believe, that you did not get all that you were entitled to, and that the funds of the hospital have not been properly disposed of. As for me, I cannot say what should be the disposition of these moneys, or how they should be managed, and I have therefore thought it best to go."

"We never wanted to drive your reverence out of it," said Handy.

"No, indeed, your reverence," said Skulpit. "We never thought it would come to this. When I signed the petition—that is, I didn't sign it, because——"

"Let his reverence speak, can't you?" said Moody.

"No," continued Mr. Harding ; "I am sure you did not wish to turn me out ; but I thought it best to leave you. I am not a very good hand at a lawsuit, as you may all guess ; and when it seemed necessary that our ordinary quiet mode of living should be disturbed, I thought it better to go. I am neither angry nor offended with any man in the hospital."

Here Bunce uttered a kind of groan, very clearly expressive of disagreement.

"I am neither angry nor displeased with any man in the hospital," repeated Mr. Harding,

emphatically. "If any man has been wrong—
and I don't say any man has—he has erred
through wrong advice. In this country all are
entitled to look for their own rights, and you
have done no more. As long as your interests
and my interests were at variance, I could give
you no counsel on this subject; but the connection between us has ceased; my income can
no longer depend on your doings, and therefore,
as I leave you, I venture to offer to you my
advice."

The men all declared that they would from
henceforth be entirely guided by Mr. Harding's
opinion in their affairs.

"Some gentleman will probably take my
place here very soon, and I strongly advise you
to be prepared to receive him in a kindly spirit,
and to raise no further question among yourselves as to the amount of his income. Were
you to succeed in lessening what he has to
receive, you would not increase your own
allowance. The surplus would not go to you;
your wants are adequately provided for, and
your position could hardly be improved."

"God bless your reverence, we knows it,"
said Spriggs.

"It's all true, your reverence," said Skulpit;
"we sees it all now."

"Yes, Mr. Harding," said Bunce, opening his
mouth for the first time; "I believe they do
understand it now, now that they've driven

from under the same roof with them such a master as not one of them will ever know again —now that they're like to be in sore want of a friend."

"Come, come, Bunce," said Mr. Harding, blowing his nose, and manœuvring to wipe his eyes at the same time.

"Oh, as to that," said Handy, "we none of us never wanted to do Mr. Harding no harm; if he's going now, it's not along of us; and I don't see for what Mr. Bunce speaks up agen us that way."

"You've ruined yourselves, and you've ruined me too, and that's why," said Bunce.

"Nonsense, Bunce," said Mr. Harding; "there's nobody ruined at all. I hope you'll let me leave you all friends, I hope you'll all drink a glass of wine in friendly feeling with me and with one another. You'll have a good friend, I don't doubt, in your new warden; and if ever you want any other, why after all I'm not going so far off but that I shall sometimes see you;" and then, having finished his speech, Mr. Harding filled all the glasses, and himself handed each a glass to the men round him, and raising his own, said,—

"God bless you all! you have my heartfelt wishes for your welfare. I hope you may live contented, and die trusting in the Lord Jesus Christ, and thankful to Almighty God for the good things he has given you. God bless you, my friends!" and Mr. Harding drank his wine.

Another murmur, somewhat more articulate than the first, passed round the circle, and this time it was intended to imply a blessing on Mr. Harding. It had, however, but little cordiality in it. Poor old men! how could they be cordial with their sore consciences and shamed faces? how could they bid God bless him with hearty voices and a true benison, knowing, as they did, that their vile cabal had driven him from his happy home, and sent him in his old age to seek shelter under a strange roof-tree? They did their best, however; they drank their wine, and withdrew.

As they left the hall-door, Mr. Harding shook hands with each of the men, and spoke a kind word to them about their individual cases and ailments; and so they departed, answering his questions in the fewest words, and retreated to their dens, a sorrowful repentant crew.

All but Bunce, who still remained to make his own farewell. "There's poor old Bell," said Mr. Harding, "I mustn't go without saying a word to him; come through with me, Bunce, and bring the wine with you;" and so they went through to the men's cottages, and found the old man propped up as usual in his bed.

"I've come to say good-bye to you, Bell," said Mr. Harding, speaking loud, for the old man was deaf.

"And are you going away, then, really?" asked Bell.

" Indeed I am, and I've brought you a glass of wine ; so that we may part friends, as we lived, you know."

The old man took the proffered glass in his shaking hands, and drank it eagerly. " God bless you, Bell !" said Mr. Harding ; "good-bye, my old friend."

" And so you're really going ? " the man again asked.

"Indeed I am, Bell."

The poor old bed-ridden creature still kept Mr. Harding's hand in his own, and the warden thought that he had met with something like warmth of feeling in the one of all his subjects from whom it was the least likely to be expected, for poor old Bell had nearly outlived all human feelings. " And your reverence," said he, and then he paused, while his old palsied head shook horribly, and his shrivelled cheeks sank lower within his jaws, and his glazy eye gleamed with a momentary light ; " and your reverence, shall we get a hundred a year, then ? "

How gently did Mr. Harding try to extinguish the false hope of money which had been so wretchedly raised to disturb the quiet of the dying man ! One other week and his mortal coil would be shuffled off ; in one short week would God resume his soul, and set it apart for its irrevocable doom ; seven more tedious days

and nights of senseless inactivity, and all would
be over for poor Bell in this world ; and yet, with
his last audible words, he was demanding his
moneyed rights, and asserting himself to be the
proper heir of John Hiram's bounty ! Not on
him, poor sinner as he was, be the load of such
sin !

Mr. Harding returned to his parlour, meditating with a sick heart on what he had seen, and
Bunce with him. We will not describe the
parting of these two good men, for good men they
were. It was in vain that the late warden
endeavoured to comfort the heart of the old
bedesman ; poor old Bunce felt that his days of
comfort were gone. The hospital had to him
been a happy home, but it could be so no longer.
He had had honour there, and friendship; he had
recognised his master, and been recognised ; all
his wants, both of soul and body, had been
supplied, and he had been a happy man. He
wept greviously as he parted from his friend, and
the tears of an old man are bitter. " It is all
over for me in this world," said he, as he gave
the last squeeze to Mr. Harding's hand ; " I have
now to forgive those who have injured me—and
to die."

And so the old man went out, and then Mr.
Harding gave way to his grief, and he too wept
aloud.

CHAPTER XXI

CONCLUSION

OUR tale is now done, and it only remains to us to collect the scattered threads of our little story, and to tie them into a seemly knot. This will not be a work of labour, either to the author or to his readers; we have not to deal with many personages, or with stirring events, and were it not for the custom of the thing, we might leave it to the imagination of all concerned to conceive how affairs at Barchester arranged themselves.

On the morning after the day last alluded to, Mr. Harding, at an early hour, walked out of the hospital, with his daughter under his arm, and sat down quietly to breakfast at his lodgings over the chemist's shop. There was no parade about his departure; no one, not even Bunce, was there to witness it; had he walked to the apothecary's thus early to get a piece of court plaster, or a box of lozenges, he could not have done it with less appearance of an important movement. There was a tear in Eleanor's eye as she passed through the big gateway and over the bridge; but Mr. Harding walked with an elastic step, and entered his new abode with a pleasant face.

"Now, my dear," said he, "you have everything

ready, and you can make tea here just as nicely as in the parlour at the hospital." So Eleanor took off her bonnet and made the tea.   After this manner did the late Warden of Barchester Hospital accomplish his flitting, and change his residence.

It was not long before the archdeacon brought his father to discuss the subject of a new warden. Of course he looked upon the nomination as his own, and he had in his eye three or four fitting candidates, seeing that Mr. Cumming's plan as to the living of Puddingdale could not be brought to bear.   How can I describe the astonishment which confounded him, when his father declared that he would appoint no successor to Mr. Harding? "If we can get the matter set to rights, Mr. Harding will return," said the bishop ; "and if we cannot, it will be wrong to put any other gentleman into so cruel a position."

It was in vain that the archdeacon argued and lectured, and even threatened ; in vain he my-lorded his poor father in his sternest manner ; in vain his "good heavens !" were ejaculated in a tone that might have moved a whole synod, let alone one weak and aged bishop.   Nothing could induce his father to fill up the vacancy caused by Mr. Harding's retirement.

Even John Bold would have pitied the feelings with which the archdeacon returned to Plumstead : the church was falling, nay, already in ruins ; its dignitaries were yielding without a struggle before the blows of its antagonists ; and

one of its most respected bishops, his own father
—the man considered by all the world as being
in such matters under his, Dr. Grantly's control
—had positively resolved to capitulate, and own
himself vanquished !

And how fared the hospital under this resolve
of its visitor ? Badly indeed. It is now some
years since Mr. Harding left it, and the warden's
house is still tenantless. Old Bell has died, and
Billy Gazy; the one-eyed Spriggs has drunk
himself to death, and three others of the twelve
have been gathered into the churchyard mould.
Six have gone, and the six vacancies remain
unfilled ! Yes, six have died, with no kind
friend to solace their last moments, with no
wealthy neighbour to administer comforts and
ease the stings of death. Mr. Harding, indeed,
did not desert them ; from him they had such
consolation as a dying man may receive from
his Christian pastor ; but it was the occasional
kindness of a stranger which ministered to them,
and not the constant presence of a master, a
neighbour, and a friend.

Nor were those who remained better off than
those who died. Dissensions rose among them,
and contests for pre-eminence ; and then they
began to understand that soon one among them
would be the last,—some one wretched being
would be alone there in that now comfortless
hospital,—the miserable relic of what had once
been so good and comfortable.

The building of the hospital itself has not been allowed to go to ruins.   Mr. Chadwick, who still holds his stewardship, and pays the accruing rents into an account opened at a bank for the purpose, sees to that ; but the whole place has become disordered and ugly.   The warden's garden is a wretched wilderness, the drive and paths are covered with weeds, the flower-beds are bare, and the unshorn lawn is now a mass of long damp grass and unwholesome moss.   The beauty of the place is gone ; its attractions have withered.   Alas ! a very few years since it was the prettiest spot in Barchester, and now it is a disgrace to the city.

Mr Harding did not go out to Crabtree Parva. An arrangement was made which respected the homeseatd of Mr. Smith and his happy family, and put Mr. Harding into possession of a small living within the walls of the city.   It is the smallest possible parish, containing a part of the Cathedral Close and a few old houses adjoining. The church is a singular little Gothic building, perched over a gateway, through which the Close is entered, and is approached by a flight of stone steps which leads down under the archway of the gate.   It is no bigger than an ordinary room, —perhaps twenty-seven feet long by eighteen wide,—but still it is a perfect church.   It contains an old carved pulpit and reading-desk, a tiny altar under a window filled with dark old-coloured glass, a font, some half-dozen pews, and perhaps a dozen seats for the poor, and also a vestry. The roof is high-pitched, and of black old oak, and the three large beams which support it run down to the side walls, and terminate in grotesquely carved faces—two devils and an angel on one side, two angels and a devil on the other. Such is the church of St. Cuthbert at Barchester, of which Mr. Harding became rector, with a clear income of seventy-five pounds a year.

Here he performs afternoon service every Sunday, and administers the Sacrament once in every three months. His audience is not large; and, had they been so, he could not have accommodated them: but enough come to fill his six pews, and, on the front seat of those devoted to the poor is always to be seen our old friend Mr. Bunce, decently arrayed in his bedesman's gown.

Mr. Harding is still precentor of Barchester; and it is very rarely the case that those who attend the Sunday morning service miss the gratification of hearing him chant the Litany, as no other man in England can do it. He is neither a discontented nor an unhappy man; he still inhabits the lodgings to which he went on leaving the hospital, but he now has them to himself. Three months after that time Eleanor became Mrs. Bold, and of course removed to her husband's house.

There were some difficulties to be got over

on the occasion of the marriage. The archdeacon, who could not so soon overcome his
grief, would not be persuaded to grace the
ceremony with his presence, but he allowed his
wife and children to be there. The marriage
took place at the palace, and the bishop himself
officiated. It was the last occasion on which
he ever did so ; and, though he still lives, it is
not probable that he will ever do so again.

Not long after the marriage, perhaps six
months, when Eleanor's bridal-honours were
fading, and persons were beginning to call her
Mrs. Bold without twittering, the archdeacon
consented to meet John Bold at a dinner-party,
and since that time they have become almost
friends. The archdeacon firmly believes that
his brother-in-law was, as a bachelor, an infidel,
an unbeliever in the great truths of our religion ;
but that matrimony has opened his eyes, as it
has those of others. And Bold is equally inclined to think that time has softened the
asperities of the archdeacon's character. Friends
though they are, they do not often revert to
the feud of the hospital.

Mr. Harding, we say, is not an unhappy man ;
he keeps his lodgings, but they are of little use
to him, except as being the one spot on earth
which he calls his own. His time is spent
chiefly at his daughter's or at the palace ; he is
never left alone, even should he wish to be so ;
and within a twelvemonth of Eleanor's marriage

his determination to live at his own lodging had been so far broken through and abandoned, that he consented to have his violoncello permanently removed to his daughter's house.

Every other day a message is brought to him from the bishop. "The bishop's compliments, and his lordship is not very well to-day, and he hopes Mr. Harding will dine with him." This bulletin as to the old man's health is a myth; for though he is over eighty he is never ill, and will probably die some day, as a spark goes out, gradually and without a struggle. Mr. Harding does dine with him very often, which means going to the palace at three and remaining till ten; and whenever he does not the bishop whines, and says that the port wine is corked, and complains that nobody attends to him, and frets himself off to bed an hour before his time.

It was long before the people of Barchester forgot to call Mr. Harding by his long well-known name of Warden. It had become so customary to say Mr. Warden, that it was not easily dropped. "No, no," he always says when so addressed, "not Warden now, only precentor."

THE END

ANTHONY TROLLOPE'S
CLERGY

ANTHONY TROLLOPE'S
CLERGY

BY MICHAEL SADLEIR

An introduction to *Barchester Towers,*
Everyman's Library, 1956

For the benefit of those readers who now for the first time
make acquaintance with the county of Barset and its capital,
the cathedral city of Barchester, let it be explained that
Barchester Towers is the second of a series of six novels which
constitute what Trollope himself called the 'Chronicles of
Barsetshire.' The first of this series was *The Warden* (1855),
the third was *Doctor Thorne* (1858), the fourth *Framley
Parsonage* (1861), the fifth *The Small House at Allington* (1864),
and the sixth *The Last Chronicle of Barset* (1867). Although
any one of these novels can be read separately and with
enjoyment, there is this advantage to a perusal in sequence—
that it enables the reader to observe the steady development
of Trollope's control of his material, and of his amazing in-
tuition as an interpreter of the human heart. This statement
is not so contradictory of my opening sentence as it may
seem; for although *Barchester Towers* is the most *famous* of
the Barsetshire Chronicles, it is not in a technical sense as
good a novel either as *Doctor Thorne* which immediately
followed it, or as *The Last Chronicle of Barset* which came ten
years later. In other words, between 1855 when he published
The Warden, and the appearance of *The Last Chronicle* in
1867, Trollope became a master of his craft.

But concentration on the Barset novels to the exclusion
of the many other admirable stories written by the same
author has led to a misapprehension which should be corrected.
There is a general impression that the clergy of the Church of
England play a predominant part in Trollope's fiction. This
is not the case, though it is easy to see how, under the powerful
influence of the Barset novels, the mistake arose. These

novels are full of clergy, as befits a series of stories concerned with a clerical hierarchy dominating a major bishopric and with the social structure of a city steeped since the Middle Ages in Church tradition and Church history. That the author of these stories wrote many others of a different kind is either not appreciated or regarded as unimportant. 'Trollope,' says the generality, 'is a novelist who wrote about parsons, and that is all about it.' Very well; let us attempt a rapid survey of Trollope's fictional output and we shall find unexpected limitations to his ecclesiastical interest.

Anthony Trollope was born in 1815 and died in December 1882. Between 1847 and 1883 were published fifty-four novels, all except two over his name. In only twelve of these novels (among which are included the six Chronicles of Barsetshire) do Anglican clergymen exercise any worthwhile influence on the plot. Even if one takes into account a sprinkling of nonconformist ministers, the prevalence of parsons is strictly limited.

The Macdermots of Ballycloran, Trollope's first novel, was a story of Ireland and contained no parson. His second novel, *The Kellys and the O'Kellys*, was another story of Ireland. Again no parson. *La Vendée*, his third novel, was a tale of the French Revolution and, not surprisingly, parsonless. With his fourth novel, *The Warden*, he inaugurated his series of Chronicles of an imaginary county called Barsetshire, in which novels he gradually presented an entire clerical society.

The Warden himself, Mr Harding, is a gentle, retiring little man, sixty years of age, unself-seeking and upright. He is Trollope's conventionalized conception of a humble servant of a Divine Master, a distillation of the qualities which ideally should endow a member of the priesthood. Admittedly the perfection symbolized by Harding is trite and obvious; but Trollope was still an unpractised writer.

After Harding we meet Archdeacon Grantly, the forceful worldly cleric, a fine organizer and business man, the Church's champion in matters temporal. He is married to the Warden's daughter, and his dismay when a usually docile father-in-law stubbornly persists in resigning the wardenship of Hiram's Hospital because a Radical newspaper-man has made innuendoes regarding the disposal of the funds of the alms-houses, is the genuine dismay of a fighter who is on the side of the Church right or wrong.

Barchester Towers, which followed immediately after *The Warden*, makes important additions to the gallery of Trollopian clerics, as well as reintroducing with a new sureness of touch some already-acquaintances. Of the newcomers, pride of place belongs to Dr Proudie, now bishop of Barchester, and his redoubtable wife. The bishop is undeniably a type—the hen-pecked husband of a virago; but Mrs Proudie, from the moment of her first appearance, has a horrid individuality of her own, and one feels that Trollope, in his unflinching delineation of a nagging shrew, had for the first time in his novel-writing career imagined a real character and brought her to life.

If we pause for a moment over the Reverend Mr Slope, it is because he is the first of a series of fortune-hunting or sancti-monious or power-hungry parson-intriguers, for the most part over-caricatured and set up as cockshies.[1] Slope, to put it bluntly, is grossly overdone; and we are so insistently invited to hate him that we end in half-pity. The same more or less applies to four venal parsons who carry on the Slope tradition in later novels—Mr Prong in *Rachel Ray*, Mr Macguire in *Miss Mackenzie*, Dr Emilius in *The Eustace Diamonds*, and Mr Greenwood in *Marion Fay*.

Very different is the case with the Reverend Francis Arabin, who becomes Dean of Barchester and marries Harding's second daughter, Eleanor. Arabin is a great favourite with his creator. 'An eloquent clergyman,' says Trollope, 'a droll, odd, humorous, conscientious man, a thorough gentle-man.' The Arabins make increasingly important appearances throughout the Barchester canon and one can almost hear Trollope purring over their good breeding, lack of malice, and general excellence of upholstery.

There remain Mr and Mrs Quiverful of Puddingdale, who precipitate a bitter and final quarrel between Mrs Proudie and her hitherto protégé, Mr Slope. They are an appealing and pathetic couple; but are completely overshadowed, by the time *The Last Chronicle* has come to completion, by the grandiose and tragic figure of the Reverend Josiah Crawley of Hogglestock.

No need for me to dwell on Mr Crawley, who is now admitted

[1] Probably Trollope inherited a taste for scarifying Low-Church clergymen from his mother, whose best-known novel, *The Vicar of Wrexhill*, is an exaggerated assault on evangelical hypocrisy, and who introduced other unpraiseworthy parsons into her long series of novels.

to be one of the monumental creations of nineteenth-century English fiction. His is the third spiritual crisis to afflict a clergyman in the course of the Barchester novels, and by far the most profound and heart-breaking. We are moved and charmed by the humility and integrity of old Mr Harding; reading *Framley Parsonage*, we are tense with anxiety over the squalid money troubles into which the suave Mr Sowerby lures the heedless Mark Robarts. But neither Harding nor Robarts can compare as human tragedies with Mr Crawley—unbending, falsely accused, bitterly prejudiced, and sunk in penury.

Before leaving Barchester, I would ask your attention for another clerical family, whose treatment at the hands of their creator constitutes an interesting example of his unsureness in these early days. Among the important personalities of the Barchester Close are the members of the family of Dr Vesey Stanhope, an absentee benefice-holder, who has for years led a life of cultured idleness in Italy, drawing on stipends he made no attempt to earn. Himself an elegant and carefully groomed figure, he has a smartly dressed wife, a fascinating waster of a son, and two daughters. Charlotte, the elder, is managing, efficient, and handsome (all the Stanhopes are very good-looking); Madeleine Neroni, the younger, is a pathetic but dangerous beauty, crippled (it is said) by the ill-treatment of an Italian husband, but still an insatiable collector of masculine scalps. Of this sensationally promising household Trollope makes no enduring use. After *Barchester Towers* they disappear altogether, and any hope of a detailed portrait of the handsome sybarite and pluralist, with his vivid and disruptive family, must be abandoned. It was not that Trollope did not realize what a good thing he had invented when he imagined the Stanhopes, but that, out of a vaguely formalized fear of contemporary moralism, he funked their exploitation.

The six Barchester novels were published over a period of a dozen years, and during these dozen years Trollope also published a series of parsonless stories: *The Three Clerks, The Bertrams, Castle Richmond, Orley Farm, Can You Forgive Her?, The Belton Estate,* and *Nina Balatka.* When he was finally free of *The Last Chronicle,* he wrote steadily on, publishing *The Claverings, Linda Tressel, Phineas Finn, He*

Knew He was Right—hundreds of thousands of words, but no clergyman of any significance until, in 1870, he gave us *The Vicar of Bullhampton*. Now this story is not by any means a faultless specimen of the Trollopian novel. It is too long and too full of transcriptions of letters; its conventional love-story is more than usually trite; and the author introduces a village girl gone wrong, making matters worse by apologizing in a special preface for doing so. But it is a book important to our present theme because its hero—who gives the tale its title—the Reverend Frank Fenwick, is an excellently sustained and sympathetic character, of a kind not elsewhere found among Trollopian tales.

Fenwick is a generous-hearted, courageous, and humorous man who rushes into battle against cruelty or meanness or arrogance without counting the cost. He is described as 'imprudent,' and the word is just. 'Imprudence' means a weighing-up of right or wrong and, once convinced that one is right, a blank refusal to compromise just in order to avoid trouble. Recklessness, on the other hand, would mean swift action on impulse alone, and that is not one of Fenwick's failings. He is above all a human parson—neither a cathedral dignitary nor a player at Church politics. He is a parish priest who really does his job, who is always ready to help the helpless, to mediate between irreconcilables, to risk insult and a broken head by forcing his way into street-corner gangs in a rough quarter of the town. The conflict between Fenwick and the Marquis of Trowbridge—between a solitary pugnacious and selfless parson and a rank-proud and foolishly domineering landlord—keeps us genuinely on tenterhooks.

After *Bullhampton* comes an alarming list of stories, not literally parsonless, but not sufficiently parsoned for our purpose—*Sir Harry Hotspur of Humblethwaite*, *Ralph the Heir*, *The Golden Lion of Granpère*, *Lady Anna*, *Harry Heathcote of Gangoil*, *The Way We Live Now*, *The Prime Minister*, *The American Senator*. But at long last (1878) from the now ageing novelist, comes *Is He Popenjoy?* This excellent if protracted story introduces us to the most detestable of Trollope's marquises. In comparison with baby-Popenjoy's putative father Lord Brotherton, Lord Trowbridge (the Bullhampton marquis) is an amiable ass and Lord Hartletop (in *The Small House at Allington*) is attractive, even as a parcel tied to his wife's apron-strings. The Marquis of

Brotherton is a peevish, sneering bully; and the consistency with which his creator maintains the quality of his Lordship's insulting letters and unendurable bad manners is novel-writing of the highest order. Into direct conflict with this horrid creature comes the Dean of Brotherton, whose daughter is married to the marquis's younger brother. Dean Lovelace is a cross between Archdeacon Grantly and the Reverend Frank Fenwick. He has great courage, a proud consciousness of his dignity and rank, an obstinate belief in the righteousness of his cause, vis-à-vis the snarling nobleman who has called the dean's daughter a foul name. The dean is pursued with jealousy and innuendo by the bishop's chaplain (a revised edition of Mr Slope) but sweeps the man aside with something of the archdeacon's flamboyant arrogance.

One final Trollopian cleric, and he a self-portrait. From *Is He Popenjoy?* we pass via *An Eye for an Eye, John Caldigate, Cousin Henry,* and *The Duke's Children* to *Dr Wortle's School* (1881). This last is a very short novel, about a successful schoolmaster in Holy Orders, who has as second in command an admirable teacher and disciplinarian called Peacocke, a well-loved friend rather than a salaried employee. This Henry Peacocke came from America with his wife, and rumours of an irregularity in the Peacocke marriage are spread about by a malignant enemy of Dr Wortle. The school begins to suffer; new entrants fall away; there are withdrawals of existing pupils. What does Dr Wortle do? He does precisely what Trollope himself would have done. He stands obstinately by the side of his friend and colleague, overcoming the gossiping women and refusing to bow down to the conventional timidity of a vintage Trollopian bishop.

Dr Wortle's School is a compulsory epilogue to any extensive reading of Trollope's novels. It completes the cycle of clerical portraits which began with Mr Harding, Archdeacon Grantly, and others, presented as pieces of social landscape rather than as personalities; which passed through ever-strengthening phases of parsonical individuality; which, in the person of the Reverend Frank Fenwick, attained to a four-square conception of the clergyman as a fighter for decency and pity and tolerance; which ended with the old novelist, sitting in front of his looking-glass, seeing himself.

In conclusion, something must be said on a subject as to

which opinion among Trollopians is divided. Trollope's clergy, even from the start, are living human beings, who walk the streets and country lanes as natural and recognizable figures of their period. But they have something more than mere vitality. The majority are *good* men, and *goodness* in a priest surely consists of something beyond decent citizenship or visitations to the sick or pulpit oratory?

What then does Trollope tell us of their spiritual function? What of the mysticism which should surely lie in the hearts of men vowed to the ministry? Of this aspect of clerical activities virtually nothing. Was he too much of a materialist to care about it? Was he, in his determination to present with fidelity the outward deportment of his clergymen, deliberately indifferent to their interpretation of their calling? Or did he shirk the subject, telling himself he was a social chronicler and not a soul-reader?

He made his own statement as to this momentous alternative on the last page of *The Last Chronicle of Barset*, where occurs the following apologia, direct from the novelist himself:

> Some have accused me of having forgotten in writing of clergymen the first and foremost characteristic of the ordinary English clergyman's life. I have spoken of them all as though their high calling was a matter of no moment either to me or in my opinion to themselves.
> I would plead that my object has been to paint the social and not the professional lives of clergymen, and that I have been led to do so, firstly by a feeling that no men affect more strongly by their own characters the society of those around them than do country clergymen, and that therefore their social habits are worth painting; and secondly by a feeling that, though I as a novelist may feel entitled to write of clergymen out of their pulpits as I may write of lawyers and doctors, I have no such liberty to write of them in their pulpits. . . . Had I written an epic about clergymen I would have taken St Paul for my model; but describing such clergymen as I see around me I could not venture to be transcendental.

Hugh Walpole interprets this declaration by Trollope as evidence of an inability (stronger than 'a refusal') to perceive that a cathedral and even a parish church can have a separate and dramatic personality apart from its complement of human beings, as has Notre Dame in Victor Hugo's novel or the great church in Huysmans's *La Cathédrale* or that in Meade Faulkner's *Nebuly Coat*. Walpole might, modesty permitting, have added 'or in my own novel *The Cathedral*.' With due respect I consider that any such romantic symbolism was foreign to Trollope's genius, and that we are still left facing the fact that the spiritual preoccupations of Trollope's clergy are unexplored.

Why is this? I venture a suggestion and leave the problem with you. Trollope did not wear his heart on his sleeve, and his private convictions were purposely kept very private indeed. Is it not conceivable that he had so profound a respect for the spiritual functions of the clergy that he would have regarded any discussion of them in a novel as sacrilege? This is going further than his own statement about pulpits; for there he admits a possible parallel between clergy on the one hand and lawyers and doctors on the other—to whom he might have added politicians. Lawyers he scarifies with energy and relish; doctors he firmly divides into quietly dutiful practitioners and fashionable pomposities with knighthoods. As for politicians, he openly declares his unconcern with their political pretensions and manœuvres, and portrays them as puppets of petticoat government, who spend such spare time as they have between social engagements sitting in the House of Commons wearing top hats, and debating measures about which they know and care little.

How different is his attitude toward the clergy! He never hints that he might regard himself as potentially a clerk in Holy Orders. Any such aspiration would have seemed to him shocking presumption; and I think that the same respectful humility toward the spiritual aspect of the priesthood —no matter what human frailties disfigured many of its members—compelled him scrupulously to keep that spiritual aspect outside what, to him, was a novelist's permissible scope.

MICHAEL SADLEIR.

1956.